Many thanks to the
United States Army,
United States Army National Guard,
and a special thanks to
Sergeant Gerry Ziegler,
Sergeant Larry LaDuca
and Sergeant Pat Henderson.

All characters in this book are fictitious and in no way represent any persons living or dead. All places of business are also fictitious and represent no places of business, past or present. Any similarities in either respect, is strictly coincidental.

Copyright, 1992

THE
MINUTEMAN
PUBLISHING
HOUSE

**The Minuteman Publishing House
P.O. Box 1389
Lewiston, New York
14092**

Printed in the U.S.A.
Cover Photographs by Russ Pettifer

HEADING HOME

by Daniel R. Rodrique

CHAPTER ONE

It was April 1970 and Bob Hills was in a foxhole praying he would survive the next thirty two days when he was due to rotate back to the real world. His eyes casually scanned the tree line that stretched across the far side of the clearing in front of him. The smells of the trees and the grass filled the air. He continued to focus on the tree line as he fought with the boredom of being there. Vietnam was one hell of a bad experience and he never would have made it, if not for having Jimmy Wheeler there to help him through it. Jimmy stood six feet tall with brown hair and big brown eyes. He was the type of guy that the girls just loved and he knew it too. He certainly had a way with them. Hills should have been so lucky. Bob was just an average fellow, five feet ten with blue eyes and brown hair. He had a small scar by the corner of his left eye, the result of a bicycle accident from his childhood. Bob Hills, was the type of person who would have no problem blending into a crowd. He was liked by most everyone who had ever met him, a character trait he undoubtedly inherited from his dad.

As Bob stood there in the foxhole looking out at the tree line ahead of him, he could visualize everyone back home in his mind. It was just as though they were right there in front of him. His mind began to wonder through space and time, to a less complicated place ...... home.

Jimmy and Bob had grown up together. They had attended the same school, played on the same ball teams, they even had the same birth date. The two were almost inseparable. Jim was the brother Bob never had. Even their parents were close friends.

Jimmy's dad, Bill, had a small construction business,

which in Bill's mind was a large and still growing corporation. He was a stocky fellow about five feet nine, with blue eyes and grey receding hair. He had big plans for both Jim and that business. Bill was a gentle, quiet spoken man with a low almost raspy voice, and eyes that smiled. Alice, Jim's mother, was a slender, attractive looking woman with short brown hair and brown eyes. She stood about five feet two which was why she always wore high heels. Alice always had a warm glow about her, with a continuous soft smile. Fred, Jim's older brother, looked a lot like Jim except that he was a little taller and perhaps slightly heavier. Jim and Fred liked each other as brothers, but never did much together, possibly because of the different personalities. They had completely different interests from one another.

Bill was going to teach Jim the business when he got back from the Nam. Fred was ordained as a Catholic Priest in 1968, and had no intention of having anything to do with his father's business, for obvious reasons. Jimmy was Bill's only hope of keeping his business dream alive. Bill talked about how the two of them were going to expand the business to something worthwhile to hand down to a grandson. Jimmy having kids; now that was something Bob used to kid Jim about all the time. Jim was never satisfied with any two girls at one time, let alone just one. He was a regular Casanova with two left feet. Wheeler used to go to the High School dances without a date , and always left with someone. That never ceased to amaze Bob, simply because Jim never knew how to dance. Jim would always say, "You don't have to dance to get to first base." Bill would just shake his head and say to Jimmy's mother, "Don't worry, he'll grow out of it." Jim used to feel that it was his duty to make up for his brother's "lack of the good life", as he called it. He often referred to his brother, with a smile, as Father Fred. It wasn't that Jim disapproved of his brother being a priest, it was because he loved to tease his brother.

Jim's parents wanted grandchildren in the worst way and Jim was their only hope. The odds were quite good of that happening with Jim, but their last names would probably be all different.

Bob, on the other hand, was head over heals in love with Sue Lucas, his sweetheart for the past four years. They had met in high school, at a dance. His good pal Wiener, as Bob sometimes called Jimmy, took one look at her that night and decided she was definitely his next victim. He turned to Bob with a fiendish look on his face until he saw the way his closest friend was looking at her, and an unspoken understanding was made. He chuckled and patted Bob on the back. "Go ahead Bob, ask her to dance. Turn on the old Hills charm. She'll be putty in your hands." he coaxed. Bob did, and that's all it took to light the flame. He touched her hand and Sue could almost feel his body temperature rise. She was a real knockout, and probably could have gone out with anyone she set her mind to, but after that night she chose him. With her blonde hair, big blue eyes and that great smile of hers', Bob couldn't help but fall in love. The moment was equally as magical for her as she gazed into his eyes. Without a doubt, a bond between the two was formed.

Bob's parents were particularly fond of Sue and treated her more like a daughter than Bob's girlfriend. She was the apple of their eye. The best way to describe Bob's parents' appearance would be to say they looked just like Ward and June Cleaver. Mike was a tall, thin, dark haired man, with a kind face and trusting smile. His full head of hair and smooth complexion, made him look younger than he really was. He was always well dressed and carried himself in a manner becoming a respected businessman. Mary was a tall, slender, soft spoken blonde that also carried her age very well. The sparkle in her eyes, showed the kindness in her heart. At one time she worked with Mike in their store. Now with the business doing so well, Mary was able to stay at home. She enjoyed working around the house and playing bridge once a week, with some of the neighbourhood housewives. Both of Bob's parents, were always understanding and willing to hear both sides of any story before drawing any conclusions. Anything that they would say was backed by logic. They were always certain that Bob or his sister, Judy, understood their reasoning for any disciplinary action they took. For that reason, Bob had always respected and looked up to them.

Like Jimmy's dad, Bob's father wanted him to follow in his footsteps and work in his hardware store. He was proud of his store, and rightfully so. It was a large store as hardware stores go; only a few blocks from the city college, close to the heart of the city. Years of hard work and a reputation as being an honest businessman, made both him and his store, valued and respected parts of the downtown community. When Bob was a young boy he would watch his father at work in the store. How important he looked, as he walked through the store, attending to anyone that may need assistance, Bob thought.

Oddly enough Bob really missed his sister. Quite often as a child, he fought with her, usually after she had gone to great lengths to provoke an argument. However, time changed their relationship and they learned to understand each other. His sister was a pretty girl, tall and slender with long brown hair and hazel coloured eyes. She worked at the hardware store until she married Tom two summers ago. They then moved to Dearborn Michigan, where Tom began work as an automotive engineer for the Ford Motor

Company. The last letter Mary had written to Bob, mentioned that Judy was pregnant and was due in early May. Often he would think of them and with a little concentration, he could still see their faces.

Jimmy never did go to college, as Bob did. However Bob only lasted one year before dropping out. That was a mistake. That made him, like so many others, a likely candidate for the draft. If he had thought things out more and taken the Vietnam situation a lot more seriously, he never would have left school.

The two friend's birth dates were not the only date that Jim and Bob had in common. Jim came to see Bob at the hardware store one day and was visibly upset. When he had told him he had been drafted, Bob felt terrible for him, but not as terrible as Bob felt for himself when he got home and discovered that the U.S. Army had not forgotten him. Bob was sure that this was nothing more than putting time in the Army and then coming home when it was done. He thought, "How bad could it really be?" He had no idea, but he was about to find out. The next thing the pair knew, they were dressed in green and going through basic training. Bob never did look good in green and the hair cut was definitely cramping Jimmy's style. It was all a very bad mistake, the two of them thought.

The sound of a radio transmission, brought Bob's thoughts back to the war. He looked over to Jimmy, who was staring at the trees without expression, and Bob asked him if he was thinking about home. He nodded and began to tell him, for the thousandth time, about the plans he was making for when he returned home. Needless to say, most of the plans involved women.

They often talked about growing up back home and their folks and loved ones that they left behind. Thinking about home was the only thing that kept anyone going there in the Nam. How Bob hated Vietnam, not that anyone sent there particularly liked it.

Staring blindly at the tree line Bob said, "What in the hell are we doing here? Why us? What did we do to deserve this?" Bob felt cheated, as though he was being punished for something he didn't do.

"Timing my friend, just fuck'n bad timing." Jim said in the same monotone voice. "But that's OK because all we have to do is last just thirty two more days and we're out of this hell hole... And the whole damn North Vietnamese Army can kiss my ass. They won't see me for dust".

Bob turned and looked at him and said, "You know what I've always liked about you Jimmy?"

"What's that?"

"You've always had a real charming way with words".

He turned to him and smiled as he nodded, " Yeah... I guess I do, don't I. Do you think I should run for mayor when we get back home?"

Bob shook his head and smiled, "Why certainly... but only if I write your speeches." His expression turned more distant, "I sure wish we were home now."

Jim gave him one of those big brother looks and said, "It's Sue isn't it. Look Bob, forget her. She hasn't as much as written you one single letter in over a year, except for a lousy Christmas Card. The least she could have done was write you a Dear John letter."

"Look, I don't want to hear this 'she,s found a hair-head' crap." Bob said raising his voice. "My folks said in their last letter that they saw her and she asked about me. She told them that she was too busy with school right now to write me or to drop over to their house. She's taking some pretty heavy courses right now. Besides, she has never been big on writing letters."

"Hey look pal, I'm sorry ..... I didn't mean to get you

upset. That's the last thing we need in this place." he said with sincerity, "We've got enough to worry about, just staying alive. I wished Charlie would attack or we would pick up and leave. Something, anything. This waiting is driving me crazy. It's got to be the worst part of being here."

"Hey you Goddamn shit-heads."

Oh shit, the pair thought, it was Sergeant Kalar and he had fire in his eyes. Staff Sergeant Kalar stood about six feet one, two hundred pounds, had piercing blue eyes, with brown hair and a mustache. Kalar always carried himself with authority. He had regular army written all over him.

"What in the hell do you two assholes think you're doing. While you"re socializing over casual conversation half the goddamn NVA could be waltzing through your tree line and kill the two of you and every son of a bitch in this fuck'n platoon." He shook his head and glared, "I'll have to get Buxton to ride your asses."

Sergeant Buxton was the squad NCO. Most of the time the men in the squad just call him Bux or Buxton. He was six foot, skinny and prematurely balding with black hair. A large gap between his two front teeth caused him to mispronounce his "S's". Any newcomers into the squad quickly picked up on it right away. It would cause them to laugh, but in silence, so not to piss Buxton off. At times the guys in the squad called him Eight Ball behind his back, just for fun.

Kalar was a different story ... everyone pretty much always call him Sarge or Sergeant to his face and never anything behind his back. He had earned the respect of each and everyone of the guys in the platoon.

Jim tried to say something but the Sarge cut him short. "Shut up. Keep your ears and your eyes open and watch the perimeter. Charlie is out there, and don't you think for one minute he's not. If you let your guard down, Charlie will have your sorry ass, I shit you not. You two dick heads have been here long enough to know at least that much. Now you leave the Nam in a body bag or on foot, it's up to you. You get lax ... you get dead. I'll be back to check on you two Bozos later, and you had better not be screwing up."

With those words of encouragement, he was off to check on the next hole, Beemer and Deluca. Deluca came to the Nam with Jim and Bob. Beemer, was a cherry. A cherry was a new guy and Beemer was certainly that. He had just arrived in country, the week before. Jim and Bob were sure the Sarge was about to give them the same hello he had just given the two of them.

Kalar was right though. He was always right. His being right was what kept most of them alive in the past.

Bob stared at Kalar as he thought back to when he first laid eyes on Sarge. It was shortly after he had landed in country. In fact, they were still on the tarmac at Da Nang. It was DAY ONE of what would seem an eternity. He was talking to a young lieutenant. When their conversation was over they saluted, then he turned and looked at each and every one of the new arrivals in the eyes.

"Welcome to Vietnam. I trust all of you had a pleasant flight from Saigon." he said with sarcasm. "I'm Staff Sergeant Kalar, I'll be your Platoon Sergeant while you're here. I am responsible for getting your little asses out of the Nam in one piece ... those of you who choose to listen to me, that is. Those that do, will in one years time, leave like the troops you see boarding the aircraft over there." He pointed to a group of tired expressionless soldiers boarding a plane. "Or for those of you choosing to be individuals, we have the BODY BAG. I suggest that you pay close attention to EVERYTHING I have to say, and do EVERYTHING I tell you to do, and WHEN I tell you to do it." He gestured towards a roll of occupied body bags. "Or that WILL be you. Think about it gentlemen, we play for keeps out here."

The sight of those body bags burned in Bob's mind, particularly the ones marked 'MEMBERS MISSING'. It was at that point Bob realized what he was really in for.

The Sergeant looked over everyone's expression to assure himself that he had made his point. "There's no need to sweat the Nam, as long as you stick to the program. You vary from my program ...... and you'll be one dead mother fuck. ....That was Lieutenant Cunningham you saw me talking to earlier. He too is new here. You will call him Lieutenant or Sir, whichever you prefer. You will not salute him in the field, unless of course you don't like him for some reason or another. This is because there are snipers out there gentlemen, and Charlie just loves killing G.I.s like ourselves. Particularly those of us who are saluted. Who knows, he might even mistake you for an officer if you're saluting the Lieutenant." Again he looked us over. "While you are here you will quickly learn that just because we are the United States Army, we are not going to walk all over these people like they do not exist. Now listen up ... because this is the way it really is and make no mistake about it. The Vietcong are not the backward peasant farmers you may think they are. They are a well disciplined, well trained, and highly motivated enemy who is more than willing to die for the cause. DO NOT underestimate them. It could very well be your last mistake. This is a one shot deal gentlemen, DON'T FUCK UP. ..... Your dog tags; you will wear one around your neck, the other on your boot lace. This is so we can identify you if you get your head blown off. ... It does happen. ... Time's ticking on people, so I'll give you the rest of the good news when we get to base camp. OK gentlemen, we've got a long drive ahead of us, so let's board the truck behind you." He pointed to a truck directly behind them, then turned to an awaiting jeep and climbed in.

The whole time he talked to them, no one moved, their eyes were fixated on him. It also seemed as if no one noticed the sounds of the aircraft landing and taking off in the background. All they seemed to hear was what the Sergeant had to say. They hung on his every word.

The men climbed into the back of the truck and drove off. Bob watched as the body bags disappeared from sight. That day, they were told how to get their mail out; instructed on personal hygiene in the field, and lastly, they filled out their last will and testament. Already Bob and Jim were wondering if they'd ever see home again. Bob didn't want to be there and he was angered that he was forced into this.

It's at times when one feels so cheated, that long forgotten events or trivia, come to mind. Such was the case with Bob. He couldn't help but think of something he had read in a magazine article once. The average age of the American soldier during World War II was twenty-six years old. Here in Vietnam, the age of the average soldier was nineteen. He shook his head wondering why Uncle Sam wanted to kill off him and his fellow Americans, who were still so very young?

In the first two weeks the platoon lost two of the guys that Bob stepped off the plane with; Koschuck and Scott. Whenever Bob saw one of the guys get killed, he'd get quiet and very distant, wondering if he was going to be next. It was hard, and it was very frightening. There was no safe place to be in Vietnam and they really didn't know who the enemy was. Neither sex nor age was a consideration to the Vietcong. They could be a fourteen year old boy, or a sixty-eight year old woman. That was the scary part. You could be feeding them candies and tending their wounds one minute, and they'd be shooting you in the back the next. No uniforms, no flags, no brass band, and absolutely no warning.

The first time Bob was in a fire fight he was terrified; terrified beyond anything he had ever felt before. He was totally conscious of what was happening around him, but it almost seemed like a dream. Bob could hear his heart pounding in his head, like a bass drum. It seemed to be beating quicker than normal. He was doing everything he was trained to do, but it was as if it wasn't him doing it; as if he was inside someone else and just along for the ride. The night was lit up by the moon and the stars, and with a little help from some good old American made flares. Bob saw a North Vietnamese soldier stop twenty meters in front of him, look directly at him and raise his rifle. As he did Bob fired his weapon directly at him. They must of fired at about the same time. Bob heard his adversary's round whiz by his head as his round caught Charlie in the centre of his chest. It threw him backwards as his weapon dropped from his hands. The look on his face was of absolute shock. The fear Bob felt was overwhelming.

For Bob, that was Day Ten in Vietnam. It was the end of the line for a young cowboy by the name of Greg Scott, from San Marcos, Texas. It was the first close look Bob had at the enemy. Charlie killed one of them and wounded two others. Guys in the platoon killed four of Charlie's and wounded an undetermined amount of them. The Cong managed to get their wounded out. Looking out at the dead, Bob thought he was going to be sick to his stomach. There was no preparing yourself for that. Knowing that just a moment ago they were living, breathing human beings. Yet through all of his mixed emotions at that moment, Bob was glad to be alive.

Bob Hills just stood there staring when Kalar came up behind him, slapping him on the back, and said, "Come on soldier they're not going to hurt you now... Remember this, it's better them than you."

They packed up Scott and their wounded and headed for a clearing where they were to meet the choppers. Sarge had radioed ahead for MEDEVAC. By the time they got to the L.Z. or landing zone, they could hear the choppers coming in.

Bob thought that after the first time it would get easier for him ..... but it never did. If anything, it just ate away at him ... slowly. It was no wonder a lot of the guys used drugs. How else could you cope with things around you. The death, destruction, and mostly ... loneliness. About the only other thing that would help were the thoughts of going home. Home to the loved ones they left behind. For Bob that was Mom, Dad, Judy, Tom and especially Sue. Her picture helped him through a lot of hard times. The dreams and hopes of the way it was going to be when he returned home to her.

Two days later his platoon, with others, were in another fire fight. This time they were dug in within the confines of their home base and the fighting was considerably worse. The sun was just going down when they came. Barbed wire was strung around the outer perimeter of the firebase, but that didn't stop those God damned Zips. They went through that barbed wire like it wasn't even there. Dying to these people seemed to mean absolutely nothing. This damn war to them was a great and noble cause, and to die for the cause was an honour. Bob and Jim sure as hell didn't share the same outlook.

They managed to fight Charlie back, but they paid a price to do it. Koschuck and Corporal Shriker's foxhole was in the direct line of entry of the V.C. and the N.V.A. coming through the wire. They didn't have a chance. That day the final casualty count on our side was three dead and six wounded, for Kalar's platoon alone. Bob had been in a foxhole with Deluca that day. Deluca, a tall, skinny guy, with a distinct southern accent, just looked at the aftermath, through his wire framed glasses, in disbelief.

"Hell's bells, Hills.......I better check my pants, I think I may have shit myself."

"Me too," Hills replied quietly,........ "me too."

There were dead Cong all around their foxhole. How they weren't killed was beyond them.

Bob Hills saw napalm being used for the first time that day. He'd never forget the stench of the burning petroleum and bodies. What a horrendous weapon. What incredible destruction. Jim was still talking about it two days later. What a hell of a way to go. It scared the shit out of them. Charlie had a lot of guts to attack their home base. The attack brought on a lot of talk about the Cong and his ability to attack in mass, when backed by N.V.A. regulars. To the men of the firebase, it was like the '68 Tet offensive they'd heard so much about. No one was interested in seeing an instant replay of that type of fire fight.

Another month of patrols, digging in, and some minor skirmishes with Charlie. Hills couldn't believe how hard they were being pushed. They were all just so damned tired. Then they finally were pulled back out of the fight for a rest and clean sheets. A whole four days for rest and relaxation, time to pull themselves back together. They drank beer, a couple of the guys smoked some shit, played some cards, and just took it easy. Although they were away from the fight, they never stopped thinking about it. They knew that they would eventually have to go back, and Charlie would be waiting.

Four weeks back home would have been a whole lot nicer

.... but under the circumstances, no one really could complain. Everyone had clean sheets, there was reasonably good food, and they were still alive.

Jim lost a hundred dollars playing poker, seventy-five of it his, and twenty-five of it was Hills. He was a lousy poker player; unfortunately he didn't think so. After those four short days the platoon was right back up to the D.M.Z. or the Demilitarized Zone.

One of the most boring details to pull was watch. You stay awake while the rest of the squad sleeps. Everyone took turns doing it. Night after night they would sit in the dark, waiting for the enemy to come. There's no one to keep you company but the sound of the crickets. The boredom would cause your mind to wonder with thoughts of being back home. Home ... it seemed like centuries ago, and light-years away. How they all wanted to be there. Then a distant noise would bring them back to reality.

Anytime the platoon went into a hostile area Bob was glad of one thing; that they had Sarge with them. If anyone was going to get them out alive, it was going to be him. He was smart and usually kept his cool. With the Lieutenant, that must have been pretty hard at times.

The Lieutenant, at the ripe old age of twenty-three, knew all there was to know about soldiering. He learned it all in R.O.T.C. and Lord knows, that would more than qualify him. Cunningham, LT as the men sometimes called him, looked like a weasel, with a long neck, a long pointed face and little beady eyes. He looked to be a little over six feet tall and weighed about as much as the average person five feet six. A good wind and he'd be history. His personality left a lot to be desired as well. If you looked arrogance up in the dictionary, you'd probably see his picture there as the example.

Bob didn't think he'd ever seen the Sarge as pissed off as

a time in September. They were dug in near a hill top and Charlie was building up troop strength down below, preparing for an assault. Sergeant Kalar was just making his rounds of the foxholes. Jimmy and Bob were together that particular day. Crouched down, he started telling them that Lieutenant Cunningham had decided to call in a fire mission on Charlie's suspected position. While Kalar was still talking to them the first rounds were fired.

He stopped talking half way through a sentence, his eyes widened and a look that would kill came over his face as he yelled, "INCOMING!" Turning to the direction of the Lieutenant, he screamed, "CHECK YOUR FIRE ... YOU GODDAMN ASSHOLE!" With those words of wisdom and comfort, off he went to finish his conversation with the young Lieutenant. By the time Sarge got to Cunningham the fire was corrected and hitting its proper target. Everyone was surprised that Cunningham even knew how to go about calling in the corrections.

Hills looked over to them to see what was happening and could tell that neither one of them was very happy with the other. Kalar turned his back to the Lieutenant and tried to walk away from him. Cunningham, insisting on having the last word, attempted to keep the Sergeant close at hand, so he could continue his defence. Lt would make a comment and Sarge would reciprocate with another, making the Lieutenant all the more angry.

They were making their way towards Hills and Wheeler's position and having a rather heated argument in a not-so-quiet whisper. Jim and Bob pretended not to be paying attention to them.

Cunningham was following Kalar at a brisk walk now and said, "Look, there were only three rounds that fell in the perimeter."

Sarge, still walking ahead of him, said, "That's three too

many, asshole. You didn't even ask for a single spotter round, shit for brains."

"Look Sarge, no one was even hurt."

"Thank fuck for that. I can't believe that no one questioned your coordinates."

"I told them I knew what I was doing. So I made a mistake. How else do you expect me to learn anything?"

"By asking, you fuck'n jerk."

"Hey there mister, you better stop treating me like an idiot. I'm your superior."

"You're not superior to shit and you are definitely a fucking idiot."

The Lieutenant grabbed Sarge by the arm and spun him around saying, "Look Sergeant, I'm an officer and you'll treat me accordingly or I'll have you court martialled." He looked at the Sarge as though he were something less than human.

That's when Sarge started pecking at Cunningham's chest with the tip of his finger, pushing him back with every peck. "Listen you simple-minded shit-head. You go right ahead and try and get me court martialled. Who knows, maybe we'll have a double court martial when they find out you tried to blow up your own position, dick-head. You kill one of my people over your goddamn incompetence, I'm going to frag your ignorant ass."

The Lieutenant now a little more cautious and defensive said, "Do you realize what you're saying? You're actually threatening my life."

Kalar, now looking right into his eyes, said, "I'm not threatening you. I'm making you a promise. So if you don't know what in the hell you're doing, you had better get someone who does, to do it for you. I'd really hate to have to shove a claymore mine up your ass ... Sir!"

Bob and Jim now knew where Kalar's priorities were,

without question ... and his men were it. Sarge turned and walked away; Cunningham didn't follow - instead he just stood there with a blank look on his face. Then looking around to see if anyone had witnessed the scene, he hurried off.

Cunningham continued to play leader, never taking into account the morale of his men. He volunteered his men for every patrol and job that would come up. Christmas was no exception. Bob's squad was in the jungle from the morning of Christmas Eve until the evening of Christmas Day. The Lieutenant was waiting for them at base camp when they returned. Kalar, with an apologetic look on his face, was standing next to him. LT was wishing them a Merry Christmas as the weary soldiers filed past. Sarge looked him up and down, shaking his head, as though Lt was crazy. It was LT's idea to send them out and all the men knew it. They were so tired that night, that they decided to celebrate Christmas the next day.

Mail had come in while Bob and the squad were out in the jungle. There were letters and packages for most of the guys. The surroundings didn't exactly scream holly, happiness, and ho ho ho, but as it turned out it wasn't so bad for Hills.

He had received two packages, three letters, and a card. The card had Sue's return address on the back. His heart began to pound and he became afraid of discovering what message awaited him, beside the traditional Merry Christmas. Though he never wanted to admit it, there was always the chance that she had met someone else and she would break it off between them. But she would do that in a letter not a Christmas card. Finally, he drummed up enough courage to open it and when he did, he sighed with relief. It didn't say much, just, MISS YOU, GET HOME SAFE, LOVE SUE. He wondered how time might have changed her. Even the way she wrote, her hand writing seemed to be slightly different somehow. But that didn't matter. He was still glad she wrote - it meant she still cared. The card gave him the reassurance he needed.

It was shortly after Christmas that Jim and Bob were able to take their well deserved R. and R. and at the same time. Kalar said he had to give it to them together, because neither one of them alone would be able to find their way back. One thing they had discovered about the Sarge was that, if he liked you, he teased the living shit out of you. R. and R. was definitely something Bob needed, at the time. He had visions of running off to a quiet retreat and relaxing. Jim insisted he knew the perfect spot for the two of them to take it easy. A place that would help them forget the war, somewhere peaceful. Next thing Bob knew they were on a plane heading for Bangkok, Thailand. For Wiener it was relaxing, to Bob it was like a cross between Mardi Gras and a gang war. Jim fit right in with the natives, it was truly incredible. You would swear he had lived there all his life. There wasn't too much over there that Jim didn't try. After all, he felt it was his duty to relax as he put it.

It wasn't long after they had arrived, before they found themselves in the red light district. Jim said that Hills should get off his chastity craze and leave that sort of shit to his crazy brother, the priest. Bob found it hard to think about making it with a hooker, without thinking about Sue. Jim was right though and Bob knew it. Bob had no idea of who she was seeing or what she was doing back home. It had been such a long time since he had laid next to a woman and after all, he was just human. Jim looked at Bob and said, "Hell, it's not like you're dating the hooker, she's only providing you with an essential service." Bob smiled and had to agree with him. Who knows if he'd ever make it home, hell live for today and with no regrets. Bob found one that caught his eye and an hour later, emerged from a room with the young Thai prostitute, feeling like a new person. Bob never thought that he'd ever stoop to paying for sex, but he never thought he'd be stuck in the bush for months on end, either.

By the time they got back from their R. and R. Jim had successfully spent not only all his money but Bob's as well. The thing that really bugged Hills was he didn't have a lot to show for it. Jim had bought himself a pair of lovely jade cuff links, not that he had any shirts with french cuffs, a cone shaped woven bamboo hat, and not to mention, the clap. That he got from someone he said he would be proud to take home to the folks.

The two were on the plane on their way back to Vietnam when Jim said, "I can't believe I went through all my money."

Hills looked at him with surprise and said, "Your money, how about my money?"

"Oh yeah ... I'll pay you back."

"Sure Jim, when? You have nothing at all left?"

He reached into his pocket and pulled out some coins. "Let's see now, one baht and sixteen satang."

Bob shook his head and said, "Great, you don't even have enough there for a Pepsi."

"Yeah well who's thirsty anyway?"

Bob pointed to his head, "Why don't you take that ridiculous bamboo hat off; you look like an idiot."

"Oh, you mean LT."

Bob smiled, "That's right buddy. Now, that should convince you to take it off."

"Actually, I rather like it." He slid down into his seat, pulled the hat down over his eyes and went to sleep.

Thinking of how he went through money made Hills glad that he was saving some for when he got back States Side.

That, of course, was if he lived long enough to spend it.

It wasn't long before they were back in the field and in the war again. As time went on, Bob Hills realized more and more just how much they were all living on borrowed time. How he prayed the day wouldn't come when he'd have to pay up that debt. That debt was a fact of life and in the Nam everyone had come to accept it, and that the time could be right around the corner. Bob was hoping that when it was his turn to face the Big Guy, it would be when he died of old age.

CHAPTER TWO

That was all behind them now. All Jim and Bob had to worry about was staying alive for the next thirty-two days. Kalar was heading their way now, to make sure that the two were alert and not goofing off.

He looked worried, and that meant trouble. He had a knack for knowing when there was going to be trouble and how bad it was going to be. He never told anyone specifics of what his hunches were, just that Charlie was coming. It was funny though, you could read it in his face, just as though you were reading a book. He was almost to Bob and Jim when distant shots rang out, like the Fourth of July. Charlie's favourite time to fight, was at night. But, like the day Koschuck and Corporal Shriker bought it, it was a half hour before dusk when the attack came.

"That's our ambush, they're here." he yelled. From the look on his face the whole damn N.V.A. was headed their way. It wasn't long before that fact was confirmed. By radio at first, soon after a few of the advancing N.V.A. troops ran into some strategically placed, claymore mines. Then the little bastards, showed their stinking faces.

First they fired rockets, followed by heavy machine gun fire more intense than anytime Bob had remembered. There was no question about it, this was a part of a major offensive for the N.V.A. and the Cong.

There were bullets and rockets whizzing past Bob and Jim's foxhole. Things were really getting crazy. The rockets stopped and the main assault began.

Jimmy's eyes got like saucers and he said, "Oh my God ..... oh .. my .. God."

It was a thick solid wall of North Vietnamese Soldiers

scurrying towards them. The two were firing at their adversaries, but their attempt to halt them seemed almost futile. At that rate they would be overrun in a few minutes. Now was a time when anger and revenge for all those Americans Bob had watched die at their hands, overcame the fear in him. He wasn't about to hide in that hole and let these damn gooks just come and kill him. If they wanted him they were going to pay for it. It was like Bob Hills became a completely different person. Perhaps he had gone temporarily mad, the kind of madness heros are made of. But at the time, it was what Bob felt he must do. Bob got partially out of the foxhole, yelled at his advancing adversary and opened up on them. For that brief moment he felt invincible. Hate and rage ruled all of his actions, the dark side of him had taken over.

Jim couldn't believe his friend's actions. He yelled to him, to get down, but Bob just kept on screaming and firing at his enemies. Jim got up and tried to pull Bob back into the foxhole, but a volley of bullets forced Jim back into the hole.

In the distance Bob could hear choppers approaching and all of a sudden their guns opened up on the N.V.A. assault force. They were cut to pieces. The little bastards had just retreated to the tree line when they were hit by a second air attack. This time it was an inferno from hell; Napalm. The blackened smoke of victory filled the sky, while screams of pain and desperation filled the ears of those who were left to hear their cries.

Bob sat staring at the awesome power of his 'Governments' military. The panorama of flames, smoke and destruction, made Bob feel small and as if his contribution to the war was insignificant. He was just starting to catch his wind and calm down from all of the activity when he realized there was someone close by, moaning. Bob spun around and there was Jimmy laying on the bottom of the foxhole, looking up at him with sad, helpless eyes. He had two bullet holes in him, one in the shoulder close to his neck, and another one in the centre of his chest.

"Bob, help me, please ... please help me. Dear God I'm dying," he whimpered, "God help me, don't let me die. Dear sweet Jesus I'm so sorry."

Bob jumped down and began to yell for a medic. He felt clumsy and useless, as he fumbled with his friend's shirt, trying to get a better look at his wounds. Bob thought he was going to be sick when he saw the blood exuding holes in his friend. "Jesus Christ Wiener, hang in there buddy, you're going to be alright. Just hang in there pal." Hills could see that Jimmy was losing a lot of blood and he had great doubt about his friend's future. "Don't worry pal, we'll get you out of here." Bob felt a chill running up his spine and couldn't stop shaking.

Jim could sense Bob's uncertainty about his condition and Jim became all the more frightened. Just then Sarge and Perelli, the medic, showed up.

Sarge looked down at the two in the hole and said in a sad whisper, "Oh shit ... no." Now yelling he called out, "Templeton, tell the Lieutenant we now have five men down, and we need that Medevac, ASAP!"

They lifted Jimmy Wheeler out of the hole so Perelli could bandage him and assess his wounds. Perelli was leaning over Jim when he looked up at Sergeant Kalar, as though to say he's not going to make it.

Hills saw the expression on Perelli's face, then got down on his knees next to Jim. He held Jim in his arms and said in a soft voice, now trying to hold back his tears, "You're going to be Okay. You'll be going home now buddy ... you're going home."

He looked up at Bob with tear swollen eyes and said, "I'm going to die, aren't I?"

"Hell no, shit you're going to be just fine." Bob said, now rocking him like he was an infant in his arms.

There was a stream of tears running down Jim's dirty cheek when he asked Hills, "Do you think God will forgive me, do you think he'll let me in? I mean we killed people over here. I didn't want to hurt anyone." Blood now ran from the corner of his mouth. "Do you think he'll still let me into Heaven?" He looked at Bob like a small, sad child asking his father for forgiveness.

Bob Hills couldn't fight the tears any more, "Shut up Wiener, you're not going to die! You're going home, you hear me, you're going home." Bob's tone of voice was now one of anger. He felt a big knot forming in his stomach, as he watched his best friend fight for his very life.

Still crying he said to Bob, "The Bible says, 'Thou Shalt Not Kill'. God I'm sorry." Just then his voice got softer and more calm. All expression on his face began to drain away. "Take ... me ... home ...Bob. Take ... me ... home." Those were his last words. His eyes closed slowly as though he were going to sleep.

Bob stared at Jim's lifeless body in his arms, never to laugh, never to cry again. Neither one of them ever thought the other would have died there in Vietnam. There were times when the two had wondered how they ever survived, but when it came right down to it, they never thought they would actually die. Bob felt as though part of him had died as well. The part that played high school pranks, went to school dances and played football. The innocence was gone. His youth, as well as his life long friend, died that day.

Sarge put his hand on Bob's shoulder and said in a comforting voice, "Are you Okay Hills?"

Hills slowly looked up towards him with swollen eyes and said, "Yeah .... I'm Okay."

Templeton was just heading towards them. Sarge turned to him and said, "Give Hills a hand getting Wheeler to the choppers."

Bob turned to them and in a quiet voice said, "No ... That's Okay I'll get him there myself. Please."

Kalar turned to Templeton again and said in a quieter tone of voice, "Police their frags and grab their weapons. We'll met you over at the L.Z."

Bob Hills picked up what was left of his best friend in his arms and looked at Sarge.

Kalar began to say something to Bob, but stopped before he could get it out. It was one of those times when you want to say something comforting, but there is nothing you could say, that would be appropriate. Kalar had that type of look, all over his face.

Looking away Sarge finally said, "Come on, I'll walk you to the choppers." Kalar put his right hand on Bob's left shoulder just to let him know he was there for him and walked next to him up to the waiting choppers. Jimmy hung loose, cradled in the arms of his friend. Wheeler's arms, legs and head hanging down, swinging, as if he was a rag doll. The front of his uniform was covered in blood, with the two bullet holes in plain sight. The Sarge just shook his head as he looked at Wiener and Hills. Kalar was no different than the rest of them in that he never got used to the senseless killing. And like the rest of the guys in the platoon, he did what he had to do to survive, except he had more than himself to worry about. Like a lioness watching over it's cubs he watched over all of his men.

Bob laid his childhood friend in a body bag and took one last look at all that remained of Jim Wheeler. In a soft compassionate voice, Bob said, "Goodbye buddy, I hope you're in a better place where you've gone....." Then the anger and frustration of loosing him became too much for Bob to control and he continued, "Damn you, how can I say good bye. ... You Son of a Bitch, you weren't suppose to die on me. Now what'll I say to your folks? How can I face them?...... Jesus .. Wiener.....Jesus I'll miss you my friend." His tears were now falling on Jimmy's chest. Bob then took his hand and held it for a moment, then stood up.

Perelli had stood by and watched until Hills was done saying good bye. Then he knelt down beside Jimmy and zipped up the black bag and tagged it while Bob watched. A part of Bob couldn't believe what he was seeing. This couldn't be happening, this couldn't be true, he thought. Hills remained until all the choppers had left and were out of sight. Now, for the first time in Vietnam, Bob Hills truly felt completely alone.

For the last month of Bob's tour in Nam he was just going through the motions. He found that things which would have bothered him before, were not as significant now. Hills wasn't worried about anyone so much as he was himself. Now more than ever, getting out was Bob's only concern.

The platoon was out on patrol one day, shortly after Jim's death. Bob's squad came across four Vietnamese bodies off the side of the road. They had been decapitated, their heads lined up all in a row like some morbid display. They didn't know who they were or why they were killed. That didn't much matter. The bodies were far from fresh, so who ever did it was long gone. A few weeks earlier, the sight of these heads and bodies would have made Bob ill, but now since the death of his friend, it meant nothing. The sight of Jim dying in Bob's arms changed Bob's outlook on the cruelties of war. All that remained in him was a great void, he'd had enough of this war. Now, all Bob Hills wanted was to go home.

Bob found that Sarge was watching him a lot now. Kalar told Hills that he had that, "I don't give a damn, I've had it with being here." look in his eyes. And that could be dangerous for not only Bob, but everyone in the platoon. The troops there term it, "Short-Timer's Fever", short-timer being someone only having a short time until their rotation back home. He was right. Bob found himself becoming irritable with people around him. He was getting to the point, where he didn't give a shit about orders. If the ememy wanted to kill him, he figured that they'd have to find him first. Whether it was the Vietcong or the N.V.A. , their cousins to the north, Bob felt someone had a bullet with his name on it. Someone was going to try to kill him and all Bob knew was that he wasn't going to go out of his way to give them a chance to do it. He'd had it with the war and he began to loose his will to fight.

They were on yet another, of what seemed to be an endless number of patrols. This time they came across a village that intelligence said could be a hot spot. Intelligence, now there was a contradiction in terms. This was not supposed to be just any village. This one, they were told, was suspected of being a V.C. supply camp. The platoon spread out forming a defensive perimeter, while the Lieutenant, or LT as Kalar called him, and the NCO's decided how they were going to execute this military manoeuvre. They had been ordered to verify the reports that the village was, in fact, being used to house V.C. supplies. Cunningham and his platoon would take appropriate actions if it was in fact true. To Hills it wasn't a very significant village, or at least not a very big one. It was located not far from the Laos border. After LT gave his instructions to his NCO's, Kalar gave his to LT. Then LT gave his revised instructions to the NCO's, and in turn they passed them on to the men. The village stood before them, about five-hundred meters away. To Bob it was like a cobra, waiting for them to get close enough to strike. If the information that intelligence received was correct, then they could be walking into a hornets nest.

Sergeant Buxton huddled his men together under protective cover and started to fill them in on what their fearless leader, the illustrious LT, had come up with.

Buxton wasn't smiling when he said, "The Lieutenant wants this squad to lead in and the rest of the platoon will be following on our flanks and taking up the rear."

Hills spoke up right away and said, "Why in the hell does it have to be us?"

Buxton now pissed off said, "Shut up Hills, you're going to do what you're told to do. I'm not any more crazy about the prospect of getting my ass shot off than anyone else around here is. Besides it's our turn, Kalar isn't showing any favouritism."

"It's just that I haven't got a whole lot of time left to go," Bob said, "and I've put in my time. I've got a hell of a bad feeling about this."

Buxton looked right in Bob's eyes and said, "You're lucky my friend, this plan was Sergeant Kalar's idea. LT, that num-nuts, wanted us to go in on our own and radio back our findings. Then the idiot was going to march in like Napoleon Bonaparte with the rest of the fuck'n platoon behind him."

"I still don't like it Buxton. I've got this strange feeling about this."

Kalar was walking towards them and had heard what Bob Hills was saying. "What's your problem Hills?"

"I have a real bad feeling about this one Sarge."

"A real bad feeling. I'll give you a real bad feeling Hills." Kalar was glaring at Bob now. "If I kick you in the nuts you'll have a real bad feeling shit head. I'm going in with

Sergeant Buxton and this squad here, so what ever happens to you, happens to me. Hell, some of you guys do ten or eleven months here and suddenly you get superstitious. This is my third tour and I'm not superstitious, just cautious; but I still do my job Hills." Looking at Bob, he saw the genuine fear in Hills' eyes. Then he put his arm around Bob's shoulder and said with a devilish smirk, "I wouldn't have you do anything I wouldn't do myself. In fact I'll be right next to my old pal Hills, here. What do you think about that Hills?"

"Great .... just fuck'n great Sarge."

Kalar looking at him said, "I thought so. Now as for the rest of you, let's get our thumbs out of our asses and start earning our combat pay."

The squad got ready to move out; reluctantly Bob followed them. But at least he felt better about it, knowing that Kalar was going to be by his side. He still had a feeling that something was going to happen to him. Perhaps it was because he only had a short time to go. How he wished he was home.

They were scattered across an open field and walking towards the village. Miraculously no one had noticed them closing in, until they got within thirty meters of the village. Then someone certainly did. All of a sudden there were children and women screaming.

Kalar, Buxton and his men, swept through the village like a swarm of locusts and in a matter of minutes, the entire village was completely over run by the platoon. The men went through every nook and cranny looking for anything that would tie them to the V.C. Then the Lieutenant came up with another brilliant idea.

LT yelled to the NCO's, "I want all the villagers in a line over here," and he pointed to one side of a clearing in the centre of the village, "then I want you to take all the children and line them up over there." He pointed to the opposite side of the clearing. "Oh, and Sergeant Kalar, I want the two lines of these gooks to face one another, too."

Kalar turned and looked at the Lieutenant as though he had finally flipped and said, "What in the hell are you doing?"

"Just do it Sergeant!" he demanded.

"Sir this better not be what I think it is."

"Kalar, trust me."

They did as he said and stood waiting for his next ingenious command.

"Sergeant Buxton, take your men and line them up in front of the children with their weapons at the ready. Now we'll get some answers."

Kalar yelled out, "Are you crazy, or just plain stupid ... you ASSHOLE!"

Cunningham now pointing his finger at Kalar said, "I've finally had enough of your insubordination Sergeant."

Kalar walked right up to him and said in a low voice, "I don't happen to give a fuck ...Sir." If looks could kill, LT would have been a dead man.

In a low voice LT said to Kalar, "I was only going to throw a little scare into them, Sergeant. Now let me handle this my own way. Now, you can just give me a snappy salute and do what I told you to do."

"Okay....... whatever you say.......But if anyone gets killed, I swear I'll see you do time in Leavenworth."

"Just do what I said, Sergeant." Cunningham said in a demanding tone of voice.

Kalar took one step back and gave LT a half ass salute and said, "Yes Sir!"

LT smirked with victory and returned the salute, when a shot rang out.

"SNIPER!" Kalar called as everyone in the platoon dove for cover.

Bob spun around in the direction that the shot came from. As he hit the ground, he saw the sniper standing there in the open with a rifle in hand. Hills started shooting and let off maybe six rounds before the sniper fell to the ground.

When Kalar saw the sniper hit the ground, he called out to the troops, "Hold your fire!"

Bob got up cautiously and with his rifle at the ready, walked over to the killer. It wasn't a sniper, not what he would term a sniper. It was just some kid with a .22 calibre rifle. The sound of the villagers screaming and crying filled his head. The rest of the guys got to their feet and kept them back at gun point. His face lost all expression as he stared at the little girl lying there. She couldn't be any more than thirteen years old. What was she doing with that gun; where did she get it? Stunned, Bob stood looking at her for a moment. Then he ran behind one of the huts and was sick to his stomach. "Oh God forgive me, I'm so sorry, forgive me." He killed some poor kid who probably thought that she was saving the lives of the village children. That son of a bitch, Cunningham. The whole damn war was just getting too crazy for him any more.

Kalar stood next to the girl looking at her, shaking his head and then kicked the rifle away from her. After a moment he walked over to Bob and said, "Are you Okay Hills?"

"Yeah ... I'm Ok. Did anyone get hit?"

"Yeah, our fearless leader."

"How is he Sarge?"

"Dead. You're hunch was right. What a fuck'n mess....That was pretty good shooting, Hills"

"Yeah well if I had realized it was just some poor kid I may not have been so God Damn quick to fire."

Bob began to turn away when Kalar grabbed Bob by his arm and spun him back around. "Listen to me Bob, you better get away from that line of thinking, soldier. What if you didn't do what you did and that kid decided to take a few more of us along with her, what then? You did what you had to do to save the lives of the people in the platoon. You remember that. If you hesitate ... you or somebody else is dead."

"Do you really think that kid was out to kill the whole damn platoon with a twenty-two calibre rifle? Hell she was just probably trying to stop that nut bar from killing the village kids."

"We don't know that for sure, Hills. LT was wrong, but so was she. We don't have the luxury of asking questions before we start firing. You remember that. Now, go help the others secure this village."

The platoon finished the operation and rounded up two V.C. suspects for the South Vietnamese authorities to question. The only reason they were suspects, was because of their violent attitudes towards American troops. Of course, if someone shot a little girl in your home town, you'd probably develop a poor attitude towards the ones who killed her, too. The village was searched a second time, but other than the twenty-two calibre rifle the kid used, no weapons were found. There was no physical evidence that the village had V.C. ties. What a waste of human life.

They returned to base camp, and found Captain Hamilton waiting for them. The captain, a tall, thin, soft spoken man, was smoking a cigar, standing outside the HQ. Hamilton was in his early thirties, 'though he didn't look it with his premature grey hair. He was always level headed and very popular with the men. The Captain seemed to be looking for someone, probably Sergeant Kalar.

Then he spotted him, "Staff Sergeant Kalar."

"Sir."

"Can I see you for a minute?"

"I'll be right there, Sir." Kalar finished giving his NCO's their instructions then walked over to the Captain.

"Yes, Sir?" Kalar said.

"I have to write a letter to Lieutenant Cunningham's family back home. Could you tell me what happened out there?"

"For the family, Sir?"

"For the family sergeant."

"What you might want to tell them, Sir, is that he was a nice man with a big heart. But that would be a pile of crap, Sir."

"Come on for Pete's sake, help me out."

"Okay. The Lieutenant was giving food and medical supplies to the villagers when he was savagely murdered by a sniper. The villagers are still mourning his sudden and tragic death."

The Captain just stared in silence for a moment then said, "That's good ... that's very good. I particularly like the part about the villagers still mourning his tragic death. Now Sergeant, just for the hell of it, what really happened out there?

"Sir?"

"Come on Sergeant, give it to me..........and without the frills."

"The way my actual report will read, Sir?"

"That's your classified report, Sergeant. Remember that. Now, what happened out there?"

"Sir, may I speak freely?"

"Hey Dan, we've known each other a long time. Now, how about it?"

"Okay Sir. The Lieutenant was a dumb fuck, Sir. A search

33

of the village turned up nothing initially. Lieutenant Cunningham had us round the villagers up and had us confine them to a clearing in the centre of the village. Then he had us separate the children from the adults, moving them to opposite sides of the clearing. He wanted the children in a single line. That's when he ordered Sergeant Buxton's men to form a firing line in front of the children with their weapons at the ready."

"HE WHAT?"

"He was going to scare the villagers into giving us information."

"And you let that idiot do that?"

"The hell I did ... Sir!"

"What did you say to him?"

"I told him that if something happened, I'd report the incident and see him do time in Leavenworth. He knew exactly how I felt about his dumb plan. I never would have allowed him to take his plan too far. Scare tactics, shit, they probably weren't even V.C."

"Okay, Okay. So how did he get killed?"

"A young kid, a girl ... thirteen maybe fourteen, popped him with a twenty-two when he ordered us to line Buxton's men up."

"I don't understand how that girl showed up with a weapon. Where did she get the rifle? How did your men miss her when they searched the village?"

"I really don't know Captain. I'll tell you one thing though Sir, that man was a real special breed of jerk, and he played it right to the bitter end. Which version are you going to tell his folks, Sir?"

"The first."

"Figures."

"What do you want me to do Sergeant? I'll admit, the guy wasn't the best I've ever seen, but things are bad enough

State Side without having people back home thinking we have people like him running around."

"So we're going to cover for him?"

"That's right. If word got out what this guy was really like, people would think we're all like that. I happen to think that for the most part, we have some pretty fine people over here. I won't let someone like him, because of his mistakes, tarnish the reputation of some damn fine soldiers. I've lost a few good friends over here. They died doing what they thought was right for the world. I won't do anything to destroy their memory. ... That will be all Sergeant."

"Yes Sir." Kalar saluted and left.

Bob overheard Kalar telling Buxton about the conversation he had with the Captain. Hills couldn't believe it. LT was the biggest goof ball he had ever met. Shaking his head he thought, at least his chances for survival had improved with good old LT out of the way. But even with LT out of the way, he was still uneasy.

The Sarge, knowing that Bob was getting more jumpy by the day, watched him all the more. He must have been afraid that Hills would do something stupid and get himself or someone else killed. Kalar saw to it that Buxton wouldn't use Hills for point and tried to keep the pressure off Bob as much as possible. Bob Hills prayed every night for forgiveness. He couldn't believe that he killed that poor little girl. The girl wasn't the only thing on Bob's mind, he kept thinking of the day when he would get his orders and he'd be heading home. Every time his squad went out on patrol he became more frightened and Kalar could see it in his eyes. Then the day came when Hills' orders to head home finally arrived.

Hills had just come back from a patrol out of the jungle. The squad had made contact but managed to come out of it with only one man wounded. It seems almost cruel to feel relieved that one of the men had been shot, but when you consider what could have happened out there, it was understandable and forgivable. Bob had sat down and started to read one of his letters from his father. He kept all the letters he got and read them over and over again. It was his way of being with family, it helped him fight the tremendous loneliness he felt inside. Hills was looking at a picture of his folks in the letter, when out of the corner of his eye he noticed Kalar coming towards him. Turning to Kalar, he could see that he was looking right at him. What ever he had to say, it was specifically to Bob.

He stopped right in front of him and said, "This is it Hills, your orders just came through. You're out of here. Come on I'll walk you to the choppers."

"You mean I'm out of here? I'm going home?"

The Sarge just shook his head and said with a smile, "That's right asshole, your out of here."

A smile came to Bob's face and he said with relief, "Fuck'n A Sarge, Fuck'n A. Finally I'm getting the fuck out of this hell hole." He sprang to his feet. Bob couldn't believe it. He had wanted out of there from the day he had arrived and now, at last, it was happening. It was really time to check out. As Jim would have said, "The whole damn N.V.A. can kiss my ass."

Bob Hills felt a lump in his throat. He didn't know whether to cry, sing, or just yell. He looked around at the guys who were trying to rest up after the patrol. Templeton and Perelli were close enough to hear what Sarge had to say. Perelli came right over and shook Bob's hand.

With a smile and a tear in his eye, Perelli said, "Listen dude, you take it easy and save us some of that beer back there in the real world."

Bob just smiled and said, "Well I'll do my best, but no

promises."

Templeton, with a low voice, said, "Take it easy, Bob."

He had a sad smile on his face. He was glad Bob was getting back, but he was wishing it was his turn to rotate instead of Bob's. You could see it in his eyes.

The Sarge put his hand on Bob's shoulder and said, "Enough of these sad goodbyes. If you don't get your ass in gear, that chopper will be leaving without you and it'll be a 'sad you're fuck'n back', instead. Now grab your kit and let's get going."

"Yeah ... you're right. I sure as hell wouldn't want that. Lets get going Sarge." Bob scrambled to grab his kit.

Kalar walked Bob over to the choppers. When they got there they stopped and he said, "Listen you take care of yourself and stay out of trouble."

Bob smiled, "You too. Stay out of harm's way."

"I'll do my best."

"Sarge are you ever going to call it quits over here?"

He just nodded his head with a sort of far away look on his face. "Yeah I've had it." He looked tired and depressed, "We can't win this war Hills, and I'm getting out before the final crunch comes down from the top. Maybe I'll put in for Europe; anywhere as long as I get the fuck out of here. Besides I've always wanted to go to Europe. No fighting; just a lot of good times. They've got great beer there too, Bob." He paused for a moment. "Look Bob, I wanted to tell you how sorry I was about Jimmy Wheeler. I know you grew up together and you were close."

Bob looked at him and said, "It's Okay, I know." Then he broke into a smile and said, "You know what he used to say about you whenever you were in a huff?"

Kalar looked at Hills with a disturbed almost hostile look on his face, "What?"

With a smile still on his face, Bob said, "You were all

upset because your panty hose were too tight."

Kalar turned away and the look on his face slowly turned into a smirk. Then he said, "That dumb son of a bitch." Looking at Bob, now in a more serious tone he said. "You did real good out there, Hills."

Bob looked at him with an uncaring expression on his face, "Yeah, right." Bob could see the hurt in Kalar's face. Hills put on a half smile and said, "Hell, we all did good out there Sarge; damn good."

He gave Bob the same half smile back and said, "You take care of yourself." shaking his hand. Then the two wrapped their arms around each other and hugged as brothers would.

Bob found himself getting choked up with emotion and he said, "I'll never forget you Kalar. You live through this you son of a bitch."

"Go on and get on the damn chopper, Hills. Get the fuck out of this damn place."

He started to board the chopper and then he turned and said, "Hey Kalar, we've always called you Sergeant, Sarge or Kalar and no one ever gave a second thought to your given name. What in the hell is your first name, Fred, George, Alice...?"

He shook his head and smiled. "It sure as Hell isn't Alice. It's Dan, Daniel Michael Kalar."

"Well take care of yourself, Daniel Michael Kalar."

Bob boarded that chopper, heading for Da Nang. Finally he was leaving that place. As they took off he looked down at the Sarge; he was waving. Then turning from the chopper, he began calling out orders to some of the troops. He looked tired - as though he was ready to call it quits himself, as he had said. He was certainly one of the best human beings Bob Hills had ever met, and he deserved to get out of that hell hole alive. Bob sure hoped he would. He was going to miss him. A part of Bob was relieved and happy to be leaving, but another part of him felt empty and sad. Everyone that did time in the Nam, left a certain amount of themselves behind when they left there. It was a sense of being torn and Bob Hills certainly felt the paradox of emotions at that very moment. He would never forget Sarge, Deluca, Beemer, Buxton, Perelli, and all the others. He especially would miss Jimmy. Bob was certain a part of Jim's soul stayed behind, when they put his remains on that chopper. Bob only wished Jimmy's last eleven months on earth could have been at home among his family and friends.

As the L.Z. went from sight Bob said his goodbyes, to the war torn country side of Quang Tri Province, to the war itself, to the Hundred and First Airborne, and to Jimmy Wheeler, the best damn friend anyone could have ever asked for. Bob Hills was going home, or at least the bigger part of him was. While he was in Nam, he had kept a rough journal of his stay there. Not to remind him of Vietnam, but rather to remember those whom he had served with there. The guys in the platoon, they were what was worth remembering. Only they knew what it was really like.

"Goodbye Jimmy. Your memory will live with me the rest of my days. I promise you I'll do what I can to comfort your folks. I only wish that I was able to do something to help you. Forgive me, my friend. I'm sure that the Lord forgave you, for any sins you had committed. Save a place for me my dear friend ..... save a place for me."

CHAPTER THREE

From Da Nang Bob was flown to Saigon where he was put on board a C-141 service aircraft. The flight took him to Manila in the P.I. then on to Hawaii and finally to Travis Air Force Base in Fair Field, California. From there Bob received a GTR or Government Travel Order, enabling him to catch a commercial flight to Fort Dix, New Jersey. There he spent the next two days going through a physical and interviews to complete his out processing. It felt good to be back in the States and his parents were delighted to hear his voice. He tried several times to get a hold of Sue Lucas, but unknown to him, her parents were out of town and she was spending her time with her new boyfriend. He gave her the benefit of the doubt and left it up to his mother to tell her, he was coming home.

Flying out of New Jersey was with little incident, other than the odd person looking at him oddly. "I guess I shouldn't have worn my uniform." he thought to himself.

He was glad when the plane landed. The long trip home was finally over. When he got off the flight he looked around for Sue and his folks. When they weren't there he went to pick up his luggage. That's when he got his first taste of how some of his fellow Americans felt about him and his involvement in Vietnam. He was waiting for his luggage to come through the conveyor when someone yelled from behind him, "Hey you.... you stupid God damn warmonger."

Bob turned around and saw a young, long haired boy, maybe sixteen or seventeen years old. He had no facial hair, but made up for it in acne. Bob looked in his eyes with a hard aggressive glare, one he usually saved for Charlie just before shooting him. The boy's face lost all expression and he turned and ran. Bob wanted to chase him down and kick the living shit out of him, but that only would have proved him to be right about Bob. Hills felt enraged. Bob thought to himself, "He had no right to say that about me. He had no idea what we went through over there and the price some of us paid." As he watched for his bags, he could feel people staring at him from behind. Maybe Bob was some sort of freak and no longer belonged with the rest of society. He grabbed his luggage and headed for the main reception area where he was certain to meet his folks.

When Bob saw them, he rushed to greet them and hugged them both. His mother, who had tears in her eyes, when she saw him, was unable to move. She was totally overwhelmed with joy. Bob thought his father was going to break his back when he hugged him. Then Bob noticed them standing behind his mother. Jim Wheeler's parents. Bill had his arm around Alice's shoulder, they were half smiling, but their eyes were so very sad. You could see it in their faces, the disappointment that Jimmy was not alive as Bob was, and home with them.

Bob Hills went over to Alice and Bill and hugged them, his eyes swollen with tears. Perhaps it was the guilt he felt for not taking care of Jim, that made Bob react to them in this manner. He never thought to prepare himself for this. It was very hard for the Wheeler's to see Bob coming back without their son standing next to him, the way they always were. Bob wished there was something he could say or do to console them. He was experiencing the helplessness Kalar had when he was caught for words when Jim died. If Fred had only been a doctor, a lawyer, or even a plumber, anything but a priest. Vietnam took away their only chance of having grandchildren. It took away their youngest son and all of their dreams for the future.

Bob asked where Sue was and his mother said that something had come up. She said she couldn't make it because of an exam she was writing. Bob detected his mother's difficulty with an answer and knew something was up, he and Sue were definitely finished. At some point in time, for whatever reason, she had called it quits and hadn't bothered to tell Bob about it. Jim was right all the time. Bob thought it best, not to push the issue any further for the time being, so he changed the subject and asked about his sister, Judy. Mike, Bob's father said she was fine and so was the baby, Kaitlyn Elizabeth. Tom, Judy, and Kaitlyn were coming down for a visit a week from Saturday.

Another flight arrived and the reception area began to fill with even more people. Mary, Bob's mother suggested they leave, so Bob gathered his things and they left the airport and headed for home. The Wheelers followed them in their own car.

In the car on the way home, Bob's parents were talking and paid no attention to the radio. Bob did, and it was all about the war in Vietnam, as well as the anti-war movement back home. It seemed like Bob had come home to a nightmare. The American people hated the war and everything about it. He was anxious to get home, so he could take his uniform off and get into some jeans. At that moment, he could only think of disassociating himself from the damn war in south east Asia.

They drove down the old street and slowly pulled into the paved driveway. The house was a large white, wooden, two storey home, with light blue window shutters which matched the shingles on the roof. There was also an attached garage with an ornate weather vane on it's roof. Neatly trimmed shrubs decorated the front of the house, as did the stone walkway which led from the drive to the front door. The house hadn't changed much on the outside since Bob had left and once inside he found the same held true. It was as though he had never left. Bob excused himself while he took his things up stairs to his old room. They had kept his room exactly the way he had left it, except for an upholstered arm chair that was placed in the corner of the room. He put his bags on the bed and walked over to the window to look out. His room overlooked the front of the house and he watched as the Wheelers pulled into the drive behind the family car. Bob looked around the eight by ten foot bedroom, at the single bed, the familiar high school pennants on the wall and the dresser with the small crack in the upper left hand corner of the mirror. God, how it seemed as though Vietnam was just a bad dream. The room's walls were painted a soft green to match his bed spread and curtains. A large photograph of himself, when he was ten, with his parents at the beach, hung on one wall. A small desk and chair, occupied one corner of the room. Next to the bed was a small table with a lamp with a light green shade. The room was small, but Bob always found it comfortable.

Just then Mary walked in. Smiling she said, "Why don't you unpack later. The Wheelers are here and they're really excited about you being home. It would mean a lot to them. You can unpack when they leave and I'll give you a hand."

He nodded, "Yeah, sure." Looking at the chair he said, "Why is this chair here? Not that it really matters."

She looked at the chair with a sad smile on her face and said, "That's where I would sit sometimes when I was alone and I wanted to be near you." She looked up at him with tears in her eyes.

He walked over to her, put his arms around her and gave her a big hug. "I'm glad I'm home, Mom.", he said in a heavy voice.

"Me too," she replied, "me too."

Bob walked over to the bed and sitting down he said, "I don't understand Sue. Except for a Christmas Card, she didn't write me a single letter. What gives? Have you talked to her or seen her at all lately."

She looked at him and said, "She isn't the same, she's changed and she's found someone else."

His first reaction was to hang on to his dream that helped keep him going in Nam. "That's impossible, there's no way," Bob said, "she sent me a card at Christmas. In it she wrote that she missed me and that she loved me."

Mary looked at him with guilt written all over her face, "I sent the card, and I had Marlene next door write that in it for me. I didn't want you to worry about her while you were over there. I thought you had enough to worry about and I knew she wouldn't write you."

He looked at her and said, "I wrote her countless letters and none of them were ever answered." Bob could see the guilt in her. "I understand. It was wrong, but I understand you were trying to help. She should have let me know though, someone should have let me know. I had the right to know where I stood, and where our relationship stood." Bob felt sick. He couldn't believe she dropped him like that. No explanation, no goodbye, just gone out of his life. He was hurt and at the same time he was angry.

"I'm sorry Bob, I didn't want to lie to you. I hope you'll never hold it against me. "she said, now worried she had done the wrong thing and it would affect his trust in her.

"Mom, don't worry. It's Okay. Let's go downstairs and see the Wheelers." He gave her a half smile.

She smiled back and the two headed down to the living room. Bob was glad he now knew where he stood with Sue, but he still wished it wasn't so.

The Wheelers were sitting down on the couch when the

two walked into the living room. They smiled and Bill asked Bob to sit down and join them. Mike brought Bob out a beer and Bob sat down in a chair facing them. Bob looked at the beer in his hand and thought, "My first beer back home, this is going to be good", and he took a huge gulp. He looked at everyone in the room and said, "It's great to be home." There was a sparkle in his eyes and he had a big smile on his face when he said it.

Bill cautiously said, "Well, we're really glad that you're back. It must have been terrible over there. I know the Second World War was pretty bad."

Mrs. Wheeler interrupted him and said, "Lets not talk about the war. Let's just forget it." She started getting emotional.

Bill looked at her and nodded his head and said, "You're right. So Bob what do you think you're going to do now that you're out of the Army?"

Bob shrugged his shoulders and replied, "I thought I knew, but now that I'm actually home I'm not sure what I want to do. When I was over there I thought I'd go back to College, but now I think I'll take a while and think about it. Working in the store sounds good, but not for a little while. I really do need a rest. A little time to get used to being here."

Mike jumped in and said, "Yes, I think that's smart. Give yourself a chance to adjust to being back and just relax. You could probably use a bit of a holiday. Then I'll put you to work." He laughed.

Bob had finished his beer and got up to get another when Mary said, "Sit down Bob, I'll get you another beer."

He turned to her and with a smile on his face said, "No, that's Okay. I've been waiting a long time to go into that fridge and help myself to a beer. Or two, or three." His smile now getting bigger all the time.

Bob had no sooner left the room and Bill got up and said, "If you don't mind I could do with a refill myself." It was always 'feel at home and help yourself' with the Wheelers and the Hills.

Bob was getting a beer out of the fridge when Bill walked in. Bob looked over and saw Bill looking at him. He knew Bill was anxious to talk to him about Jimmy.

"I needed a beer. Could you grab me one while you're there Bob?" Bill said, trying to put Bob at ease.

"Sure thing."

He grabbed an extra beer and handed it to Bill. Looking up, Bob looked directly into his sad eyes. Bill looked as though he was ready to burst, but just couldn't get the questions he was dying to ask, out. Then he did, "Bob, I know this isn't a good time, but I have to ask you this. Did Jimmy suffer when he died? I know it's not a fair question to ask you and I hate to put you through this, but I've got to know.... please."

Bill's tear-swollen eyes looking at him and the nervousness in his raspy voice nearly broke Bob's heart. He thought about what Jimmy would want him to say. Bill must have been waiting since the news of Jimmy's death, to ask Bob about it. So he told him what he wanted to hear, to put his mind at rest, "No.... he didn't suffer Bill. He died in my arms. He was hurt pretty bad, but we got to him right away and pumped him full of Morphine. He went quickly and peacefully."

Bill made a poor attempt to hide the tears and said, "Thank God for that, at least." He put his hands over his face. "God, how I miss him."

"I'm so sorry Bill. There was nothing any one of us could have done for him."

Bill, now trying to smile through the pain, said, "I know you did all you could. Thank you, I know that it must have been hard for you to talk about it.... I really do appreciate you telling me about it.... I had to know.... Thanks."

Bob half smiled and pointed to the door saying, "Come on, let's join the others before they send in a search party for us. Dad will think we're in here drinking up all his beer."

Bill, again wiping his eyes with his hands and trying to smile, said, "Yeah you're right, he would think that."

They went back into the living room to some smiles and laughter. The two sat back down and Bob took a big swallow from his beer bottle. Bob looked at his father and Bill and said, "So tell me, is Del's still around." Del's being a small neighbourhood bar.

Mike said, "It sure is, but I don't think you'd recognize Del at all. He went on another of one his diets and gained thirty-five pounds."

Everyone began laughing as Mike showed Bob with his hands, just how big Del's stomach was.

There was some more small talk that lasted another hour or so, then the Wheelers left for home. Bob could see it in Bill's face as he was leaving that he was glad Bob had talked to him about Jimmy. As the Wheelers were walking out the door, Bill turned and gave Bob a smile that expressed his thanks. Bob smiled and nodded his head in response. Bob was glad that he was able to set his mind to ease.

Bob then went into the study to give Sue a call. Mike's study was large with dark walnut wainscotting and a dark green felt wall-covering on the top half of the walls. There were brushed-brass wall lights which matched the lamp on the edge of the dark oak desk. Next to the lamp was a black office style telephone. The desk blotter mat was dark green with a rich dark leather boarder. This room was Mike's pride and joy, with it's wildlife pictures on the walls and it's large bookcase filled with leather bound books. Bob sat in Mike's black leather swivel chair and picked up the phone. He dialled Sue's phone number. His heart was pounding, and he was frightened of what she would have to say. With every ring the knot in his stomach got bigger. Then a voice answered the phone. It was Sue's mother.

"Hello Mrs. Lucas, it's Bob. Is Sue home?" he said nervousness in his voice.

"Bob? Bob Hills is that you? " she said with surprise, "Are you home now?"

"Yes I am, Mrs. Lucas." he replied, "How is everyone there?"

"Fine, just fine. I'm so glad you're home safe and sound. I was so sorry to hear about Jim. It must have been terrible over there." She had honest concern in her voice.

"Is Sue home Mrs. Lucas?" he repeated himself.

"I'm afraid she's not Bob. She spends a lot of time at the school newspaper." Her words now becoming slower and more thought out, "Bob, she's seeing someone else. She's changed. She's still a wonderful girl, but she's involved in the newspaper, an anti-war group, and it's all she ever talks about."

"I guess that just about says it all. Maybe I should have stayed home, grown my hair long and worn love beads, instead of going to Vietnam to fight for my country." Bob thought of how he was putting Mrs. Lucas in the middle of everything and said, "I'm sorry, it's not your fault. Maybe it's nobody's fault."

"Bob, I don't know what to say, and it's gotten worse since the Kent State incident." she said sympathetically.

"I heard about the Kent State shooting. The Ohio National Guard firing at those college students. The media is calling it a massacre. What a mess." he replied. "I wonder if she's holding that against me as well. God I wish she would have written me a letter to tell me where we stood." He realized that he was putting her in the middle again. "I'm sorry. I appreciate you talking to me, Mrs. Lucas, and for being honest with me."

"That's Okay, Bob. Ted and I have always been very fond of you. We feel terrible about what has happened between the two of you. I'm sorry she never wrote you to let you know. That wasn't right at all. Well, I better let you go now Bob, but I must tell you that I don't think you'll get anywhere talking to Sue. Goodbye, it's nice to know that you're home and well. Take care and all the best Bob."

"Goodbye Mrs. Lucas, and thanks again." He gently hung up the phone and stared at it a moment.

No matter how many people tell you that your relationship with a person is over, you still hope that it isn't true and that things will work themselves out. Bob was sure that once she saw him and remembered all the good times they had shared, she would change her mind. After all, what in the world could he have done to hurt her so badly?

Bob walked into the kitchen to get another beer and found his mother by the stove.

"Look Bob," she said with a smile, "I made baked ham for you, with scalloped potatoes, asparagus spears, and cauliflower with a cheese sauce. Dinner should be ready in about forty-five minutes. Oh and look," she reached into the fridge and pulled out a bottle, "champagne, your father thought of this. Here, I'll get you a beer and you can sit in the living room and talk to your Dad." She put the bottle back into the fridge and pulled out two bottles of beer and said, "Here, you had better take one out for your Dad as well. He must be finished drinking the one he has by now."

He looked at her and smiled, she was so happy. It did him a world of good just to see her that way. He thanked her and kissed her on the cheek. Bob started towards the living room and he could hear Mom humming to herself. That made him smile again, but at the same time he couldn't help but think of what Bill and Alice Wheeler were feeling. Seeing Bob coming home they way he did and seeing Jimmy coming home in a box, must of been a real test in their faith in God and the way he works.

Bob was caught between the emotions of seeing his parents' joy and that of the heartbreak of losing Sue. It was difficult but he had to hide the hurt for the sake of his parents. This day was as every bit their's as it was his. So he spent the rest of the day talking to them and getting caught up on what was going on for the last year or so. Bob phoned Judy to let her know he was back. It was good to hear her voice again, even though there were times he wanted to strangle her when they were growing up. Those times seemed like yesterday, as he thought about them.

They finished off the day by sitting down in front of the television to watch the news. Most of what dominated the news was Vietnam, the invasion of Cambodia, and the Anti-War Movement. Kent State was still fresh in everyone's mind, and there was still a lot of talk about it. What was to have been a peaceful demonstration, left four dead and ten wounded. Two of those killed were by-standers, one of whom, was an ROTC enrollee. Bob still couldn't understand why those people were killed; that truly bothered him. It certainly didn't help things at all. It turned people against the government all the more. It was as though people had grouped together and resisted all authority, especially that of the government itself.

The Hills called it a day after the eleven o'clock news. Bob had problems falling asleep that first night. He thought about those poor bastards back in Nam and how they were spending their evening. And about Sue, and how she had let him down for reasons that were still unknown to him.

He finally fell asleep, but it only lasted until about four

thirty. Bob woke up and found his mother and father in his room. Bob was half asleep and Mike was asking him if he was alright. Bob had been yelling in his sleep, and his sheets were soaken from sweating. It was Vietnam. He just couldn't get it out of his head. His dreams and mind had taken him back to the jungle, for a brief visit with those he had left behind. The look in his eyes told the entire story.

The next morning Bob was up by ten. Mary was in the kitchen making breakfast. Bob could smell the left-over ham cooking in the frying pan and fresh coffee was perking. Mike would have been long gone to work by that time.

Bob headed for the bathroom, had a quick shower and got dressed. It felt so good to be back into his jeans. Mary was calling to him now, asking him how he wanted his eggs.

"Scrambled," he replied, "with cheese and make that four eggs. I'm starved." Scrambled eggs with cheese was his favourite breakfast and she sure knew how to make them just right. She was a great cook, it was a wonder why Mike wasn't fat.

Mary was sitting at the kitchen table sipping a coffee when Bob walked in. His breakfast was waiting on the table for him. He sat down and began to eat when curiosity got the better of her and she asked him what it was really like in Nam. He supposed it was only human nature. People want to know first hand about things they see on the news. He was reluctant to say anything, but she insisted. Bob finally gave in and began telling her some of the things that he had seen, trying not to be too graphic because he knew his mother had a weak stomach. Poor Mary, after three minutes of Bob talking about some of the less horrible details of Vietnam, decided she had, had enough. Bob smiled and shook his head. He was certain the subject would never come up again.

She turned to him and said, "You know your father was sort of hoping that you might want to work in the store, and perhaps become a partner in the business some day. He really does want you to carry on the business when he retires. He has a lot of faith in you and your ability."

"I know he does. I had wanted to talk to him about that. I'd love to if he wants me, but I thought it might be a good idea to take a few business courses at the college first. I think I'll take a couple of weeks off first, before I decide to do anything. I need a chance to plan things out."

"What are you going to do about you and Sue?"

"Nothing much I can do. I intended to see her and ask her about it, but you can't force someone to love you. Besides we live in two different worlds now. She has her type of friends and I have mine."

"I'm sure you'll find someone else, Bob. At least you're home and alive. Nothing else really much matters."

"Yeah, well, I don't think I'm going to be in any great hurry to replace her with anyone steady. I need a break from everything right now."

After breakfast Bob headed out to the hardware store to see Mike and to see if the old place had changed at all. On the way there he noticed the odd poster for an anti-war-rally and march. The march was to be held the next day, starting at the college and was to end at City Hall with speeches. Sue would probably be there, no doubt. In any case, he was going to find out what one of these rallies was all about.

As he approached the store he saw that it looked just as he remembered it. It was a large store with a wide variety of merchandise. There were plate glass windows across the front of the store displaying various goods. Setting up the displays was one of the jobs he enjoyed doing in the past, particularly at Christmas time. As you walked in there were five cashier stations on the left hand side, and a small dividing wall on the right to funnel traffic through to a revolving chrome gate. The store was broken into four main departments: hardware, homeware, sporting goods, and gifts. Bob remembered how magical the inside of the store looked during the holiday season, when it was all decorated, inside and out.

Mike had a staff of about twenty-five part and full-time employees whom he knew all by name and without having to refer to their employee badges, which they all wore. They all seemed to be quite content working there, and Bob didn't think he could remember a single employee not liking his father. Mike was just that type of person. That was the Ward Cleaver in him.

Bob spotted Mike talking to one of his employees in sporting goods. It was John Perry, who had worked in the store for the past five years and was Mike's assistant manager. John was a tall, thin, and pleasant sort of fellow. He was always well-groomed, and tastefully dressed. John looked his age of forty- three. Bob went to over to them and managed to catch them off guard.

"So what's going on here. We can't make any money with the two of you standing around talking." Bob had a big grin on his face while he said it.

John turned and shook Bob's hand, "Bob, it's good seeing you. How's it feel to be home again?"

"Great," Bob replied, "just great. How is the family?"

"They're doing just fine, thank you. I'll be sure to tell them you asked."

Mike smiled and said, " Excuse us, John. I'd like Bob to meet some of our new employees."

John just smiled and nodded, as the pair walked away.

"Well, I'm glad to see that John's still here. I've always liked him. Is Mrs. Hathaway still working in the office?"

"She sure is, and so is her daughter. She works in homeware. She's quite a good looker too." Mike looked at him with a grin on his face.

"Oh really." Bob was sure Mike's idea of good looking was probably a little different than his.

"Really Bob, she is."

"Great Dad, I'll just take her into the back room and jump her."

"Very funny. That's not what I meant. She seems like a really nice girl."

"I'm just kidding. But what I probably don't need right now is a really nice girl. I don't need someone to tie me down."

"Well, give it time Bob, just give it time."

"By the way, do you know any really bad girls?"

"Ha, ha. Come on I want you to meet one of our better part-time employees."

The two approached a good looking young man with medium length blonde hair stocking shelves. He was wearing loafers, casual beige slacks and a short sleeved, plaid cotton shirt with a button down collar.

"Jim, I'd like you to meet my son, Bob. He's just returned from Vietnam."

"Hi Bob, it's a pleasure meeting you. I'm Jim Mueller." He put out his hand to shake Bob's.

"Jim is one of our part-time employees Bob. He goes to the college here in the city."

Bob shook his hand and said, "Really Jim? What are you studying there?"

"Journalism," he said.

"Well, maybe you know Sue Lucas?" Bob said with a casual smile.

"I certainly do. She's on staff with me at the college newspaper. I just started working there last week. How do you know her?"

"Sue and I used to be old friends. We would go out once in a while."

Mike looked at Bob and shook his head while rolling his eyes. Jim never noticed Mike's reaction.

"Oh yeah?" Jim was obviously surprised.

"Yeah, well it's a small world. Well it was very nice meeting you, Jim."

As they walked away Mike said, "You sure down played Sue back there. I sure hope you learn to forget her."

"Don't worry, I will get over her." Just then Bob grabbed Mike's arm and stopped him. "Who's that?" he asked, looking at a cute redhead talking to an elderly woman in homeware. The redhead was wearing tight navy blue slacks and a powder blue, light weight, short sleeve, V neck sweater. Her clothes showed off her perfect body.

"Oh, her... she's the one you were going to take into the back room and give a good thrashing to. ... Remember her? You know the one."

"Ha Ha, very funny. That's Mrs. Hathaway's daughter? She is absolutely gorgeous. Has she got a boyfriend?"

He laughed, "Right. So much for a broken heart. No, she doesn't have a boyfriend, or at least I don't think so. Come on, I'll introduce you to her."

Bob grabbed him by the arm again and said, "Hey, I'll never ever doubt your taste in women again."

"Yeah well remember this, it only takes one good one like your mother to keep you on the straight and narrow. But sometimes it is hard not to notice."

They walked over to her just as the elderly woman was walking away. She turned and looked at them.

"Lynn, I'd like to meet my son, Bob." Mike now looking at Bob said, "Bob, this is Lynn Hathaway."

They exchanged hellos and shook hands. Her hand was

so soft to the touch and she looked great. Bob could just imagine what Wiener would say if he had have been there.

"Lynn is one of our full-time employees. She's been with us a little over a year now."

"It certainly is a pleasure to meet you, Lynn."

"Nice to meet you, Bob."

It was hard not to stare so Bob jumped in with something else to keep the conversation going, "God, you are one beautiful woman." Bob's father's jaw just dropped to the floor. He looked at him as if Bob was growing a second nose. Bob thought to himself, "Boy am I ever smooth, just like an avalanche". Lynn's giggling gave away exactly how smooth he really was. Now, all Bob needed was a crack in the floor to crawl into.

After having made such an idiot of himself, he suggested that he and Mike go for lunch.

"It was very nice meeting you Lynn."

"Thank you Bob, it was very nice meeting you."

They exchanged smiles and Lynn carried on with her work. Mike and Bob started towards the exit at the front of the store when Mike said, "Well there beautiful, where did you want to go for lunch?"

"Very funny. Nowhere, I just had breakfast. I just had to get out of there after making such an ass of myself."

Mike smiled, "You have a point there. Where did you get that line? Jim Wheeler?"

Bob smiled, "Yeah, well that was his style. Except it use to work for him." Bob stood there staring into space for a moment, with a sad smile on his face.

"You miss him, don't you Son?"

Bob found it difficult to speak. "Yeah, I'll never forget him. It does help to talk about him though. Best friend I ever had."

"How about going for a coffee and doughnut?"

"Coffee sounds good."

"You buying, Bob?"

"Sure."

They stepped out to a doughnut shop a few doors away. When they got there the place was only half full and they had no problem finding a seat. The two went to the doughnut counter and ordered their coffees. When they got them they found a booth and sat down.

They had a window seat and could see the hustle and bustle of the traffic going by. There were students walking by carrying their books. The college was only a few blocks away. The men sipped on their coffees and talked, mostly small talk. Then Bob spotted them. It was Sue and her new boyfriend. You could tell who he was by the way they looked at each other.

Mike noticed who Bob was looking at and said to him, " Forget her Bob. Put it behind you."

"Have you ever met him?"

"Yes, in fact I have, once. He actually seems like a very nice fellow, Bob."

"When did you meet him?"

"About a year ago, shortly after you went to Vietnam. I ran into them on the street. They had only started seeing each other then. Just let it lie."

"Well now is not the time to talk to her anyway. I'll just sit back and bide my time."

"Bob, just let it lie."

"I don't want revenge. I don't hate her. All I want is an explanation. Why didn't she write to tell me what was happening? I had a right to know."

"I understand what you're saying, Bob. I guess you deserved at least that."

They finished their coffees and left. Bob walked Mike back to the store and thanked him for coming out for a coffee. Bob had enjoyed his father's company, but most of all, his honest concern for his feelings.

"So, where are you off to this afternoon, Bob?"

"Oh, I don't know. I thought I'd have a quick beer at Del's. See if the place has changed any."

"Sounds good. I wish I could go with you, but I've got too many things to do around here."

"Well I'll see you at home for dinner then. Have a good afternoon. Thanks again Dad."

"You too. Have one for me."

As Bob walked away he could hear the bells from the college bell tower, ringing in the background. Again, Sue returned to his every thought.

CHAPTER FOUR

Del's Bar was a well established neighbourhood bar located in the downtown area of the city, not far from Mike Hills's store. The building itself was brick in construction and was built sometime in the twenties, which accounted for some of the ornate wood trim. The front windows were leaded glass and added to the charm and character of the building. The only thing about the outside of the building that was new, was the fluorescent beer sign in one of the windows. As you walked in, there was a long bar on the right with an equally long leaded glass mirror hanging behind it. A row of assorted liquor bottles that ran almost the entire length of the bar's back counter, were displayed directly in front of the leaded mirror. There were about a dozen bar stools that were neatly placed in front of the bar. The narrow room also had ten tables capable of seating four persons each. There was a jukebox on the left, neatly tucked in a corner next to a cigarette machine. The kitchen was hidden from view behind the bar. It was the type of place almost anyone would feel comfortable in.

Bob walked in through the front door, and scanned the bar with his eyes. Del, who was behind the bar, and a man sitting at the bar, where the only ones there. Bob thought to himself, "It sure is quiet in here. All the more beer for me."

Bob smiled when he saw Del, thinking of what was said about him the night before. Del was about five feet eight and more than slightly overweight. He was bald on the top and had silver grey hair that he kept neatly trimmed on the sides. Del was smiling as he always did. He used to always remind Bob of a clean-shaven Santa Claus. The other person who was seated at the bar looked familiar, but Hills just couldn't place his face. He was a big muscular looking fellow, with brown hair and a beard. His hair and beard were neatly trimmed giving him a professional look, even though he wasn't wearing a suit. He was wearing a pair of casual slacks, with a nice sports shirt and casual leather shoes. From the looks of him, it was obvious that he cared about the way he appeared in public.

Del spotted Bob as he was walking in the door. "Bob. Well I'll be, welcome home."

"How's it going Del? It's good to see you again. The place hasn't changed much. It still looks good."

"Thanks. So how's the family Bob?' Del said still smiling.

"Fine thanks." Bob continued to walk to the bar.

"That's good."

When Bob reached the bar he sat down and said, "So how's business these days?"

"Not too bad. I saw your father a week ago. He seems to be keeping pretty busy himself." He pointed to the fellow sitting two stools away. "You remember Jack McDougal? He used to work with your dad at the hardware store."

"Right, Jack I didn't recognize you with the beard. How have you been?" Bob reached out and shook his hand.

"I can't complain."

Del putting a coaster in front of Bob and said, "So what will it be? I've got a Bud with your name on it."

"Sounds good to me Del, and how about one for Jack here too, if you don't mind."

He opened two Buds and set them in front of the two men. "Here you go boys, on me. I have to restock the beer cooler. You two have a good chat and I'll be right back." Grabbing an empty beer case he headed for a door at the far end of the bar.

"Thanks for the beer Del." Bob called.

"Yeah, thanks for the beer."

"No problem boys. Enjoy and I'll talk to you in a few minutes." He went through the doorway.

"So Jack, where do you work now?"

"Lafferette Ford - I work in the used car lot as a salesman. I've got the day off today. You still in college?"

"No, actually. I was just released from the Army."

Jack looked at Bob, "Nam?"

"Yeah, that's right."

Jack just shook his head, "The fuck'n Nam."

"You left the hardware store to join up, didn't you? If I remember right, didn't you enlist in the Marines?"

"Yeah, I was in the Corps." He lifted his bottle of beer as if to toast. "Here's to Parris Island, to Vietnam."

"Parris Island?"

"Parris Island, South Carolina home of the U.S.M.C. Recruit Depot." Jack had a forced smile on his face when he said it.

"Basic. Seems like a century ago."

"Yeah, well I remember it pretty clearly." Jack now with a distant look in his eyes, "Marines ..... Pray.

This is my rifle.

There are many like it, but this one is mine.

My rifle is my friend.

It is my life.

I must master it, as I must master my life."

Between sips of beer Bob asked Jack, "So where did you serve in-country?"

"Nam? The First Battalion, Seventh Marines. I was there to hit the beaches on the Batangan Peninsula near Quang Ngai. Among others places." Jack was now looking his beer over, as though he was somewhere far away and in a different time. "Batangan Peninsula; they called it, Operation Piranha. That was in September 1965. ... Now that was real Hell. I was glad just to get my God damn ass out of there in one piece. ..... How about you?"

"I was with the 101st Airborne. I spent pretty much all of my time there near the north, just south of the D.M.Z. in Quang Tri Province. I went over there with a buddy of mine, Jim Wheeler. Not voluntarily of course; we were drafted."

"Jim Wheeler. The name sounds familiar. I think I remember him now. A tall, good looking kid, with brown hair, a real ladies man by the way he acted."

"That's him."

"Yeah of course, he used to come into the store and give you a hand whenever your dad had you doing something for him. He even worked there part-time for a while."

"That's right. He worked there for about three months, then got a job driving a parts truck for Kensington's. Six months later we were drafted." Bob said without any expression.

"How's he doing now?"

"Not very good I'm afraid. ... K.I.A. He was killed a month short of coming home."

Jack was quiet for a moment. "Sorry to hear that. He seemed like a really nice kid."

"Yeah, he was a hell of a good guy."

"A month to go; that's the pits. I remember what it was like my last month there. I was irritable, didn't want anything to do with being there fighting that damn war. Not that I was crazy about it before. It just seemed to be getting worse. You guys only had to put in twelve months, the Marines had to put in thirteen. A lot could happen to you in that extra month. I almost went nuts in that last month."

"Sounds like Short-Timers' Fever. That's what we used to call it. I think just about everyone who was in combat over there must have experienced that."

"Not old Gunny Hainy, there was a rock of a man. Korean vintage. A real Marine, through and through. I don't think he was scared of anything, or at least he never showed it. You didn't know who to fear more, Gunny or Charlie. He got us through though, or at least most of us."

"Yeah, we had one of those too, except he would know when to let up on you and when not to. He was a good man and I don't think for one minute that I would have survived Nam if not for someone like him being there." Raising his bottle now Bob said, "Here's to your Gunnery Sergeant Hainy and Staff Sergeant Kalar. May they live forever."

Jack raised his glass and said, "Yes, and may they both get laid every one of those days."

"Jack, do you ever think about those gooks you fragged over there?"

"Do you mean, do I have any regrets?"

"I mean, thou shalt not kill. You know."

"Are you pretty religious Bob?"

"I don't think I'm any more religious than anyone else. But while you're over there you tend to think about it."

"So you're asking me if I ever wondered if my soul is damned because I killed the enemy. Yeah, well, aside from them trying to kill me I guess I really had nothing against them."

"Jim, when he died over there, died in my arms. Before he died he asked me if God would forgive him and let him into heaven. It just sticks in my mind is all."

"Hey I know. You've got to have the attitude that you did what you had to do. It was either them or you. Better you killing them than you making the trip home in a damn body bag. We had a guy over there by the name of Tony Tavano. Tony went through basic with me, he was always well-liked by the other guys. Even the instructors liked him. He always did well on any of the courses. He was one of their aces. Nobody knows how they're going to react in a combat situation, until you're actually in one. That's when you know. Tony, well he was a very strong Catholic, a stronger Catholic than maybe he even realized. He told me, just before our first fire-fight over there, that he wasn't sure if he could kill another human being. Well, when the time came and we were in the shit, a real nasty fight, he did what he was trained to do. When it was over he sat in his foxhole and cried asking God to forgive him. He turned his weapon on himself and fired. We found him lying on his side, the rifle barrel still in his mouth." Jack looked as though the memory was tearing at him.

"It's hard not to think of the guys that you knew, who had died there, and for what? So some college kid can call you a warmonger. It's just not fuck'n right, Jack."

"Well, it seems as if a lot of people have had it with the war. And that damn Kent State shooting. They should shoot the dumb son of a bitch responsible for that."

"The part that gets me is that we went over there to fight this war for our country and we came back to a lot of resentment. Why is that? I don't understand."

Jack looked Bob right in the eye and said, "Because we never won the fuck'n thing, and we probably won't. Half the public thinks we shouldn't be there; and quite frankly, they're probably right."

"Do you ever dream about Nam? Like waking up in a cold sweat, in the middle of the night."

"Oh sure, lots at first, but you get over it eventually; sort of. You can't expect to go through something like that and not have it affect you. Like most of us you'll learn to live with it. And it does get better."

"Well, let's forget the war and talk about something else, anything."

"Sure Bob, lets talk cars. If you need one just look me up. I'll fix you up with an honest deal, the most car for your dollar. Anyone who went through that place deserves a break and I'll see that you get it." He reached into his pocket and handed him one of his business cards.

"Thanks Jack. I'll do that." Bob put the card into his shirt pocket.

"Hey Bob, I mean it, I'll show you our cost sheet. And if you ever need to talk about the shit that happened in-country, just give me a shout."

"Yeah, thanks I'll keep that in mind."

Just then Del walked back in the room. "Well guys, ready for another one?"

Bob smiled and said, "Sure as long as I'm buying and you're joining us."

Del laughed, "Can't argue with that, Bob."

Jack smiled and said, "Thanks, Bob."

Del reached into the cooler and pulled out three Buds. He set them down in front of them and opened the bottles. With a grin he said, "Here's to you, Bob, welcome back."

They toasted and took a drink. Just then four men walked in and sat down at a table near the front entrance. Del put down his beer and went over to them to take their order. They were laughing and joking with him. Obviously they knew him and he knew them. All the men were well-dressed and ranged in age from about twenty-five to about thirty-five.

"Who are they?" Bob asked Jack.

"Police."

"Police?"

"Yeah. Sometimes they use plain-clothes men, and sometimes they use uniformed men. They're just coming off shift."

"Yeah but what are they policing?"

"The College. They spread around the outer campus perimeter and wait for things to happen. Then they move in."

"Is it really that bad?"

"Oh no. Not really. There's been just a few minor incidents, but they managed to get them under control quickly and with as little fuss as possible. And I might add, without the help of the State Police and The National Guard. As long as they handle it at their level, the students won't get all up in arms."

"It's still hard to believe."

"It looks worse than what it is Bob."

"I sure hope so. They're not that far from the store. I'd hate to have them go on a rampage."

Jack laughed, "Well I don't think they're going to have a race riot if that's what you're worried about. Maybe just a peaceful hanging or something innocent like that."

"Right and they'll have one of us as the guest of honour." Bob finished his beer and started to stand up.

"Bob, you're not leaving now, are you?"

"Yeah, I think so Jack."

"Let me buy you another beer before you leave."

"No thanks. I'll catch you another time."

Jack shook his hand and said. "Take care of yourself, and hey ... keep an eye out for hostiles."

"Why, do you think I'll be harassed by a big bad long hair." Bob said with a smile.

Jack looked at Bob with a serious look on his face, "Hey, they're not all bad; in fact most of them are pretty good. But there is the odd asshole out there looking for trouble. Just keep a low profile."

The smile drew away from Bob's face. "Okay Jack, I will. Thanks." He had a feeling Jack was speaking from experience, so Bob took heed.

"See you around, Bob."

"See you, Jack."

As Bob was walking out, one of the cops turned his head and looked at him. His general appearance reminded Bob of Kalar, even the way he looked at you, as if he were trying to read your very thoughts. The look in the policeman's eyes was very intense. Neither one of them said anything and Bob kept walking.

"Leaving us?" Del called to him.

"Yeah, I'm afraid so Del." Bob said with a smile.

"Well you take care Bob, and thanks for dropping in. It was good to see you again."

"Thanks Del."

And so Bob walked out. He had decided to go back to the store and see how his father was doing. Besides, he wanted to get another look at this Lynn. Bob was thinking about what Jack had said about keeping a low profile. He couldn't believe how going to Nam had changed his life. Hell could it really be all that bad, he thought. After all it was his country too.

Bob who's head was still in the clouds, had just rounded the corner of his father's store when he ran into three people. Literally. It was Sue, her boyfriend and some short fellow with long blonde hair. The little blonde guy looked like he was rebelling against the world the way he looked at Bob. He had a baby face complexion and angry blue eyes. It didn't take much to see he was a real hot head.

Bob's head turned and he looked right into Sue's eyes and said, "Sue!"

She just looked at him with silent surprise.

"Watch where the hell you're going." said the blonde-haired kid. He looked to be seventeen or so and what a big mouth he had, one that just wouldn't quit. This had to be one of the jerks that Jack was warning Bob about. He was looking at Bob with fire in his eyes. If he would have tried something with Bob, it really wouldn't have been any contest. Bob would have crushed him.

"Take it easy Kevin, he didn't mean it." Sue's boyfriend said to Bob's surprise. It looked as if Bob's father was right about him.

Bob looked at the boyfriend and said, "Excuse me ... I'm sorry." Bob found himself almost unable to speak. He looked him over. The fellow was tall, wore wire-framed glasses, had dark medium length hair and a beard. He looked to be about Bob's age.

"Oh that's alright. Think nothing of it, no harm done." he said with a smile.

Sue, still looking at Bob, finally spoke, "Terry, this is Bob. I told you about him."

He looked at Bob now, with equal surprise. Now looking him over he said, "Bob Hills."

"Yes." she said.

"You damn murdering warmonger." Kevin, the blonde haired militant, barked.

"Shut up, Kevin!" Terry said, now getting angry. Then he looked at Bob, extended his hand to shake his and said with sincerity, "It's nice to finally meet you Bob." He knew that Sue hadn't told Bob about them and he carried that guilt as though it was his own. He was glad that the record was finally being set straight.

Bob was looking for a reason to dislike him, but he wasn't having much luck. It would have been so much easier if he had been an ignorant jerk. At least he was replaced by a nice guy, Bob thought. He put his hand out and shook his.

"I can't believe this shit." Kevin said.

"It's nice to meet you Terry." Bob said, then turning to Sue, "Did your mother tell you I had called?"

"Yes she did."

"I've got to talk to you Sue." Bob said in a quiet voice.

"I've got nothing to say to you Bob."

"Sue," Terry interrupted, "you owe him some sort of explanation."

"I don't owe anyone anything."

"Yes you do." Terry rebutted, "You dropped him without giving him as much as a Dear John letter. He doesn't even know why or when you did, only that you dropped him."

"Bull shit!" Kevin said, gritting his teeth.

"Kevin! Why don't you mind your own business?" Terry said, now becoming all the more irritated with Kevin's remarks. If Terry had believed in violence, he would have punched Kevin right there and then.

"Sue, please talk to him. The two of you can go to the coffee shop and talk there. It's best if the two of you get what's bothering you off your chest now. Then this whole thing is done and over with, once and for all."

"Okay. But this finishes it." she said in a soft voice still staring at Bob.

"Come on Kevin. We'll meet you back at the newspaper office, Sue." he said referring to the college newspaper.

Bob and Sue walked over to the coffee shop. Along the way they spoke very little and when they did it was about their families. When they arrived, Bob went up to the service counter to get the coffees, while Sue found them a place to sit. Bob turned around with the coffees in his hand to find, ironically, that she was sitting in the same booth that he had sat at only two hours earlier that morning when he first spotted her. Bob walked over and sat down with the coffees.

"Well, Terry seems like a very nice guy." Bob said trying hard to break the ice.

"Look Bob let's forget about Terry and talk about us. You wanted to talk to me, so let's talk." She was very defensive and abrupt.

"Sue. What did I do to you?"

"Nothing. Everything."

"Nothing, everything? What kind of an answer is that?" Bob was getting upset.

"Look Bob, it's not what you've done to me personally, but rather what you've done period."

"I don't understand."

"Bob it's what you've become."

"I haven't changed Sue."

"Yes you have."

"How?"

"Your morals Bob."

"What do you know about my morals? You haven't had any contact with me in over a year."

"You went there didn't you?"

"That's right I did."

"There you have it Bob, you went there and didn't give it a second thought."

"And what choice did I have?" Trying hard to hide his anger and frustration.

"You could have gone to Canada."

"Oh great Sue. And would you have come with me?"

"In time, when I finished school."

"In time, Sue?"

"In time Bob."

"So I was suppose to go to Canada and play Nanook of The North, and hope to hell that you show up a couple of years later. Now that would have to be true love."

"Well I guess you'll never know how true that love may have been Bob. I may have surprised you."

"Then again maybe you wouldn't have." Bob couldn't believe his ears. He was almost speechless.

"Listen Bob, you wanted to talk. Now I'm trying to be as

honest with you as I can."

"Honest! Why weren't you honest with me about our relationship and why are you trying so hard to get me to hate you?"

"I'm not Bob."

"Why didn't you write to me Sue?"

She looked at him and then at the table, not to see his reaction. "Because it was immoral for you to be there."

"What!" Bob found himself making a conscious effort not to yell. He was absolutely furious.

"You had absolutely no right to be there Bob."

"I had no choice, and don't give me this 'go to Canada' crap."

"And why not? A lot of people have."

"Because if I had gone to Canada I would never have been able to come back home. I do have my father's business here. Some day I may own it. I have a future here, damn it. Or didn't you even give that a second thought?"

"How do you know that you wouldn't be able to come back for sure? The government might see that they were wrong someday and give those who refused to fight a pardon. My God, they're our own people, with strong moral convictions."

"Do you actually think for one minute, Sue, that President Nixon, or any other President is going to give some sort of amnesty to anyone that dodged the draft or deserted? No President in their right mind would ever do that. If he did, the government would never again be able to put together another Army ... for whatever reason."

"Amen to that Bob.... amen to that." she said with a sneer and much sarcasm.

He just looked at Sue with a blank expression on his face and said, "Let's just hope that it's not on our turf the next time then."

Sue was silent for a moment then said, "How about all those innocent people you helped kill over there?"

"Sue, those so-called, innocent people were trying their damned best to kill me."

"Do you blame them? That's their country you invaded."

"I hardly invaded their country single-handedly and as far as I'm concerned they can have the damn place."

"Yes, but you were still there helping to destroy their home. All of your own free will."

"Free will? Aren't you listening to a damned thing I'm saying? I was drafted Sue. What did you want me to do, desert? Somehow I find it difficult to picture myself spending time in Leavenworth."

She paused again then said, "Bob, I've got to ask you something, and I need a straight yes or no answer. Did you kill anyone in Vietnam?"

Bob couldn't get over the nerve she had. He was angry and ready to put her though her paces. "Yes."

"You actually killed someone."

At that point he couldn't give a shit if he ever saw that self-righteous bitch every again. "One? Hell no, there was a pile of them. Why I was so busy killing them I didn't bother to keep count."

"I don't understand you Bob."

"I didn't think so."

"There's no way I could ever love someone I knew took another human life."

He looked at her with disappointment for the way she so quickly judged those people that served in Nam. "And I could never love someone like you who feels the contempt that you feel for people like Wiener. They're no more murderers than you or your radical friend Kevin."

"I'll have you know that Kevin's brother was killed in Vietnam. He was a journalist."

"Yeah, well if he was anything like Kevin, then he probably was killed interviewing the wrong side." He went to stand up.

"How dare you say that about him like that."

"Easy, the same way you talk so freely about the people who served in Vietnam, the Republic of." This was it, she was going to get both barrels right here and now. "The same way you and your bull shit ideals demean the name and memory of fine individuals like Jim Wheeler. Remember him? We used to spend most of our time together. You, me and Wiener ... remember? You use to say what a nice guy he was. Or has your memory gone for a fuck'n walk like your heart and conscience. You really think your shitting on people like me is going to make a big difference in the way this country is run, don't you. Your fight is with Nixon, not me. I don't run this country and neither do the poor bastards who were thrown into that damn war. You had better wake up, asshole. Your contribution isn't worth a shit because things aren't so black and white as you seem to picture them. There's a hell of a lot of grey in between that you're not seeing. Look at the whole picture before you open your big mouth. I'm at least glad you had the good sense to find yourself someone nice and sensible like Terry. If first impressions mean anything, then I'd have to say I'm impressed. I also have to say, he can have you, good riddens and thank fuck." Bob got up and started to walk out of the coffee shop, leaving Sue staring at her coffee. Then he stopped to look at the expression on her face.

She sat in silence, thinking about all that was said. Bob supposed she was wondering if perhaps she had been too hard on him the whole time. If less blame should have been put on him and more on the circumstances. Perhaps the blame for all that was said and done, could be retracted with an apology. After all it wasn't his fault that he was sent over there. He made mistakes , but then again who hasn't? Even her. She might have judged him and his actions unfairly. She might never love him again, but she did feel pity for him. The expression on her face showed her every thought. The very thought of what she might be thinking, made Bob absolutely ill.

Bob turned and walked out and began making his way back to the hardware store to see his father. He couldn't get Sue and the way she thinks out of his mind. He was glad that they had a chance to speak their minds. At least everything was out in the open now and he could now let go of what they once had. But he also walked out of there thinking about Vietnam and the close bond they all really did have over there. Bob felt more acceptance over there than he did coming home. He wondered if it would ever again be the way it was before going to Nam. Everything had changed so much. He wondered if he had come home at all.

CHAPTER FIVE

Sue made her way back to the College Campus and to the office of the newspaper. Terry and Kevin were waiting there for her.

It was a large room with tall windows covering the far wall. The venetian blinds that covered them were open which made the room very bright. Against the wall on the right was a large cork board, almost completely covered with newspaper clippings and photos. On the wall on the left were peace posters, a picture of Martin Luther King Jr., and one of the Apollo 13 space crew led by James Lovell Jr. On the same wall was an organization chart of the newspaper. In the centre of the room were five desks, three of which had phones. As you entered into the room, there was a bank of four filing cabinets against the wall where the door was located.

Sue walked in and sat down at the desk nearest the room entrance.

"Well, what did the goof have to say?"

"Shut up Kevin." Terry said with anger in his voice. "That's between the two of them."

"Hey, sorry man," Kevin said, "I didn't mean to pry."

"Just lay off her, Kevin."

Sue sat quietly looking out the window. Just then Jim Mueller walked in.

"Hello everybody." Jim said cheerfully. Looking around the room he noticed everyone's mood. "Oops sorry." he said thinking he was interrupting a bad conversation.

"Oh that's alright," Terry said. "Kevin, you haven't met Jim yet. He started working with us last Wednesday. Kevin Patterson, this is Jim ..... Mueller." Terry had almost forgotten Jim's last name.

"That's right. Hi Kevin, it's nice to meet you." Jim put out his hand and the two of them shook.

"Nice to meet you too, Jim. We could always use the extra help around here."

"So are we ready for the rally tomorrow?" Jim asked with enthusiasm.

"Damn right," Kevin said, "We've got to let those warmongering politicians know how the American people feel about their bull shit war."

Terry looked at Kevin and said, "I can see we'll get some impartial reporting from you."

Jim turned to Sue saying, "Speaking about war, Sue, do you happen to know Bob Hills?"

Sue looked at him with surprise, "Yes I do. How do you know him?"

"I met him at the hardware store where I work part-time. I mentioned that I was working here as well and then he asked me if I knew you."

"He's a warmongering asshole!"

"Will you get off his case Kevin." Terry said, still annoyed by Kevin's continuing remarks.

"To tell you the truth, he actually seems like a nice enough guy and his father is very well liked and respected by everyone in the store." Jim said.

"He is," Sue said, "he just has different morals than some of us."

"Sue used to go out with him before he went over to Vietnam, just in case you were wondering." Terry said.

"Your kidding?" Jim was surprised.

"And if he was over there, he's guilty of murder. My brother would have been able to tell you that," Kevin said to Jim with hate written all over his face.

Still surprised Jim asked, "Your brother was in Vietnam?"

"That's right. But he wasn't one of those baby butchers, he was a journalist. He came home for Christmas in sixty-eight and told me one night about some of the things he saw and what he figured was going on over there: things concerning U.S. troops. My brother hated that war but he felt there were things worth finding out about, for the sake of the American Public. He went back a week after New Years. That was the last time I ever saw him alive. Four weeks later, the State Department informed us of the accidental death of my brother. He was murdered by those bastards."

"I'm sorry. I'm really sorry Kevin." Jim had felt as though he had reopened an old wound. In actuality it was a wound that had never begun to heal.

"Yeah well, he died doing what he believed in," Kevin said staring at the floor with a faraway look in his eyes. "And I hold the government and especially ... the Army responsible for his death."

"I'm sure your brother wouldn't want you to carry all this hate around with you over his death," Terry said in a concerned tone of voice.

"He'd want me to carry on the fight to stop this senseless war!" Kevin said defensively.

"Look, would the two of you stop," Sue said, "It's not like us to get on each others' nerves like this. So let's say we try not to aggravate one another any more. We have to worry about covering the Anti-War rally tomorrow.

"Yeah you're right Sue. I'm sorry Kevin."

"That's Okay Terry. I've got a big mouth sometimes. How about if Jim and I head over to the Student Centre and see how the signs are coming along?"

"Good idea. We'll catch the two of you there later." Terry said with a smile.

Kevin and Jim left and the room fell silent for what

seemed to be several minutes.

Finally Terry said, "Well, how did it go between you and Bob Hills?"

"I thought you told Kevin that the conversation I had with Bob Hills was between me and Bob, alone."

"Come on Sue."

"Okay. He said some things that made me think that maybe he wasn't totally to blame for going there. There were circumstances that left him with little choice."

"Yes well, I think that probably was more the situation. I don't think he or anyone else really wanted to go over there and take a chance on getting killed."

"But if everyone that was supposed to go refused, what choice would the government have but to pull out of the war. They couldn't jail everyone.

"Sue that is an ideal situation but you know that would never happen. Not everyone is going to refuse to go."

"He said that if he had gone to Canada, he could forget any chance of taking over his father's store when his father retires. He said that the store was his future."

"You know his situation was not a simple one to decide on, certainly not when you take that into consideration. He did have a lot to lose if he didn't go."

"Yes, but he did go over there and he did kill innocent people."

"Sue, how do you know he killed anyone?"

"I asked him."

"I don't think anyone went to Vietnam with the idea of wanting to become a mass murderer. I really think that, once over there, they had no choice but to defend themselves. It was probably kill or be killed. It must have been a real hell there."

"Why are you always defending him, Terry?"

"Because I feel sorry for him Sue. He had to experience

something that no one should have to. Now he's going to have to live with those scars forever."

"I must have hurt him," Sue said just short of tears, "I must have hurt him so bad." She looked up at Terry. "But I could never love him again."

"I'm glad that you can at least see his side now, Sue. That makes you one fine person and I'm proud of you. Besides our fight isn't with the poor bastards that went over there, but with the government itself."

"You're right, and for the way I've treated him I'm truly sorry." She said staring out the windows now.

"Hey, I've got the feeling he's the type to forgive you and in time maybe you could be good friends again. He does seem like a good fellow." Terry said, trying hard to comfort her now.

Still staring out the window she said, "I don't know about him forgiving me. A lot was said when we talked and a lot was done in the past. Without even thinking about it, I turned my back on everything and everyone that was important to him. I acted as though there was absolutely nothing between us, ever. A close friend that we had died over there, and I didn't even acknowledge his death. I'm afraid it's far beyond forgiveness."

There was nothing Terry could say that would help. She was probably right. "Come on Sue. Let's go to the Student Centre and see what's happening."

From the Coffee Shop Bob went directly over to the hardware store to see Mike. He was in the main office looking over the inventory report sheets. Mrs. Hathaway was sitting at her desk going over some invoices.

Dorothy Hathaway was a tall, slender, good looking woman, with bright red hair. She was wearing the half glasses she had always worn. They looked like someone took a pair of regular glasses and cut the top half off. They enabled her to show off her beautiful blue eyes. It was quite obvious where Lynn had gotten her good looks from.

"Hello Mrs. Hathaway."

"Bobby, how nice to see you again. Are you glad to be back and how are you feeling?"

"I'm fine and yes I'm very glad to be back. I met Lynn earlier, she seems very nice." Just then he thought of what an idiot he had made of himself.

"I heard." She broke into a big grin.

Bob's face lost all expression as he turned fire engine red. Then he tried to look away, as if nothing had happened.

"Son you're back." he had a puzzled look on his face, "How come you're so red? Are you alright?"

Dorothy started to laugh.

Mike, not hearing what Dorothy and Bob's conversation was earlier, just looked at them both and shook his head.

"Oh yeah, I'm Okay. Actually I was hoping that I could have a bit of a chat with you, if you're not too busy."

"Sure ... How about in my office? It's a little untidy. I hope you don't mind."

"That's Okay Dad."

They walked into a smaller adjacent office. He wasn't kidding about the mess it was in. There was a snowblower in front of his desk, assorted electrical boxes and switches still in their packages scattered across his desk top. In one corner of the room was a pile of toys and in another was a stack of toaster ovens, each one a different model. From the looks of things, Bob would have thought he had moved the stock room and they were sitting in the middle of it.

"Sit down Bob."

Bob went to sit down in a chair facing the desk and almost sat on a stack of papers.

When Mike noticed the chair, he spoke out right away. "Here I'll take that for you."

Bob handed him the stack of papers and he scanned the room for a place to put them. Finally he decided to put them on top of another stack of papers on top of his filing cabinet.

"These are new products and I've I got year-end to take care of right now. That's why the place looks the way it does. I like to check out the display models before having them put out. Normally I do this in the stock room. This is an example of miscommunication. So what's on your mind?"

"At this point I think I need more of a listener than anything else."

"Sure."

"I ran into Sue and her boyfriend Terry."

"Oh," Mike's eyes widened, "Okay."

"You were right about Terry, he really seems like a nice guy. It was because of his insistence that Sue even talked to me. She's really changed. She thinks Jim and I became some sort of monsters. She's got visions of us waltzing through Vietnam slaughtering old women and babies. She basically told me she didn't write me because of my lack of morals."

"That's what she told you?"

Bob nodded his head, "Yeah. That's what she said. Then she asked me if I had killed anyone over there. She did her best to lay a guilt trip on me."

"And what did you say." It seemed as if he too wanted to know, though he tried not to show it.

"The truth ...... Yes I had. You should have seen her face- it was sheer disgust." Mike's expression was of surprise. Bob guessed it was only human nature to be curious about the terrors of the war. It was like the child that anxiously awaits the opportunity to watch a horror movie, then turns away when finally faced with the very scenes that they waited for.

"Well, it's pretty hard to go off to war, especially in the infantry, and not kill anyone, Son. I'm just glad that you weren't the one killed."

"Well, it's not as if I wanted to kill anyone or that I enjoyed it. That's something that will stay with me forever, and I'll have to learn to live with that."

"Don't think about it Bob. And don't worry about Sue. It'll work out, Son."

"Yeah, well, I don't feel so bad now that we've got it all out in the open. I just wished that she had, had the decency to have written to me."

"Sounds like you're getting over her pretty fast."

"Yeah well, I haven't much of a choice. Besides, she's not crazy about what she thinks I've become and I'm not too crazy about what she's become. Life goes on."

Mike smiled, "I bet you that Lynn's starting to look a lot better now."

"Now? Did she ever look bad? ... Hey, by the way, did you tell Mrs. Hathaway about what I had said?"

"Me? No way. I was sitting right here when Lynn walked in and told her mother about it. She didn't know I was here. She did say you were cute."

"Get away." Bob said with a smile.

"Honest."

"Fuck'n A."

Mike looked at Bob with a strange look on his face, "Where did you pick up that snappy phrase?" The one thing that Mary and Mike always prided themselves on, were the manors of Bob and Judy. They always felt that they could take their children anywhere and never have to give their children's conduct a second thought. Bob's "fuck'n A" comment, took Mike totally off guard.

"Sorry. That one I picked up back in the Nam."

"Well that's one you could have left behind. I don't mind so much if you use it just around me, but try not to use it around your mother. It would probably kill her to think that one of her children would use that kind of language."

Bob smirked. "Okay."

"Come on, I'll take you over to Del's for a beer on our way home for dinner."

"You buying?" Bob said with a smile.

"Sure, why not."

On their way out of the store, Bob noticed Lynn talking to one of the cashiers. She was beautiful and he felt he simply had to ask her out. Bob grabbed Mike by the arm and said, "Just wait here a minute, I'll be right back."

Mike looked at him, then looked over to where Bob's attention was focused. He just shook his head and grinned.

He walked back into the store and approached Lynn. When she was finished talking to the cashier Bob said, "Excuse me Lynn, could I talk to you for a minute?" The cashier smiled and left. "I was wondering if ... perhaps you'd like to go out. Maybe tonight if you're not too busy?"

"I don't know? You're the owners son and it may not be such a good idea."

"Why not?"

"The other employees might think that I'll be getting special treatment in the future."

"Lynn, I'm not your boss and my father would never allow his business to operate like that. He values his staff too much to do that. I'm sure everyone here knows that."

"I guess you're probably right."

"I know I'm right, or I wouldn't have asked."

"Sure, where to?" She said with a smile.

"I thought a movie would be nice. If you don't mind? There's a comedy I'd like to see, called M*A*S*H. It's supposed to be pretty funny."

"Sounds great. What time?"

"Let's say seven."

"Great, see you tonight Bob."

She smiled and looked at him with those big blue eyes of her's. Bob had almost forgotten to ask her for her address. "Oh, Lynn, where do you live?"

She had a smirk on her face, "Fourteen sixty-three Farmington." She turned and walked away glancing back, she still had a smile on her face.

Bob walked out of the store with a grin on his face that Napalm couldn't wipe off. Even after all that he had gone through in Vietnam, there was still a small spark of the little boy in him. Perhaps not all his innocence was lost.

"I don't believe it."

"What's wrong Dad?"

"When I talked to you first thing this morning, you were all broken up about Sue. Now I'd bet you don't even know her last name."

"Lucas, Sue Lucas. There you go."

"Now that's surprising."

"Give me more credit than that. I'm merely trying to take my mind off the past."

"I don't blame you Bob. Let's face it, she's pretty damn good looking. But you've got to admit, a little bit of Jim Wheeler has rubbed off on you."

"Sure."

"Come on Bob, let's go have that beer."

"Oh, by the way. Do you need the car tonight?" Bob said.

"No, but I'll bet you do." he said with a smirk.

Bob was looking forward to getting out for a beer with his father, just the two of them. It was going to be a real treat, particularly with him buying. Spending time with family was something Bob had really missed, and there was little doubt that Mike was looking forward to their time together, every bit as much as Bob was.

Once at Del's they found a quiet corner table and ordered a pitcher of draft. Del brought it over and remarked how nice it was to see the two of them in together. He left them and they began to talk. Most of the conversation was about the business, then the subject eventually turned to Vietnam. Again curiosity got the better of Mike, and he wanted to find out what the war was like. And unlike Mary, he didn't turn it off when it got gory.

It was hard for Mike to comprehend the fear and uncertainty of fighting in Vietnam. The hardest thing for him to understand was the use of civilian women and children by the enemy. Bob told him about the young girl that he had killed in the village where Lieutenant Cunningham was shot. Horror was written all over Mike's face, but he quickly saw the guilt that Bob was carrying around inside himself. He put his hand on Bob's shoulder and said that he had acted exactly the way he was trained to act; he had done nothing to be ashamed of. Bob told him that he sounded just like Sergeant Kalar. He told Bob that it was logic that was doing all the talking, and not just him, or Sergeant Kalar. Mike said he had no choice.

He then told Bob how hard it was on his mother, watching the news at night, wondering if her son was alright. Knowing Mary, it wasn't a surprise to him. Bob was now glad that it was all over for her, now that he was home. It felt good to talk to his father and get a lot of what he was holding in, off his chest. Bob was very different from a lot of other vets, in that he talked about it, where most other vets simply held it inside. It was Bob's way of dealing with the war. They finished their conversation and their beer, and then left.

After they got home from Del's, Bob decided to call an old friend of his and Jim's, Larry Butterfield. He was as wild a guy as anyone could possibly be, but he had a heart of gold. Bob phoned him at his parents house and his mother answered the phone.

"Mrs. Butterfield?"

"Yes."

"This is Bob Hills."

"Bobby Hills," she said in a heavy southern accent, "I haven't seen you in over two years. How have you been, Son?"

"In the Army, Ma'am. Is Larry at home, Mrs Butterfield?"

"He doesn't live here any more."

"Did he get his own place?"

"Not quite. Larry got married to Barb Selth and they have a little baby girl now."

"He's married with a family?" Bob was dumbfounded.

"Yes, and the baby's so cute."

"When did this happen?"

"Last September."

"You mean when his wife had the baby?"

"No. That was in February."

Bob just shook his head. This was just like Larry to get himself into a situation like this. "Could I have his phone number, Mrs. Butterfield?"

"Sure Bob, it's 734-5873."

"Thanks Mrs. Butterfield."

"You're very welcome Bob. It's been nice to hear from you again. Talk to you later."

"Goodbye Mrs. Butterfield." He hung up.

Bob dialled the number Mrs. Butterfield had given him, but there was no answer. Bob had the feeling that even if he had managed to get a hold of Larry, it wouldn't be the same. With a wife and a baby it couldn't be, and he wouldn't expect it to be. Bob was sure there had been a lot of changes in the last couple of years and he was bound to discover them over the next short while.

After dinner, Bob helped clear the table, then showered and changed for his big date. He was really looking forward to seeing Lynn again. She was one foxy lady. He couldn't figure out why she didn't have a boyfriend. Looking the way she did, she certainly should have. At the moment he was glad she didn't.

At seven o'clock, he showed up at Lynn's place to pick her up for their date. It was a small, but cute home with light blue aluminum siding and white shutters. The yard was big though and well-manicured, with a neatly kept flowerbed along the front of the house. There was a detached garage with a paved driveway as well.

Bob pulled into the drive and turned the car's ignition off. He felt a little nervous as he approached the door and rang the door bell. Lynn answered the door.

"Hi Lynn." She looked good in her tight bell bottom jeans and white blouse.

"Hi Bob."

"Are you ready to go?"

"I sure am. I've just got to get my jacket. Come on in."

Bob stepped into a small foyer where a coat closet with by-fold doors was located. The foyer led into a small but nicely decorated living room. The far wall of the living room was papered with a small flowered print wall covering in the blue tones. The other walls were painted a soft powder blue. The furnishings were colonial and the fabric on the coach, chair and ottoman were in the blue tones as well. The floors were all hard wood.

"Can I get you a drink of something before we leave Bob?"

"No thanks. We had better get going or we'll miss the early show."

Lynn reached into the closet and pulled out a navy blue

corduroy jacket. "Let's go."

"Where are your folks tonight Lynn?"

"Oh, they're out shopping."

"Are you sure you don't mind seeing M*A*S*H tonight?"

"Oh sure, I heard it's pretty good. Let's go."

They locked the house up and headed out for the theatre. On the way there they chatted about family, but mostly about the movie they were about to see. As it turned out, she was a real fan of Elliot Gould and Donald Sutherland. That was a relief. Bob was worried that she might not like the movie. He really wanted to make sure that she had a good time that night so she'd want to go out with him again.

When they got there, there wasn't more than a hand full of people at the ticket booth. Bob noticed the odd guy looking at Lynn, even those with dates. He had to grin and thought to himself, "Eat your heart out pal." Jimmy would have been so proud of him.

As they went to walk into the theatre Bob spotted Sue and Terry walking towards the ticket booth. Terry hadn't noticed them, but Sue sure had. She took a hard long look at Lynn. Bob also noticed that she wasn't smiling. As Lynn and Bob walked through the theatre doors, he heard Sue tell Terry that she had a headache and she wanted to go home. Bob turned around to see Sue grabbing Terry's arm and pulling him away. Bob was pretty much certain that Sue hadn't noticed that he had seen her. In any case, he really didn't care.

Once inside Bob bought some popcorn and soft drinks for them, then they found their seats. They sat close to the back and off to one side. He wanted to be as secluded as possible. Bob was surprised to find so few people in the theatre that night, but then he decided it was probably because it wasn't the weekend. In any case, they had managed to get there just in time. They had no sooner sat down when the movie began.

Bob enjoyed the movie very much. The critics were right, it was hilarious. But even more, he enjoyed the company. He found Lynn witty and fun, not to mention very attractive. It made him feel special just being around her. He could get lost in those big blue eyes of her's. The more he looked into them, the more he wanted her. All of her. He had hoped it wasn't too obvious.

After the movie was over, they waited for the credits to finish before getting up to leave. By that time almost everyone had left the theatre. They walked out of the theatre to find a large line of people waiting to get in.

They looked at each other and Bob said, "I guess we came at the right showing."

"I guess we did." she said with a smile.

"How would you like to go out for a coffee and doughnut somewhere?"

"Sure. I'd like that Bob. But just a coffee for me thanks. I have to watch my waistline."

Bob just smiled and looked her waistline over. "Nothing wrong with your waist."

"If I start eating doughnuts there will be, though. Come on, let's go."

There was a coffee shop not far from the movie theatre. It was only half full and they had no problem finding a quiet corner to have a coffee and some conversation.

"So Lynn, what do you do besides work at the hardware store?"

"You mean hobbies and interests?"

"Yeah."

"I dance."

"Dance, you mean like rock'n roll?"

She laughed, "Not quite. I belong to an amateur dance

troupe here in the city."

"Really? That's great. What kind of dancing?"

"Ballet. I've been doing it since I was a little girl. My mother got me into it when I was six."

"That's impressive."

"Well there are some people that think it's kinda corny. My last boyfriend broke up with me because of it."

"Why's that?"

"He felt that it was taking up too much of my time. He called it corny and I called him a jerk."

Bob looked at her very defensively. "Well I don't think it's corny. Not at all. In fact, I've got to give you credit for sticking with something all this time without quitting. Even if it's not what everyone else considers the 'in thing' to do."

She smiled, "Thank you."

"No. Thank you. Thank you for making tonight so enjoyable. I loved talking to you and hearing about what you think and enjoy doing in your spare time. I find it very interesting."

"So Bob, what are you going to do now that you're out of the Army?"

"I'm not sure. Probably work in the store and learn how to run it. Maybe some day take it over and give my father a chance to retire. Lord knows he's worked hard enough for it. I know he'll never want to sell it out of the family. How about you? Do you ever have dreams of dancing professionally."

"Yessss," she said with a smile and some excitement, "that's always been my dream."

"Well Lynn I can only toast your inevitable success." Bob offered a toast with his coffee cup.

She smiled and toasted, "Thank you again."

Her smile was equally as hypnotising as her eyes. Bob

had to have her, he thought. He couldn't believe how smooth he'd become. It must have been all that time he had listened to that bull shit of Wheeler's that was finally paying off.

"I'll have to come out to one of your performances. That is, if you don't mind?"

"I'd like that. I'd like that very much. Thank you."

Bob wasn't sure if he'd like ballet, but seeing her jump around with tights on couldn't be all that bad.

She seemed delighted with his enthusiasm. Bob just smiled. Jim would have been so proud of him. Even though he was telling her exactly what she wanted to hear, he really couldn't help but admire her for her. Not just for the way she looked, but for the way she was inside. She was so full of hope and dreams. He felt a little guilty now, for the way he was thinking.

They finished their coffee and Bob took her home. He pulled into the driveway behind her parents car, and walked her to the door. He could hear the television from the porch. Her parents were obviously still up.

"Would you like to come in for a while?"

"No thanks. I'm pretty tired."

"You're sure?"

"I'm sure Lynn. Thanks for coming out with me tonight. I hope you had a good time."

"Yes, very much."

"Well, we'll have to do it again soon."

"Sure."

"Maybe Saturday night?"

"Sure, sounds good." She leaned forward and kissed him gently on the lips. "Good night, Bob."

"Good night Lynn."

She turned and unlocked the door and looked back at him as she walked in. Still looking at him, she smiled gently, then softly closed the door. That was it, he was hooked. So much for the Jim Wheeler influence.

When Bob got home he was met with an unexpected surprise. Mike was still up and met him near the front door entrance. He was just walking from the living room towards the kitchen.

"Hi son. Did you have a good time?"

"Yes I did."

"Oh, by the way, Sue called. She wanted you to call her when you got in."

"When did she call, Dad?"

"Oh, around eight, maybe a little earlier. I'm not quit sure. It couldn't have been more than an hour or so after you left to pick Lynn up."

"Well, it's kinda late now. I'll give her a call in the morning sometime."

"Sure, whatever. Your mother was the one talking to her." Mike said, now in the kitchen.

Great. Bob wondered what that was all about. Obviously he was right and she hadn't noticed that Bob saw her. He wouldn't trust her now. She undoubtedly was up to no good. Besides, he really liked Lynn. So, with those thoughts, Bob went to bed.

It wasn't long and Bob was in a deep sleep. Once again, he was away from home and in the rice paddies and jungles of Vietnam. Buxton, Perelli, Templeton and Sergeant Kalar were all there, as big as life. They were laughing and talking; then Bob looked away. A sudden silence caused him to look back and they were all gone. Then when he turned around yet again, he found himself and the others back in the village, on that dreadful day. He was caught up in everything around him, as he watched on. There was that God damned Cunningham ordering Kalar to have Buxton's squad line up in front of the village children. Bob knew what was going to happen next but he couldn't stop the chain of events. Then it happened. The shot rang out and, as if in slow motion, Bob spun around, firing his M-16, not missing a single detail. The sounds of his rifle firing thundered in his head. Then the girls lifeless body was thrown back and to the ground, hitting hard with a thud. Still moving very slowly, Bob approached her. The upper part of her body was sprayed with blood, her face was expressionless and her eyes closed. He leaned over her, half in shock, taking a closer look at the young girls face. He wanted to say he was sorry, then her blood rimmed eyes opened wide and looked right at him. He was still being drawn closer and closer to her. Bob screamed in terror, then felt someone's strong hands holding his upper arms near the shoulders.

"Bob! Are you OKay? It's me, your father!"

Bob's eyes, now open, found his father holding his arms and gently shaking him. Bob's mother was standing by the door, looking at Bob in sheer terror. He was sitting bolt upright in his bed now, sweating heavily.

"I'm alright."

Mike, still shaken up, said, "You were screaming."

Bob's mother never said a word. She just stared.

Bob looked at the clock, it was four-fourteen. "I'll be alright. Go back to bed. I'm sorry I woke you."

"That's alright." Mary finally said. "Are you sure you're Okay. Maybe I can get you something?"

"No, I'm fine. Go back to bed."

They left the room. Bob laid back down but couldn't sleep. He was afraid to. Better than an hour had passed before he was able to close his eyes again. How he wish he could forget Vietnam. Bob just wanted to leave it behind him, along with the guilt and hurt. How he wished that girl had lived. It wasn't fair that someone so young had to die.

CHAPTER SIX

The next morning Bob was up early. He was still shaken about the dream he had the night before. Mary was making Mike's breakfast and Bob thought it would be nice to have a coffee with him before he left for work. Mike was getting dressed so Mary was alone in the kitchen when Bob walked in.

"You're up early. Are you feeling Okay?"

"Yeah. I'm fine Mom."

"Can I get you some breakfast?"

"No thanks."

"You've got to eat something."

"Maybe just some toast."

"Coffee's ready if you want some."

"Yeah, it smells good." Bob got up, went over to the kitchen counter and poured himself a cup.

"So how was your date last night?"

"Great. I really like Lynn."

Mary smiled, "That's nice. I've talked to her a few times at the store and I've always found her to be pleasant."

Bob thought to himself," I hope that talking with Lynn isn't all that I do."

"Sue called for you last night. She sounded pretty disappointed when I told her you had gone out for the evening. She seemed to be so very sincere when she said that she was hoping to talk to you. I felt so sorry for her. You know I think she might still care about you."

"I doubt that."

"Bob. I think you're being a little hard on her. I realize it's over, but really."

"She's an idiot, Mom."

"Bob!"

"You really like her, you think a lot of her, don't you Mom? She's a regular angel isn't she?"

"Yes I do and you shouldn't be so hard on her. Have a little compassion, Bob. I thought a lot about it last night and I'm sure it was hard for her to accept your going away for those two years. If you could have heard her last night ..."

Bob cut her short. "She saw Lynn and I going into the theatre last night just an hour before she called you. Sue knew where I was and that I was not alone. So much for sincerity, wouldn't you say?"

His mother said nothing. She just stood in the centre of the room with her mouth wide open.

"I thought she didn't notice that I saw her. Don't worry Mom, she's not fooling anyone. If she calls back, just be pleasant and say that I'm out for the day, evening, whichever. Whatever you do, don't let her know that you're on to her. For the time being I'll let her play her silly game."

"Well I guess it's fine for her to dump you for some stupid reason, but you're not expected to find anyone else yourself." She was visibly upset.

"Just let it slide, it's not important."

"What do you mean, it's not important?"

"Just let me handle it, Okay?"

"Well I certainly hope you're not planning on seeing her. I wouldn't give her the satisfaction if I were you."

"I'm not going to see her. I'll take care of her when and if I have to."

"Bob, I've got to tell you, I really do like Lynn. She seems to be more your type and she's not some schemer."

Bob smiled, "Yeah well, I sort of thought you'd think so."

Just then Mike walked in, "So what's so funny Bob. You look like the cat that just ate the canary."

"Nothing!" Mary snapped, still upset over what Sue had

done. Or perhaps that she had fallen for Sue's little mind game.

"What's going on? You're smiling, and you, you're in a big huff."

"Sue ... that Sue. Do you know what she did?"

Mike looked very cautiously at her, "No ..... what did she do Mary?"

"When she called last night so sweet and innocent, she had already seen Bob with Lynn at the show."

"So why did she call?"

"Oh Mike. Can't you figure it out? She's out to shit disturb, the little bitch."

Now Bob was sitting there with his mouth wide open. That was the first time he had ever heard his mother swear. He thought to himself, "Fuck'n A Mom, give the little bitch a what for."

"Well, I'm sure your son knows how he's going to handle it Mary, and I think we should let him do just that. If she wants to cause problems between Bob and Lynn, or anyone else for that matter, it'll catch up with her. Whatever goes around, comes around. Don't worry about it."

"Yes well, I still think she's got a lot of nerve." She was now trying to calm herself down.

"Well," Mike said with a smile, "I'm starved. Where's breakfast?" He sat down at the table, rubbing his hands together, looking around with anticipation.

"Oh darn sweetheart, I've burned it. I'm sorry. Here, why don't you have a coffee and I'll get you some toast. You wanted toast as well, didn't you Bob?" She placed a cup of coffee in front of him and walked away.

Mike stared at the coffee with surprise and disappointment written all over his face.

"Hey Dad, you're probably in a hurry, let's go to the coffee shop and I'll bye you a doughnut."

Mike looked up at him, still wearing the same look on his face, "Good idea. Let's go. It'll give your Mother a chance to get over having been fooled by another woman." He gave her a big, sloppy looking smile.

"Oh, get out you two."

When they got to the coffee shop, they picked up their coffees and doughnuts, and sat at the same table they sat at the day before.

"I should have my name printed on this seat." Bob said with a smile.

"What are you talking about?"

"This is the third time I've sat here in the last twenty-four hours."

"Well if you like doughnut shops so much, maybe you should consider becoming a cop."

"Very funny. Speaking of cops, there goes some now."

Across the street were the same plain-clothes police officers Bob had seen the day before.

"How do you know they're police?"

"They were in Del's yesterday. They're probably getting ready for the peace march this afternoon."

"Yeah, and it's going to pass right by the front of the store too." He looked concerned.

"I'm sure there won't be any problems, Dad."

"Oh, I'm sure you're right. This certainly isn't the first one we've had. There's usually isn't a problem. Knock on wood." He rapped his knuckles on the table. "I just keep thinking about our plate glass windows and some over excited kid throwing something. You never know."

"Don't worry. There's police around in case there's trouble, and you do have insurance."

He nodded, "You're right. So what are you up to today? Anything in particular?"

"I was thinking about going over to see Jack McDougal

about a car. I've got more than enough money saved up from the Army and I do need a car."

"Don't drain yourself dry. I'll lend you the money."

"No. I have the money and I want to do this on my own."

"If you need any more money, let me know."

"I'll be fine."

Mike took a bite of his doughnut and after a moment said, "Do you think Sue was really out to cause some shit?"

"Yeah, I honestly think so. She certainly has changed. I just can't figure out what caused her to change so damn much."

"Well then Bob, you're probably just as well to stay right away from her."

"One thing I learned in the Nam is, If you see trouble, try to stay away from it. As long as I'm not backed into a corner, I'll do just that."

"That sounds like good common sense to me. Not to mention a good rule to live by."

"Over there, it was the only rule to live by."

"Yeah, I guess so."

"Oh Dad, before I forget, thanks for letting me use the car last night."

"That's Okay. So ... what kind of car were you looking for. Don't tell me, a Corvette Stingray."

"Yeah right, I wish. Actually, I really like the looks of the Camaro."

"They are nice. Are you going to buy it used or are you going the whole nine yards and getting a new one?"

"Used. This way I'm paying cash for it and I won't have to go into hock for it. I'm hoping it won't eat my entire bank account up."

"If you want to buy a new one, or you need any extra money, just let me know, Bob."

"Thanks Dad but I'd rather do it this way. I do appreciate

the offer though."

"Okay. But if you do change your mind, just let me know." Mike looked at his watch. "Hey, I've got to be going. If you need the car, take it. I won't be needing it this morning."

"No thanks. The car lot is only over on Harper. The walk will do me some good."

They got up and started to walk out of the coffee shop when Bob said, "Well, you have a good morning. I should be in to see you this afternoon."

He gave Bob a gentle slap on his shoulder. "You too. Lots of luck car hunting. See you latter Bob."

Once outside he started towards the store and Bob went in the opposite direction, heading towards Harper Avenue. Bob was tempted to walk him to the store and see if Lynn was there, then decided that it would be best if he didn't. He wouldn't want to seem too obvious.

It took him about twenty minutes to walk to the car lot, but it was a nice day and he really didn't mind the exercise at all. Lafferette Ford was one of the larger car lots in town, so they had a good selection to choose from. Jack wasn't in the lot, and Bob wasn't looking around much more than two minutes when he was approached by an older, heavy set, balding gentleman. Bob wouldn't think that anyone would feel comfortable buying a car from someone who smiled as much as he did. It was like he knew something the customer didn't.

"Hello there." he said, still smiling.

"Hi."

"Nice day. Too nice to be working."

"Yeah that's for sure."

"So, what can I sell you today?"

"Actually I'm looking for Jack McDougal."

"Oh ... Okay." The smile momentarily left his face.

"Jack's in the office, I'll send him out to see you. Unless of course you'd rather talk to him in there."

"Out here would be fine, thanks."

"Fine. He'll be right out."

He headed for the office while Bob continued to look around at the used cars. The cars were mostly Ford products, but that only stood to reason. Bob heard his name called and he turned around. It was Jack.

"Bob, I'm glad to see you made it in to see me." He put his hand out and they shook. The smile on his face looked considerably more genuine than his co-worker's.

"I thought I'd take you up on that offer you made me about buying a car."

"Sure. What are you looking for?"

"A Camaro."

"What, no Ford?" he said with a grin. "Camaro, I think we've got a few to show you."

"Great Jack."

"Is colour important?"

"Depends. If you've got a powder puff pink or a passion pale purple one, I'm not interested."

He began to laugh and shook his head. "I know what you mean, besides we keep those for our hippy customers. But I do have one that's metallic blue. It's only a year old and has low mileage. I know it's in good shape and I think I can talk the manager into giving it to you for three hundred dollars over our cost. His son was in Nam."

"Great, let's take a look at it."

They walked over to this dark metallic blue Camaro. It had power windows, power door locks, an AM FM eight-track stereo system, black leatherette interior, dash clock; it was beautiful. This car was definitely Bob and the smile on his face showed it.

"Well, are you interested?"

"I sure am Jack."

"Stay right here, I'll get the keys and we'll take it out for a spin."

Jack went off to get the keys while Bob looked over the car a little more. The more he looked it over, the more he wanted it. Bob sat in the driver's seat picturing in his mind how he would look cruising down the street. "I'd bet the ladies would just love it," he thought to himself. Finally Jack came back.

He climbed into the passenger seat and handed Bob the keys.

"Let's go Bob. You're driving."

Bob started it up. It sounded great. You could hear the power. Bob put it into gear and started to pull away. This car definitely had Bob's name on it. The two men took it around the block a few times and returned to the lot.

"Ready to sign on the dotted line?"

"Yeah, I'm ready. But what's the price tag on this machine?"

"Come on, I'll show you."

They walked into the showroom. It was a large room with a number of desks on an inside wall. The desks were only separated by five feet high room dividers. In the centre of the room were several new cars on display. Off the main room was a big office with large glass windows looking over the showroom.

Bob pointed towards the larger more private office and said, "That must be your office, right Jack."

"Oh right. I'm just lending it to Pat, my boss, for a while. I wish. He's the person I'm going to persuade to sell you the car for cost, plus three hundred dollars."

He opened up a black book that had a listing of all the cars and what the dealer had paid for them. He found the listing for the Camaro and showed Bob what he had found.

"Normally the customer would never see this book but you're not just a customer. Here is what we paid for it," he pointed out the dealers purchase price of the car, "we'll just write up the offer at three hundred dollars more than this and I'll take it in to him. Is the price Okay? I don't want you to get in over your head."

"No problem Jack. It's worth all of that and more. Let's write it up. Do you want a deposit?"

"Whatever you have Bob."

"How about fifty in cash."

"That should be Okay."

"You couldn't be getting much commission on this deal Jack."

"You're right. Actually I'm not getting any."

"Well that's not right Jack."

"Forget it Bob. Besides, it's a one time deal. You can buy me a beer at Del's."

"You got it."

He wrote the offer up and Bob signed it. Gathering up the papers he got up and left for the private office, papers and cash in hand.

"I'll be right back Bob."

While Bob sat there waiting, he looked through some new car brochures sitting on Jim's desk. Every couple of minutes he'd stop looking at the brochure, to look at the time on his watch. He wasn't interested in the cars, Bob was merely killing time. After about fifteen minutes, Jack returned with a big smile on his face and the papers in his hand.

"Well Jack, how did we make out?"

"No problem. He's pretty good when it comes to vets. He seems to feel we deserve some sort of break."

"It's nice to know someone appreciates us."

"I think Pat's son being a vet helped. He was a Captain in the Army serving with Military Assistance Command in country in sixty-three. He was out in the field once too often and was wounded. He almost died. When he got out of the hospital his C.O. asked him to sign up for another tour, because his time was up. He said no and resigned from the service altogether. After serving over there, he decided that the Army wasn't what he wanted in life."

"Well, be sure to thank Pat for me, will you Jack?"

"You'll be able to do that yourself. He wants to meet you this afternoon when you pick the car up. He's going to have the car checked over to make sure it's clean and the tires are properly inflated; the whole bit. We've got to make sure that we treat you right now, don't we?"

"That's great. What time should I be back?"

"Say about three. Bring a cheque and we'll have the paperwork and car ready."

"Sounds good Jack." Bob stood up and shook his hand, "See you this afternoon. Thanks."

"Glad I could help."

Bob left Jack and headed back towards the hardware store. On the way back he came to Del's. It was noon by that time, so he decided to drop in for lunch. Del served the best cheeseburgers in town.

There wasn't anyone sitting at the bar, so Bob sat himself down in front of the draft taps. There were only four others in the bar. They were all seated together at a table at the front. Del was busy wiping down the bar.

"Hi Bob."

"How is it going Del?"

"Good. What'll it be?"

"Do you still make those great cheeseburgers?"

"You better believe it." He was all smiles.

"Well I'll have that and a Bud."

"Coming right up."

"Thanks."

Del put an opened bottle of Budweiser in front of Bob. "I'll get Judy to get your cheeseburger on for you. Did you want fries with that?"

"No thanks."

Bob was thinking about the car and sipping on the Bud when Del came back out.

"So what's new Bob?"

"Not too much. I saw Jack McDougal this morning."

"Oh yeah? Where was that?"

"Where he works."

"No!" Del said with a smile. "Did you buy a car?"

"Yep."

"You're kidding. What kind?"

"A Camaro."

"How do you like that. A Ford Camaro."

"No Del. The Camaro is a Chevy product." Del was obviously not too knowledgeable about cars.

"Oh yeah, that's right. I know the one now. They're pretty sporty though."

"It sure is. You'd like it Del. All power doors and windows, AM/FM eight track stereo system."

"That'll make the girls turn their heads, I'll bet."

"I sure hope so."

"So what colour is it?"

"Dark metallic blue."

"Del," a woman's voice called from the back, "your cheeseburger's up."

"I'll be right back Bob."

Sounds crazy, but Bob would dream about those burgers when he was in Vietnam. He'd also dream about cheesedogs, french fries, milkshakes, ice cream cones, and ice cold coke. These were things that people tend to take for granted, here in the States. Bob was glad to be back and able to enjoy these things, and whenever he felt like it.

It was something he wouldn't take for granted any more, it was absolutely wonderful.

Del returned with the most impressive cheeseburger Bob had ever seen. He couldn't help but smile.

"I've got to check on the table at the front. Enjoy your burger Bob."

"Thanks Del."

When Del returned to the bar he asked, "Well, how's your cheeseburger?"

"Fabulous."

He laughed, "Now that's a new one. Bet you didn't get too many of those over there."

"You got that right."

"You ready for another beer?"

"Sure."

Bob finished his burger and sipped on his beer.

"Didn't take you too long to finish that cheeseburger Bob. You must have been pretty darn hungry."

"It's like this Del. When something you're eating tastes that good, it's hard to put it down."

He just laughed and shook his head. Grabbing a cloth and some spray cleaner, he went off to clean tables. Bob had finished his beer by the time he had returned.

"Will there be anything else Bob?"

"No thanks Del. I'm going to head over to the store to see my father."

"Well tell him I said hello."

"I sure will Del." Bob paid for his lunch. "We'll see you later. Thanks."

"Take care Bob."

Bob walked out and as he did, he notice the time on the clock behind the bar. It was two minutes to one. Bob was sure to catch his father coming back from his lunch. Bob certainly enjoyed his. Beer and a good cheeseburger, now that was what made this country great. What more could you ask for?

On the way to the store Bob stopped off at a drug store for Certs, just in case he ran into Lynn. He didn't want her to smell beer on his breath. As Bob stepped back outside he could hear a large crowd of people, yelling and chanting slogans of some sort. It seemed that the closer he got to his father's hardware store, the louder the crowd got. He had a gut feeling that it meant trouble. It was one of those feelings he hadn't experienced, since the Nam.

CHAPTER SEVEN

Bob had just rounded the corner when he spotted the crowd marching right in front of his father's store. He cautiously made his way to the front entrance where he could see his father and some of the employees watching the crowd from the front window. Mike had not noticed Bob as yet. Bob was reaching out for the door when he suddenly felt a hand firmly grab his shoulder and spin him around.

It was that little twit Kevin. He now grabbed Bob by the front of his shirt with both hands and began shaking him. Bob was caught off guard and wasn't sure how to handle the situation.

"You warmongering son-of-a-bitch." He cocked his head back then spat in Bob's face. "That's from the Anti-War Movement, GOOF!"

Bob was hunched over, covering his face. He thought he was going to be sick. Then Bob let his right arm drop to his side, forming a tight fist. Bob felt rage like he hadn't experienced since being in the field, back in Nam. "How dare he humiliate me in front of these people like that," Bob thought. What gave him the right? All of a sudden Bob let out a yell and planted his fist right on Kevin's nose. The force of the blow sent Kevin flying backwards to the ground.

"There you go, you punk asshole, that's from the One Hundred and First Airborne: ALICE!"

Now Mike noticed his son, along with everyone in the store; not to mention the police who were now surrounding him. They especially noticed the incident. They grabbed Bob, and Terry grabbed Kevin. Kevin, the fool that he was, struggled to get free. You knew what he wanted to do from the fire in his eyes. Bob thought it best not to make a move.

"Kevin, you idiot! What in the hell, did that prove?" Terry was furious. For a moment Bob thought Terry was going to belt the little jerk himself.

Kevin pointed at Bob and screamed, "I want that bastard charged. He hit me."

Those officers not holding Bob, were busy trying to hold back the crowd that had formed around the two. Bob heard some say, "Stand clear, out of the way." Changing his focus of attention from Kevin to the voice, Bob saw that it was the officer that looked him over at Del's the other day. He was staring Bob in the eye and he didn't look overly happy.

Pointing at Bob he said, "Okay Joe Louis, you want to fight, you're going down to the station ... and get that clown over there too. If he wants to press charges, he's going for a ride as well." The officers were beginning to take Bob away when he said, "And don't put them in the same car, they might try to kill each other. Now wouldn't that be a shame."

Bob looked over and spotted his father staring at him, just a few feet away. He seemed to be in shock.

"Hi Dad. You wouldn't want to come downtown and pick me up, would you?"

Kevin was still yelling and screaming at Bob, particularly now that the police were taking him in as well. Bob was glad that he at least got one good punch in. It really looked good on the dumb asshole.

When they got to the police car, one of the officers that had Bob by the arm, held him against the car with his hand behind his back. The other officer pulled out a pair of handcuffs from a pouch on his belt.

"Hold it fellows, you don't need those, I won't be giving anyone any trouble."

"Sorry, it's department policy. Besides, why should we trust someone who tried to start a riot?"

"Hey, I was the one that was grabbed. You must have seen it. I was only trying to get into the hardware store. The only reason I was grabbed by that crazed maniac was because I served in Nam and he knows it."

"Yeah well, Pal, we'll sort all that out later at the station. Come on, watch your head."

He put his hand on top of Bob's head and eased him into the back of the cruiser. Bob could see Kevin in the cruiser ahead. He had his head tilted back and some bandages pressed against his bleeding nose. Then the cop that was at Del's that day, walked over to the car ahead. He talked to the policeman that was driving and sent them on their way. As they drove off with Kevin, the officer turned and walked up to the car Bob was in.

He leaned over to talk to the driver and said, "They're going to the hospital to get the kid's nose looked at, I think it's broken. Take the champ here, downtown and I'll meet you there in a little while."

The policeman behind the wheel nodded and drove off. Bob felt like a common criminal. Here he was, cuffed in the back of a police cruiser, being held for something that he had no control over. He sure as hell wasn't going to let that little bastard get away with spitting on him, just because he was unlucky enough to go to Vietnam and get his ass shot at. This simply wasn't fair. As they drove to the station, people walking along the street would stop to see who had been arrested. Bob was humiliated. He loathed Kevin for this. That son-of-a-bitch had no right to grab an innocent bystander in the first place.

Before Bob knew it, they were at the station. He was

taken inside to a large reception area and over to a long counter. There Bob was uncuffed and they started to process him. From here he was taken to an office area and seated at a desk. This they called the booking room. An officer there took down some information. It seemed to take him forever. He typed with two fingers and even at that slow pace, he kept making mistakes. Bob would have bet anything that this guy had failed typing in school. Next, Bob was taken to what they called a holding cell.

It was a large cage-type cell with several people already in it. Bob looked around the cell; it was a depressing sight. The first of three guests there was a tall, thin hair-head with a moustache and a complexion problem. His bell-bottom jeans were torn and dirty. From the looks of him, his long scraggly hair could have done with a cleaning as well as the rest of him. The second guy was the biggest baddest looking black man Bob had ever laid his eyes on. He must have stood six feet-four and probably weighed out at about two hundred and forty pounds. He was wearing tight black pants and a tight fitting black T-shirt that showed off his "Charles Atlas" physique. Bob thought to himself, "I wouldn't want to piss this guy off!" A third guest was a wino who was laying on the floor in the corner of the cell, sleeping, the crotch of his pants soaked with urine. Bob was thrown in with these other 'socially unacceptable' low life.

He turned to the policeman who was just locking the door. "Hey, it stinks like piss in here."

He looked at him, "Well where in hell do you think you're at? The Holiday Inn."

The black guy burst into laughter. Then the officer left them unattended so that he could get better acquainted with his new friends. Again Bob swore he was going to get Kevin for this. They didn't even ask him if he wanted to make a phone call. It didn't matter, Mike would be there by now anyway.

The hair-head walked over to within a few feet of Bob, and asked, "So what are you in here for?"

"I got into a fight at a peace rally."

The black guy started to laugh , "Well honky, I'z didn't think you was no Mass Murderer." He continued to laugh.

The hair-head was taking all of this very seriously. "Right on, I can dig it. I know what kind of damn goofs the pigs can be. I've been there." From the looks of him, more than once Bob would have bet.

"Yeah, except that the fight wasn't with the police, it was with one of the demonstrators."

With that the black guy, holding his sides, broke into a riotous laughter.

The hair-head gave Bob a hard look. "What did you say?"

"If you cut your hair you'd probably hear a whole lot better. I punched out a demonstrator."

"YOU GODDAMN GOOF; you're no better than the pigs!" He was furious now.

"The damn demonstrator came after me, shit-head, I didn't go after him."

"You're just a damn filthy pig." He glared at Bob.

"You two honky mother fuckers are the funniest jive ass turkeys, I'd ever seen. Yous a regular Laurel and Hardy. Ha, Ha, Ha ... Yes sir, a regular, Norton and Ralph Cramdin, mother fuckers." The black guy was laughing all the harder.

The hair-head started towards Bob, with fighting written all over his face. As he walked, he turned his head and yelled, "SHUT UP NIGGER!"

Before Bob knew it, he was standing right in front of him, glaring. Then, this huge black hand grabbed him by his shirt and lifted him right off his feet.

"What'd you call me, mother fucker?" The black guy

wasn't laughing now.

The hair-head was an easy two feet off the floor, looking down with terror written all over his face. Somehow, what was happening to the hair-head made Bob forget the shit deal he was getting, and made him smile.

"Hey brother, I'm sorry. Put me down, will ya."

"You ain't my brother. Yous too ugly to be related to me. Why don't you sit you jive ass down, over in the corner with your real brother. And shut the fuck up before I kick your mother fuck'n head in, honky lips."

Then he threw the hair-head across the cell like a rag doll, onto the floor in the corner. He rolled over and there was blood from a scrape along the side of his face.

The hair-head now looked as if he was going to cry. "I'm sorry man, I'm sorry."

The black guy said in a demanding tone of voice, " Yous sorry my ass. Now that's your brother.", pointing to the wino. "Now kiss your brother."

The hair-head looked at the wino with widened eyes. "Like hell. I ain't kissing nobody."

"Ain't your Mama bring you up right. Now you kiss your brother or I'll kick your jive ass. KISS YOUR BROTHER!"

Just then a policeman walked in. "What in the hell is going on in here? There's no need for all the yelling. Hills, the detectives want to see you." Then he looked over to the hair-head. "What in the hell happened to you?"

"That big black bastard over there, picked me up and was throwing me around. Just ask him." He pointed to Bob.

Bob looked at the officer and said, "I don't know what he's talking about. He tripped and fell. This black gentleman over here didn't do anything."

The black guy was all smiles. "That's right, listen to the man."

The Policeman opened the cell door, "Come on Hills, we

don't have all day. And as for the rest of you, you had better stop screwing around."

As they were walking out of the cell block the black guy let out a little chuckle and said, "Don't you go worrying about us in here, we'll keep ourselves amused. Won't we, Shirley Temple? Hey, I'm talking to you, mother fucker. What are you waiting for? Kiss your brother."

They closed the door behind them, leaving the hair-head at the mercy of the black guy. It seemed that Bob was right about not wanting to piss the black guy off. Too bad the hair-head didn't think of that. Somehow Bob had a feeling he'd wind up kissing that wino. Bob was smiling from ear to ear.

There was a corridor which led to a number of offices. Bob was taken to one of them. Inside was the officer from Del's. He was busy looking through a file.

"Sit down Mister Hills. I've been told that you have been read your rights. Do you understand those rights?"

"Yes."

"I'm Detective Russel. There has been a charge of assault laid against you. What do you have to say about that?"

"Yeah, well I can explain all that, Sir."

"Great, I love hearing how people accidentally, almost start a full scale riot. I bet you were in Detroit in the summer of sixty-seven too."

"Hey look, I was only trying to protect myself. He grabbed me first."

He looked at Bob for a moment in silence then said, "I know. You can count your lucky stars that my partner and I happened to see the whole thing."

"Then why was I arrested."

"What do I look like to you? A referee at a hockey game. I'm a cop. I didn't have a choice. He wanted to prefer charges against you, and it was well within his right to do so. So I had to have you brought in."

"So I had to be humiliated as though I was a common criminal. Hell, I'm a war vet."

He looked at Bob with a blank look on his face. "So?"

"What do you mean by, so?"

"Just that, so. It's admirable that you fought for your country but that doesn't give you any special privileges, remember that. If you hadn't hit him, you wouldn't be here now. Hell, you're just on a 'poor me' kick. You think it's so hard being a vet? Try being a cop, Pal. People call me pig, goof, gestapo, nazi, you name it. Yet if some creep pulls a gun on that same person that calls me all those names, I'm expected to lay my life down to save him. You have one bad incident, hell, I have one or more every day. There's a lot more people out there that hate cops, than veterans from that GODDAMN WAR."

"I guess I'm feeling sorry for myself."

"You sure are."

"Hey Detective, it's just that I felt that I was getting a pretty rotten deal, Okay."

"Look," he checked the name in the file in his hand, "Bob, right?"

"That's right."

"Listen Bob, it's not my place to say but if I were in your shoes, I'd be considering laying charges of my own."

"You mean like counter charges?"

"Something like that. You have sufficient grounds and the right to lay charges against him. It's up to you if you wish to exercise that right."

"That sounds good to me."

He smiled and shook his head. "You also have two police officers that witnessed the entire incident. But you had better promise me that you'll stay right away from him and these demonstrations. You hear me? Keep your nose clean."

"Yeah, well it was an accident that I was even there. I was on my way into a store at the time."

"I know. Bob, I'm going to release you, but first you'll have to swear out a complaint against your friend Kevin Patterson. Meanwhile we'll process him and he'll find himself in a holding tank with Big Henry."

"Who's Big Henry?"

"He's that big negro fellow you met in the tank."

"Won't he be surprised? It won't take him long to say the wrong thing." Bob could picture Kevin taking turns with that other hair-head, kissing that old wino.

"Actually Henry is a pretty good guy. Henry may be in our jail right now, but he's well liked by pretty much everyone on the force. We had no choice in arresting him, like we had no choice in arresting you. I'll tell you a little story about our big black friend in there, he helped a cop once who was getting beat up by a few punks. He probably saved his life. Come on and I'll get the paper work out of the way and you can leave. Your father has been waiting the whole time for you to get processed."

"Tell me something Detective. You don't seem to be overly fond of this Kevin yourself. Why is that?"

"Let's just say we have had a few problems with him in the past. He's a bit of an agitator."

"Thanks for your help, Detective."

"No problem. I don't like seeing people being railroaded by people who use the system the way people, like this Kevin Patterson do. From what I could see, I'd have to say he started it."

Fifteen minutes later, they had finished the paperwork. Kevin, much to his surprise was taken from one of the small offices to the front desk to begin processing. You could hear him yelling all over the Station House. Shortly after,

Bob was walking out of the Police Station with his father.

"Are you Okay, Son?"

"Ya, I'm alright, but I'm not sure if the other guy is. I think I broke his nose."

"I saw the whole thing and so did quite a few other people in the front window with me. We noticed him as soon as he stormed over to you. He was the one who grabbed you. It wasn't as if it was the other way around. None of us could figure out what you did to upset him, or why they would arrest you. I think I would have done the same thing if I was grabbed like that during one of these demonstrations. Hell, people get all worked up and you never know what they might do. He deserved what he got."

"Mom will be disappointed."

"Let me take care of her, she'll be Okay. You were just defending yourself from a crazy nut."

"I'm having the crazy nut charged."

"Good, and so you should. Let's go home, I could use a nice stiff drink."

"Hold it. We can't."

"What do you mean, we can't?"

"When all this happened, I was on my way to tell you about the car that I have bought."

"So you did buy a car after all?"

"Yeah. What time is it?"

"Three-thirty."

"Dad, can you give me a ride to the bank, and to pick the car up at the lot?"

"Sure, I guess so. Hop in the car and let's get going. I still need that stiff drink."

They went to the bank then headed over to the car dealer. Bob didn't see Jack at first, but the car was sitting in front of the office when they got there.

"There's the car Dad, check it out. I'm going into the

office to find Jack."

A few minutes later Bob returned with Jack. "Jack, do you remember my Dad?"

"I sure do. How have you been Mike? It's really good to see you again."

"Good Jack. It's nice to see you again, too. So this is the car? It sure is a beaut'. It seems to have enough gadgets in it. What's this thing over here with the radio Jack?"

"That's your eight track tape player, Mike. It's stereophonic, you have two speakers in the front and another two in the back. The sound is really quite impressive. So, Bob, I wasn't sure if you were coming back today, but now that you're here I guess we can go to my desk and finish this off."

"Nice car, Son."

"Thanks a lot Dad, I'm glad you like it. Jack would you happen to have the keys on you?"

"I sure do Bob, here you go." Jack handed Bob the keys and he handed them to his Dad. "Here you go, finish checking the car out while we finish off the paperwork inside."

Mike smiled and said, "Good idea."

Jack and Bob stepped into the office while Mike got in behind the driver's seat. He put the key into the ignition and turned it on to accessories, then tuned the radio into Radio Free Elevator, a station reserved for the elderly. A few minutes later, Jack and Bob stepped out to find Mike feeling right at home behind the steering wheel.

"Hey Son, here are my keys. How about if I take this one home and you follow me." He handed Bob his keys.

Bob looked at the keys in his hand and said, "Gee ..... why.... sure, Dad."

"You don't mind, do you Bob?"

"No, not at all Dad." Bob turned to Jack, "Well, thanks

again for everything Jack." he shook his hand.

Jack smiled, "Thank you Bob. We'll have to get together for a beer over at Del's; I still owe you one from yesterday. Listen-you take care of yourself."

"Sure, and I would like to get together for a few, except it's me that owes you the beers. Take care Jack."

Mike was revving the engine, "Oh, hey Jack, it was nice to see you again after all this time." Mike held his arm out the window and shook Jack's hand."

Bob had the strangest feeling that he'd lost his new car and that his father had gained one. He pulled out of the lot and Bob followed. Needless to say, he took the long way home. It seemed like they went by way of Omaha.

When they finally got home, Mike beeped the horn to get Mary's attention. She came out; took one look at the car and said, "I hope you're not getting any ideas Mike."

"It's Bob's, Mary. How do like it? Pretty snazzy, don't you think?"

She walked over to take a closer look at it and said, "It's gorgeous. I love the colour."

Bob hopped out of the old family bucket and said, "What do you think Mom? There's even an eight track tape player in it. The stereo has four, real quality speakers, as well."

She turned to Bob and smiled, "I love it."

Mike said, "How about if I take you for a little ride Mary? Just around the block."

Bob thought to himself, around the block, right. That should take in most of the State.

"Not now, Mike. I've got dinner on the stove right now. How about later?"

"Okay. Is that alright Bob?"

Bob was standing there looking at the smile on his father's face. What could he say? "Sure, make it after dinner Dad. Just don't be too long, I thought I might show it to Lynn if she's not too busy."

They went into the house just as the phone began to ring. Mary answered it.

"Bob. It's for you."

Bob went into the study and picked up the receiver. Covering the mouthpiece he yelled to the living room, where Mary was hanging on to the phone, "I've got it." She hung it up and he answered. "Hello."

"Hi Bob. It's Lynn."

"Oh, hi Lynn."

"Are you Okay Bob?"

"Yeah sure, I'm fine."

"I saw the whole thing Bob. I can't understand why he went after you like he did. He simply went crazy. You were just defending yourself."

"Lynn, all I want to do is forget the whole thing ever happened at all."

"I'm sorry Bob. I understand completely."

"Don't worry about it, I'm not. Say Lynn, what are you doing this evening."

"Not too much. What do you have in mind?"

"I bought a new car. I thought we would go out for a drive, and then maybe out for a drink somewhere."

"Sounds great."

"Say about seven."

"Sure Bob, sounds good. Well, I've got to go. I'll see you a little later."

"See you tonight. Bye." Bob hung up the phone and walked back into the kitchen where his parents were.

Mike turned to Bob and said, "So who was on the phone Son? Not Sue I hope."

"No. It was Lynn."

Mary smiled. "I like her Bob." It was her way of reinforcing her disapproval of Sue. The distrust was deep rooted now.

Mike turned to Mary. "Mary. Let's face it, you like her because right now your so upset with Sue, not that you don't think Lynn isn't a nice girl."

"Oh Mike, it's because I really like her."

Mike looked at Bob and said, "So Bob, does this mean you're going out tonight?"

"Yeah, I'm picking her up at seven."

"Well Mary, we better hurry and have dinner if we're going to go out for a drive in the new car."

Bob smiled. Mike certainly was one of a kind. There couldn't be two more nicer people than Mike and Mary Hills. What a pair they made. They were the type of people that would make anyone's heart smile.

Kevin definitely wasn't smiling, he was furious. When he was released from the Police Station, he went straight to the college news office. Jim Mueller was the only one in and was working on a story when Kevin got there. He stood in the door entrance, his nose heavily bandaged and taped, his eyes showing his rage.

"Where's Terry?" He demanded.

"I think he's gone home Kevin."

"Home? Hell! The fuck'n pigs arrest me and he decides to go home."

"Arrest you? I thought you were the one that was charging him? What happened?"

"Yeah right. The pigs decided to pull some sort of a switch. I was the one charged."

Kevin grabbed the receiver off the phone and dialled Terry's home number. He sat on the desk top, looking like a bomb waiting to explode. Jim just sat there watching him as if Kevin were a madman who might go on a killing spree.

Terry answered the phone at the other end, "Hello."

"Terry?"

"Yes."

"It's me Kevin. Did you hear what happened?"

"I saw it, remember? I was there."

"I was charged."

"What?"

"I was charged, damn it."

"I don't believe it."

"Believe it."

"Where are you now?"

"At the news office, on campus. I came here as soon as I was released from there."

"Well what happened at the Police Station?"

"The bastard basically laid the same charges on me that I laid on him. The Police went along with him and charged me. Can you believe that shit?"

"You did grab him, Kevin."

"GODDAMN YOU TERRY! Will you stop sticking up for that murdering goof!"

"I'm not sticking up for him, but I know that if I were in his position, I'd do the same."

"Well, he's not going to get away with it. There's no damn way, I won't let him."

"Kevin do yourself a favour. Go home and get some rest. Give yourself a chance to calm down. Whatever you do, don't go looking for trouble. You've got to play the game by the rules. The whole thing will work it's own way out."

"My brother played by the rules with assholes like him, and where did it get him, Terry?"

"Look Kevin, If it's revenge you're after, you're going to find yourself in more shit than you can handle."

"He's not getting away with this Terry."

"Kevin, promise me you won't do anything and I'll talk to you about it in the morning."

"Can I drop by and see you tonight?"

"Sue and I are supposed to be going out. If you feel you really have to though, of course you can."

"No, that's Okay. But I sure hope that you'll be more sympathetic of my position in the morning."

"I will be Kevin. I'll talk to you in the morning. Just go home and stay out of trouble."

"Okay, see you in the morning." Kevin hung up the phone.

Kevin stood up, staring at the floor; he seemed to have his temper under control.

He looked over to Jim. "So, Jim, what's the big story you're writing about?"

"It's the coverage on the march today."

"Oh yeah, let's see."

"Sure, here you go." He handed Kevin the report he had just finished typing.

Kevin read the report and as he did he became furious again. He threw the paper back on Jim's desk. "Why in the hell would you refer to my assault as a minor incident? Where in the hell did you learn that type of journalism?"

"Terry told me to refer to it like that."

"Why?"

"Because he didn't want to tarnish the event with a violent action. He said it would tend to take away the credibility of what the movement was doing. It was only one incident between two people."

"Jim, I was attacked. And how about the credibility of this paper? We have an obligation to report news. That was news."

"He said that it was a personality problem between the two of you and it wasn't to be included in this story."

"Bull shit."

"He said that if we were going to make any headway at all, it was going to be through peaceful demonstrations."

"This is crap."

"Sorry Kevin, but that's the way it's got to be written. What can I do?"

"I'll tell you.... write the truth."

"He is the editor Kevin. So I've got to do whatever he tells me to do."

"I'm getting out of here. This place is starting to turn my stomach."

"Sorry."

"Don't worry about it, you're just doing what Terry the whimp tells you to do. See ya later."

"Take care, Kevin."

Kevin left the office still upset over the arrest and the lack of support he thought he'd received from Terry. It seemed to Kevin that lately he and Terry had grown so far apart that there was little to no communication. He remembered a time when the two of them were very close friends. But since the death of Kevin's brother, they began to grow apart. Slowly at first, but now more noticeably than ever.

It was six-thirty and Bob was waiting for his parents to return from their transcontinental test drive of the Camaro. He found himself pacing the living room floor and looking out the front windows. Bob had been doing this for the past half hour. Finally they pulled into the drive. They laughed as they got out of the car and slowly walked towards the house. Bob went out to the front porch to greet them.

"So what do you think of the car?"

Mary was quick to answer, "I love it."

Then Mike said, "I hope we're not making you late for your date with Lynn."

"Oh no, it's alright Dad, but I do have to get going right away."

Mary smiled, "Have fun."

"I will. See you later."

Bob hopped into the car and as he was pulling out of the

drive, he said to them "You two have a good evening." He waved then drove off to Lynn's."

When he arrived, she was ready and waiting for him. He had no sooner pulled into her drive when she walked out the door, locked it and was walking towards the car.

"Hi, Bob."

"Lynn, I hope I'm not late."

"No. No one is home and I was anxious to get out." She spoke to him through the open car window and looked over the outside of the car. Getting into the car, she carefully looked around trying not to miss any detail. "This is some car you've bought. I love the colours."

"Thanks."

"So where are you taking me."

"I thought we would take a drive around the town and then go out for a drink somewhere."

"Sounds great except that I'm not of legal drinking age yet. Not until August."

"Sure but you could probably pass for older than you are. No one will ask you."

"If something happened though, we'd both be in shit. My mother would crucify me, then she'd go straight to Mike with it."

"I never thought of that."

"We could always drive around for the next three months. I'd be old enough then."

"Right Lynn, I'd probably run out of gas by the time that happened."

"You've got a point there. I wouldn't mind seeing another movie if it's Okay with you Bob."

Bob pulled out of the drive and started down the road. "Sure. What movie did you have in mind?"

"Alice's Restaurant. I didn't get a chance to see it when it first came out, but now it's back and I kinda want to see it. It'll be my treat."

"Well I can't argue with that. If that's what you want to do. Alice's Restaurant? To tell you the truth, I don't think I've ever heard of it."

"Don't worry. You'll love it."

"Well who are the stars in it, Betty Crocker, Aunt Jemima, and Uncle Ben? Produced and Directed by Sara Lee?"

"Ha, Ha, very funny." Then she said with a smirk, "Just drive the car, Mister."

Bob reached over into the glove box and pulled out a Credence Clearwater Revival tape that he had bought on his way to pick her up. Giving Lynn a devilish grin he said, "How about a little music my dear?" he put the tape in the player and turned it on.

"Oh, C.C.R. great! I love their stuff. What other tapes do you have?"

"Just the one right now. But I'm sure my father will take care of that. It won't be long and we'll be cruising to the sound of Mantovani and Lawrence Welk."

"Come on Bob. Your Dad's a great guy."

"Yeah, I know. I like Lawrence Welk anyways."

"Ha, Ha. You start playing that Lawrence Welk stuff and you can forget me."

They listened to the only tape that Bob owned and drove around the downtown streets for about thirty minutes. It was great driving with the windows down and the stereo playing. He could have done that for hours and never have tired of it. But she did want to see that movie and it was time to go, before it got busy.

It was a pretty good movie. The big stars of the story were Arlo Guthrie, Pat Quinn, and James Broderick. Bob had guessed wrong earlier, even though he still thought Aunt Jemima would have played a good part. Lynn liked it more than he did, but the company was nice, so he didn't mind.

After the show Bob asked her if she wanted to go out for something to eat. She declined, saying that it was too late and that she had to be into work early tomorrow to help finish off the year end inventory. So Bob asked for a rain check.

On their way home he found that they were paying more attention to themselves than to things around them. She was beautiful and he couldn't keep his eyes off her. It wasn't until they were stopped at a red light that Bob noticed him. They were in the right lane. In his side view mirror, Bob noticed an old tan Ford in the left lane and one car behind. He was adjusting his mirror when he saw Kevin there, behind it's steering wheel. He was just sitting there, looking at the two of them with hate. Bob rolled his eyes, shook his head and pretended he wasn't there.

The light changed, Bob pulled away and drove Lynn the rest of the way home. While Bob was driving, he tried to keep an eye out, just in case Kevin decided to follow him, but it didn't appear that he had. When they arrived, Bob walked Lynn to the door and they kissed. After about two minutes of goodbyes she went inside. Bob drove home and when he got there, parked in the garage, locking the door when he closed it. The garage wasn't something that they always locked; but it was something that he did without thinking about that night. Bob was surprised that Mike's car wasn't around. They must have gone out, possibly with the Wheelers. Bob went in without giving anything outside the house a second look or thought. Down the street, there was a tan Ford parked in the shadows, between two street lights. A car that was not there a moment ago. In it a hatred was growing, building like a balloon being blown up and getting ready to burst. Little known to Bob Hills, that balloon was going to burst in his own front yard.

About an hour later, Bob sat in the comfort of his living room, having a beer and watching the late show. John Wayne, as always, was being his usual heroic self, when a car pulled into his driveway. Then, there were voices shouting and Bob could hear his mother. She was upset over something. As he approached the door, he could hear that the car was still running. When Bob walked outside, he found his mother holding her face, and crying. Mike was standing next to the car, headlights still on and staring at the garage. He called out to them, asking them what was wrong. As Bob walked towards them, he noticed that something was printed on the garage door. Large letters painted with a can of red spray paint covered the large door. The words read " A M U R D E R E R L I V E S H E R E ! ".

Bob went over to his mother and put his arms around her. She was shaking and crying uncontrollably. "My house."

Bob whispered to her, "Don't worry, it'll be alright. I'll get some paint from the store and clean it up, tomorrow. It'll be fine. Don't worry."

As she cried she said, "Why my home? Why us? Why? Why? I don't understand."

Mike said in a voice choked with emotion, "What kind of animal would do such a thing? To paint that on a persons house. Damn it, damn it all."

Bob was enraged by the sight of what some narrow minded, self righteous, vigilante did to his family. He knew that he was the target and what the message meant. It was either Kevin or people that Kevin knew.

By now the neighbours were looking out their windows and coming out on their porches to see what all the commotion was about. Bob left his mother long enough to shut the car's lights and ignition off, then locked the car up.

Bob coaxed his parents into the house, and got them a drink to calm them down. He thought about calling the Police but decided to leave it. The damage had already been done, and there wasn't anything that could be done now that couldn't wait until the morning. Mary sat in her chair shaking and sobbing. It was hard for her to accept that anyone could lash out at her or her family. To deface the home that she loved so much.

Mike looked at Bob and said, "Why would someone write something crazy like that on the garage door? What kind of a sick joke is that?"

Bob looked at him and said, "It's no joke."

Raising his voice he said, "Then what's it suppose to mean? Why are they doing this to us?"

Bob said in a quiet voice, "It's not directed at either one of you. It's being directed at me."

"Why you?" he said.

"Because, Dad, I fought in a war that some people felt I had no business fighting in. So, in their minds, I killed some innocent people."

"That's ridiculous and I don't buy it."

"Buy it. It's not ridiculous to these people, Dad. They probably felt justified in doing this."

Mary still sitting in her chair, mascara running down her face said, "I'm tired, I think I'll go to bed." She got up and slowly shuffled off in the direction of the staircase.

"Good night, Mom."

She turned around and said in a soft, sad voice, "I'll talk to you in the morning. Good night." Her eyes were still puffed from crying.

Mike remained up long enough for one more drink, then he went off to bed himself. Bob looked at him as he left the room, and said to himself, "I'm going to get whoever was responsible for doing this to my family." Bob had a good idea who it was. Tomorrow he was going to work on proving it. If not to the authorities, at least to himself. When he finds out for sure who he, she or they were, they'd pay, he'd see to that. Bob had another beer, then went to bed.

Bob found it difficult to doze off but the affect of the beer finally overcame the power of hate that rushed through his body and he fell into a deep sleep. Two hours later, he woke up in a cold sweat. He had been dreaming about the Nam again. His pulse raced and his breathing was shallow, just as it was the previous nights. This time he was the only one who was awakened. How he hated to go to bed at night. Bob was afraid to sleep........ terrified to dream.

The next day, Bob was up early. Mary said nothing; while Mike sat at the kitchen table sipping on a coffee. He was skipping breakfast that morning. No one felt much like eating. Bob told Mike that he would take care of the clean-up. First, he was going to call Detective Russel and let him know what had happened. They had a coffee together before Mike left for work, then Bob went into the study to call the police.

The station switchboard answered the phone and Bob asked for Detective Russel. He had managed to catch him at the station before he left for the College.

"Detective Russel here."

"Hi. This is Bob Hills, I was in yesterday over the peace march incident. Do you remember me?"

"Oh, you mean the near riot. Is that you Joe Louis? How in the heck are ya, and what can I do for you?"

"I had visitors last night."

Suddenly Russel became serious. "What happened?"

"They wrote, "A MURDERER LIVES HERE!" across my parents garage door, in big, bright, red letters. What can I do about it?"

"Paint it."

"Paint it?"

"That's right. Actually, Hills, there is very little you can do about this. Did you or anyone else happen to see the vandals that did it?"

"No, not that I know of."

"That's what I thought, and that's why you can't do anything about it."

"But I'm pretty sure that it's my little buddy from yesterday, that did it."

"Look. Unless you caught whoever did this red handed, there is nothing we can do about it. We just cannot go around accusing people of a crime without proof. And even if we did find out who did it, it's only a misdemeanour at best. If I were you, I'd just keep it low profile and try not to let this bother you. If whoever did this knows that it bothers you, they'll be at you all the time. Just let it die."

"And if they won't let it die?"

"If they persist, then we'll follow up on it."

"So that means whoever did this to my family is going to get away with it."

"Look, the Police Department hasn't the manpower to look for vandals. We're too busy with killers and rapists. I take it I'm the first person you notified?"

"Yeah."

"Well a black and white going out there last night wouldn't have done much more good than this. I mean what are they going to do? Put out an A.P.B. on some nut with a can of spray paint? Not likely."

"So that's it?"

"Look, again if you saw them, we could do something about it. As it stands now, it could be anyone from the kids in the neighbourhood, to the old lady down the street. Who knows? Meanwhile, if you want to do something, take a picture of the damage. Make sure that you record the details on the back of it or on a separate sheet of paper."

"Okay, sorry for bothering you."

"Hey ... it's Okay. If you run into any more problems, give me a call right away. And don't do anything stupid. I want to nail him, not you."

"Thanks again. I appreciate everything. Goodbye."

Bob hung up the phone. It seemed as though the bad guys had chalked up another one."

Bob did as the detective suggested and got out his father's Polaroid camera. Bob took a picture of the garage door, looking around he could see no other physical evidence. Then he got the Camaro out of the garage and drove over to the hardware store. Bob needed to get some things to clean the mess up.

When he got there, he headed straight for the paints. Jim Mueller was stocking shelves.

He looked over to Bob and said, "Bob, your Dad said you'd be coming. I was suppose to keep an eye out for you. He had me put some things aside for you. It's all here in this bag. I've all ready put the paint through the shaker. There's a roller, brush, tray. and some varsol. This should be everything you need for the job."

"Thanks Jim." Bob made a poor attempt to smile.

"Hey Bob, I heard some bits and pieces of what happened at your place last night. It's a shame and I'm sorry it happened," he said with sincerity.

"The person or persons who did this had no business trying to hurt me through my family, Jim."

"What did they write on your garage?"

"Something about me. A murderer lives here, to be more exact. All in bright red."

"That's nuts. Do you have any idea who did it?"

"I've got an idea."

Jim shook his head, "Who ever did it is in bad need of professional help."

"I think your pal Kevin did it."

"Hey Bob, he's no pal of mine. He's a little to hot-headed for my liking. He was upset yesterday though. From the looks of all the tape on his nose, I'd say you broke it. I can't say I know him well, but he seems to be the type to carry a grudge. Listen, if I knew for sure that he did it, I'd let you know. But I can't say for sure."

Bob bent over and picked up the bag and said, "Thanks Jim. Did my father take care of this or should I have it checked through the cash?"

"Your father's already taken care of it."

"See you later Jim. Oh, and thanks again." Bob quietly turned and walked away.

Bob was headed towards the exit when Lynn caught sight of him. She hurried over to talk to him.

"Bob."

"Hi Lynn."

"Bob, I heard. I was in the office when your father was telling my mother. I can't believe someone would do that. They have to be sick."

"Everyone seems to think the same thing. But it's only paint and I can have it cleaned up in no time. It was more emotionally upsetting for my mother than anything else. I'm just on my way to clean it up now." Bob made a gesture towards the bag he was holding.

"It's still too bad."

"I would rather just forget the whole thing happened, if you don't mind. Well, I better be going. I've got to get home and paint the garage door."

"Okay, call me tonight." She gently pulled him over to her and kissed him on the cheek.

"Hey what are you trying to do, Make the rest of the

staff jealous?" Bob asked smiling. He held her hand for a short moment, "Tell my father that I'll call him later. And I'll call you tonight." He left.

Bob went home and painted the garage door. He was just cleaning the painting equipment when Russel showed up.

"Hello there, Mr. Hills."

"Well if it isn't the Cavalry. How are you Mr. Russel?" Bob said with a smirk.

"Why Robert, I see you've taken up home painting and decorating. How very nice."

"Very funny. What brings you here?"

"I was on my lunch break and I thought I'd come over and see the fancy artwork, but I guess I'm too late. You've already painted over it."

"Yeah, well it didn't exactly enhance the neighbourhood. People were getting nervous about property value."

"Did you take any pictures of it?"

"I sure did, a Polaroid. Do you need it?"

"Yeah, I'd better file an Incident Report and I'll need the picture for it. Did you find any other damage?"

"No."

"Take my advice and leave the police work to me. Oh, and stay away from Mr. Patterson."

"Okay for the tenth time... but he better leave my family alone, or I'll have his ass."

"That's not what I wanted to hear. I want you to stay out of trouble and let him hang himself. I was planning on talking to him this afternoon."

He took a statement and the picture. Before he left he gave Bob his card with instructions to call him at work if anything else happened.

"Thanks for dropping around Russel."

"No problem Bob. Stay out of trouble and I'll talk to you if I find anything out." He got into an unmarked police car and drove off.

That afternoon Jim Mueller went to classes, then to the college newspaper office. When he got there, only Terry was in. This gave Jim the opportunity to get some things off his chest.

"How's it going, Jim?"

"Not too bad Terry. And you?"

"Oh pretty good. So what's new on the home front?"

"Nothing much, I guess."

By the tone of voice that Jim used, Terry could tell something was bothering him. So he asked him, "Jim, is there something wrong? Because if there is and it's about the newspaper, I really should know about it."

"Terry," Jim said with some reservation, "Kevin was in last night."

"Yeah. Was that when he called me at home?"

"Yes, it was. He was pretty upset when he read my story on the rally, too."

"Why? Did he want a story on how, HE almost changed a peace rally into a riot?"

"He doesn't see it that way, Terry."

"I know. That's the part I find so scary. I don't know him any more. Ever since his brother's death, he's become bitter and almost violent."

"Do you know Bob Hills?"

"Not personally, but I know who he is. Why?"

"Someone painted something on his garage door last night."

"What are you talking about?"

"Someone took some red spay paint and wrote, "A Murderer Lives Here". It really upset his family."

The look on Terry's face turned to disgust, "That stupid fucking idiot."

"Terry, we don't know for sure he did it. Besides I want

you to pretend that I didn't tell you any of this. I don't want to be involved in anything."

"Don't worry Jim, I don't blame you. It'll all catch up with him eventually, though."

"Do you think that he really did do it, Terry? That's a pretty crazy thing to do."

He just nodded his head then looked up at him, "Yes ... yes I really do."

"It's not our place to say anything because we don't know for sure if he did it. You know Terry, if I did know for certain that he was responsible for the vandalism I'd probably go to someone with it. If he'd do that, it's only a matter of time before he would do something much worse. It's his temper. One day it's going to get the better of him, then look out."

"I know what you mean about going to someone about this. If you sat here doing nothing and something worse happened, you'd be just as guilty as he was."

"Let's hope this whole thing blows over. Meanwhile Terry, why don't you humour him and try to go along with what he says. Then slip in some common sense about handling situations. Maybe he won't feel so rejected and he'll listen to what you have to say, and straighten himself out."

"You mean like, when the cops have treated you wrong, we'll file a complaint and forget about slashing the tires of a police car?"

"That's right, something just like that."

"I'll talk to him first chance I get. Now lets get some work done around here."

Just outside the college campus perimeter were the police keeping watch. Detective Russel was talking to another officer near the main entrance. The other cop, his partner Detective Carter, was a tall, heavy-set fellow, with a round face and a balding head. Carter was eating a bag of peanuts at the time, when Russel spotted a familiar face walking in their direction. There was no missing all that tape on his nose and his two black eyes. Russel just smiled.

As Kevin drew near, Russel said with a grin, "Please excuse me Carter. There's someone I've just got to say hello to. I'm sure he could use a little cheering up."

"Don't be long, I want to go and get something to eat."

"The way you eat, you should weigh three hundred pounds. Finish your peanuts. I'll be right back."

Russel approached Kevin. "Hello Mr. Patterson. And how are we feeling today?"

"Take that smirk off your face, pig. I've got nothing to say to you, or any of your kind."

"Oh, come now Mr Patterson, can't you see I'm only trying to help you?"

"Oh yeah," Kevin said looking at him with contempt, "and how's that pig?"

"I'm here to give you a little advice."

"I don't need your advice."

"Hey, it's free, besides your going to get it anyways. This situation between Mr. Hills and yourself is not good for either one of you. Now, if one of you decides to take the law into your own hands and gets caught, it wouldn't look good for that individual. That person would definitely find themselves in some pretty serious trouble."

"I don't know what your talking about, pig."

"It's like this. If I catch you with a can of spray paint on your person, I'm going to shove it up your nose, Picasso."

"I still don't know what you're talking about. See I can't hear you, pig. I'm not listening."

"See Mr. Patterson, that's because a guy like you can only think about one thing at a time. Right now you're probably thinking about sex." Russel was still smiling,

"You're probably wondering where you're going to find your next great big, strong, muscle bound man to shove his parts up your ass. Ain't that right, you sweet thing?" He patted Kevin gently on the side of his face. "Oh, and you're using way too much eye liner. Your eyes are starting to turn black. Catch you later handsome."

Russel turned and walked away with a big grin on his face, leaving Kevin standing there in a frenzy.

Kevin yelled to him, "Hey Gestapo, this is harassment! I'll complain to your superiors! You fuck'n goof! I'll have your job asshole!"

The other policeman finished the peanuts, walked over to Russel and said, "Must be a friend of yours. You seem to have that affect on a lot of them."

"Thanks partner."

"You're welcome. So what did you say to him to get him so wound up?"

"Nothing."

"He yelled at you like that for nothing?"

"Actually Carter, he wanted your phone number and I wouldn't give it to him."

"Very funny, wise-ass. Let's go for a break and get something to eat."

CHAPTER EIGHT

That afternoon Bob went to Del's just to get away from what was happening for a while. He couldn't believe the shit that was going on. All he was trying to do was mind his own business. Bob walked in and sat up at the bar. The place was quiet; Del was there alone. He asked Bob how he was doing. Bob did his best to hide his anger and frustration, telling him that everything was just fine. Bob asked Del for a Budweiser and he brought it over.

"Thanks Del."

"You're welcome. Oh, yes, if you want something from the kitchen, you'd better hurry up and order it. It closes for the afternoon in a few minutes."

"No thanks, Del. I had something to eat not too long ago. Besides, it's only a couple of hours until dinner." The time on the clock behind the bar was three-thirty.

The front door opened and Jack walked in.

"Bob, I've got something for you. It's in the car." He sat down beside him. "Del, I'll have a Bud if you don't mind and I'll pay for these two beers."

Bob raised his bottle and smiled, "Thanks Jack."

"You're welcome." Del put an open bottle of Bud in front of him and Jack picked it up and took a sip. "I dropped by the store just now to see you. I thought I'd catch you there. I was talking to Mike."

Del walked away to clean some tables.

"Yeah, so what did he have to say?"

Jack looked at him with concern, "He told me what was happening. The rally and the vandalism."

"Yeah well, Jack, I just happened to be in the wrong place at the wrong time."

"Keep a low profile Bob."

"I think I know who did it."

"Bob, if I were you, I'd let it slide and pretend that nothing ever happened. You don't need this kind of trouble."

"That, Jack, is precisely what I fully intend to do. But if someone attacks my family again, and I catch them, I'll have their sorry ass."

"Just remember, you're not in the Nam now and that's no Vietcong you're dealing with."

"Yeah, you're right Jack."

"Remember, if you need to talk about anything, just give me a call."

"Thanks, I'll keep that in mind. And don't worry, I think I'll manage to keep my nose clean. I'm not too big on jail."

"Did you talk to the police about it?"

"I sure did. There isn't a lot anyone can do about it. At least, the way it sits right now."

"Why not?"

"They said, unless you catch them in the act, there is little to nothing you can do. And even if you did catch them, it's only a misdemeanour."

"That hardly seems fair."

"Well that's the system for you."

"Yeah, and the system stinks."

Bob raised his bottle, "I'll drink to that Jack. The system should make allowances for vengeance."

Jack laughed, "Sure. That'd be something alright."

"Sure Jack, damages plus ten minutes alone with the bugger, to kick the little mother's ass." Bob had a big smirk on his face.

"Listen Bob, wait here while I run out to the car and get you your floor mats."

"Floor mats?"

"Yeah, Pat was going to have them thrown in and they were never put in the car."

"Hey, that sounds good."

As Jack was walking out, Russel and Carter walked in and sat at a front table."

Del walked over to them and said, "So where are your other two friends?"

Russel said, "Oh they're coming. They should be here any minute now."

Del smiled. "So what'll it be?"

Carter just grinned, "Oh, we'll have four drafts and a couple bags of potato chips, bar-b-que."

"Make those beers, coffees. We're still working."

Carter looked at Russel and said, "My, aren't we good little public servants."

"Yeah well, we're not too far from the college campus and I'd hate to get caught drinking."

Carter was now pissed off, but couldn't argue the fact about drinking with Russel. Just like Kalar, Russel was usually right. "Whatever you say, partner. And Del, don't forget my chips."

Russel just looked at Carter. "Bar-b-que chips and coffee, you're disgusting. And you eat enough to feed any third world country that I know of."

Del laughed and headed back towards the bar.

All of a sudden another plain clothesed officer ran in. "Russel, Carter. There's trouble over at the R.O.T.C. facility on campus! Let's roll."

The two of them sprang up from their chairs and Russel said, "Oh shit!"

"Hell, you're not kidding, I never got my chips." Carter complained.

They darted out of the bar. As they left, Jack walked in. "What in the hell was that all about?"

"An emergency," Del said, "some sort of trouble over at the College."

They could now hear the sirens, outside. They were from both the Police and the Fire Department vehicles. They passed right by the front of Del's.

Russel and the other officers drove onto the campus grounds straight to the R.O.T.C. building. Much to their surprise there were only a few people standing around. There were flames on the outside of a brick wall of the three-story building. The building had large windows across the front, making it a good target for vandals.

Russel approached the bystanders and asked, "Did anyone see anything, anything at all?"

Nothing was said and they began to walk away.

Russel turned to Carter who was no standing beside him and said, "That's great. A building's solid brick wall is on fire, for no apparent reason, in broad daylight and nobody saw a thing. This I don't believe."

Just then a female student started walking towards them, her books in hand. She looked to be nineteen or so, slender with long brown hair.

Carter nudged Russel, "We got company. Maybe a witness."

Russel looked over, "Let me do the talking, you'll be asking her for chips."

"Ha, Ha. Some partner you are. I'm going to see what the firemen have to say anyways." Carter started walking towards the crew chief. The fire was pretty much out by now.

When she reached Russel, he said, "Yes, can I help you?"

"Actually," she said, "I think I can help you."

"You saw this happen?"

"I sure did. I was standing in front of my dorm room window over there." She pointed to a building approximately forty yards away, with an unobstructed view of the R.O.T.C. building.

"So you had a clear view of the person or persons involved in this?"

"What makes you so sure someone did something?"

"I hope that you're not going to play games with me. That brick wall didn't ignite all on it's own. Miss?"

"Okay. I was just curious as to why you would blame someone without knowing if a person was even involved. It could have been a freak accident. And, It's Ms. Sharon Foster; and yes, I saw the whole thing."

"Ya right. Did you recognize the person or persons who did this?"

"There was only one guy; but I couldn't recognize him because of the rubber mask he had on."

Russel started taking notes and asked, "Can you describe what the person looked like?"

"Sure, no problem there. The person was a male, slim, wearing jeans, a blue plaid shirt, and a Richard Nixon mask."

"Why do say the person was male?"

"You don't have to be a detective to figure that one out. No tits and he ran like a quarter back."

Russel looked at her with his jaw wide open, "You might have a point there. Good thinking."

She looked at him and smiled. "Thanks."

"Would you mind walking over here where the man was. Show me exactly what you saw."

"Sure thing."

The two of them walked over to the R.O.T.C. building.

She stopped him, "He was standing here, he reached into a paper bag he was carrying and pulled out a bottle with a rag in it. He then threw the bag on the ground and pulled out a lighter from his pocket. He lit the bottle then ran in this direction; threw the bottle at the building and ran off in that direction there." She motioned in the direction of the Student Centre.

Russel looked around on the ground then said, "Well I don't see any bag. What hand did he use to throw the bottle with?"

She thought for a moment then acted out his motions. "His right, I'm positive it was his right."

"Good. Was he wearing gloves at all?"

"I believe so."

"But you're not sure?"

"I'm pretty sure, because his hands looked dark."

"Could he have been black then?"

"Oh no, some of his hair was sticking out of his mask at the back. And it was blonde."

"Yes, well there aren't too many blonde-haired, black people walking around. So his hair must have been, say, shoulder length?"

"I'd say so officer."

"Is there anything else you can remember, anything at all? No matter how small a detail you might think it to be."

She thought and shook her head. "Nope, that's it."

"Well I appreciate the help Ms. Foster. Do you have a number where you can be reached?"

"Yeah, sure, it's 275-3097. But it's to be used only for official police business."

"Have no fear. My wife would kill me if I phoned you for any other reason. Meanwhile, here's my card; it's got my work number on it. Call me if you happen to remember anything else. But be sure to call me only on official police business."

"Dream on fellow." She walked away.

Russel thought to himself, "What do I look like, some sort of masher?"

Then he noticed a College Security Officer walking towards him. He was wearing a light blue uniform, complete with a peak cap. The man was about six feet tall, with brown hair, clean shaven and had a rugged, outdoors look to him. When the officer reached Russel, he put out his hand to greet him.

"Hello there. I'm Captain Gregg Kiser, I'm with College Security Services."

"Russ Russel."

Gregg looked at him with surprise written all over his face. "Detective, Russ Russel?"

"My folks liked the name, Russel."

Gregg ,trying to act as though he wasn't taken off guard by his name, said, "It's a nice name."

"Thanks."

"So, have you found out anything?"

"Well Gregg, we're after a right-handed, slim male caucasian,wearing blue jeans, a blue plaid shirt, and he looks like the President."

The Security Captain just looked at him with a blank expression for a moment, then said, "Like as in the President of the United States?"

"He wore a mask." He nudged Gregg on the shoulder.

"Anything else, Russ?"

"Yes. He used a molotov cocktail, he can't throw for shit and he's an idiot."

"Why would you say he's an idiot?"

"It's like this, Gregg. When someone firebombs a building in broad daylight, like he's done, it's not gutsy - it's stupidity. Hell, he even missed the friggin' window by seven feet. The window is only five feet across, by eight feet high. All he managed to do is scorch some bricks."

"It doesn't sound like an attack by the I.R.A. when you put it that way."

Russ laughed, "Yeah, not very professional at all."

"Is that it?"

"That's it, Captain."

"Are you going to have your people check for prints on the bottle pieces, Russ?"

"Oh sure, that'll be checked, but they won't find much. The student I talked to seems to recall him wearing gloves. There should be a paper bag around here somewhere as well. It might have prints."

"That's too bad about him wearing gloves. What's the name of the witness?"

"Sharon Foster. She saw the whole thing from the building right over there."

The two men walked towards the fire engines to examine the damage done by the fire bombing, when they were approached by Jim Mueller. He was carrying a note pad, eager to get the scoop on the terrorist attack.

"Hi, my name's Jim Mueller, and I'm with the College Sentry. That's the student paper."

"Jim, I'm Captain Gregg Kiser and this is Detective Russ Russel, with the city police."

"I'm here to find out what happened. Can either of you tell me anything?"

Gregg was the first to offer any information. "At three fifty-two P.M., my office was informed that the R.O.T.C. facility was on fire."

Jim, enthusiastically, started to record everything that was being said. "Were there any witnesses?"

Russ Russel jumped in, "No there weren't. So if you come across anyone, please let us know."

Jim looked as though he knew he wasn't going to get a lot of cooperation from Russ.

Russ nudged Gregg. "Listen, I've got to get going. If I find anything out, I'll let you know. Here's my card in case you come across anything, Okay?"

Gregg took his card and smiled, "Thanks for all your help Russ. It was nice meeting you."

Russ nodded. "It was nice meeting you ... ," he paused and looked at Jim, "both." He had almost completely ignored Jim Mueller. He turned and walked away.

Jim carried on with his interview with Gregg Kiser. Gregg now knew enough to keep the existence of any witness to himself and to Russ. He also knew that cooperating with the student paper would be appreciated by the Dean of the college. Jim fully intended to praise Gregg Kiser for all his help, and did so in his article. Jim got his article and Gregg was going to look good to his superiors.

Bob got home at four-thirty; in time to catch Mike just getting home for dinner.

"Hi Dad."

"Hello Bob. I see you got the garage door painted over OK."

"Yeah, I finished it this morning."

"Thanks, Bob."

"Don't thank me. It's because of me that this crap has happened."

"Don't say that, Son."

"It is true. But let's say we put it all behind us. The door is painted and we can just forget it ever happened."

"That's a good idea. Let's go inside and see what your mother's up to."

They walked into the house and found Mary in the kitchen.

She turned to them and said, "So, what do you two want for dinner?"

"Gee, Mary I thought it would have been ready. I have to go back to the store later."

"Hey Mom," Bob said with as much sincerity as he could,

"I'm cooking dinner tonight. And it won't take long either. But I've got to be left alone in the kitchen."

Mary was quick to say no, but Bob insisted and ushered the two of them out into the living room. He made the two of them promise to leave him alone while he prepared his culinary delights.

Bob had no sooner returned to the kitchen, when he got on the phone to the Galloping Gourmet himself... Fast Freddy, of the Fast Freddies Pizza Parlour fame. Fred himself took Bob's order. A large pizza with extra cheese, pepperoni, mushrooms, bacon and hot peppers. Mary wouldn't be too crazy about the hot peppers, but she could always pick them off. After all there were two of them that loved them and only one that didn't. It had been a long time since Bob had a pizza. To add to the surprise he asked them to deliver it to the back door.

Bob heard a knock at the kitchen door, it was Mike. Bob grabbed some pots and pans and began to rattle them, as though he was busy cooking. He was asking for a beer for himself and a glass of wine for Mary. Bob got the drinks and brought them out to him.

"How's dinner coming, Son? I'm starved." Mike said with a smile, trying to look in the kitchen. "That's funny, I don't smell anything yet."

"Come on, get out of here; let a genius work." Bob pushed him back from the door.

He left, and Bob got on the phone to talk to Lynn. Mrs. Hathaway answered. They exchanged hello's and how are you's, then after a short conversation, he asked to speak to Lynn. She placed the telephone receiver down on the table and called to Lynn. Bob could hear her quite clearly in the background making a cute comment. "Oh Lyyyynnnnnn, it's for yooouuu. It's your heart's delight, Bob Hills." Bob could just visualize a smirk on her face. Now, he could hear Lynn in the background, "Mom, I wish you wouldn't do that. He might hear you." It was apparent that she was not pleased about being teased. She picked up the receiver, "Hello."

"Hi, it's me, heart's delight." Bob knew that he was just adding salt to the wound, but he couldn't resist.

"Oh, I'm going to kill her."

"Hey, come on Lynn, she's only teasing you. You should hear my Dad with me. And I very rarely ever want to kill him."

"Ha, Ha. So how's your day been?"

"Oh not too bad. I got the garage door painted over. Then I went out for a quiet beer this afternoon."

"Sounds as if you had a nice afternoon anyways."

"Yeah, it was good."

"Do you think you could come out to see me dance tonight?"

"Sure. What time?"

"We start at seven."

"And how long are you there for?"

"We usually practice for a couple of hours. So we should be finished by nine."

"How about if I meet you there at about eight." Bob didn't think he could take much more than an hour of ballet.

"Sure. That'll be fine."

"Where do you go for your practices?"

"The downtown YM-YWCA."

"Great. I'm looking forward to seeing you dance."

"I only hope you don't get bored."

"I won't. See you at eight then, OK Lynn?"

"Fine Bob, bye for now."

Bob hung the phone up and he could hear his parents talking in the living room. His father was saying that maybe they could go on a vacation. It had been a long time since they had gone anywhere, and he felt that the store could pretty well run itself for a week. Mary was agreeing with him. Bob smiled and nodded thinking the idea was a good one.

Then Mike yelled out to him, "Hey Bob, how's dinner coming. We're getting hungry out here."

He grabbed some pans and started to rattle them on the stove again. "Great Dad. No problem."

Just then, he noticed someone approaching the back door, so he rattled the pans some more to muffle the knock. It didn't take him long to answer the door and pay for the pizza. Bob tried to be as quiet as possible. The pizza was placed on the counter, then he got the plates, napkins and utensils out. He went to the dining room and arranged the table as elegantly as he knew how. If the guys in the platoon could see him now, they'd be impressed.

Mary said, "I certainly hope you're not going through too much trouble."

"No trouble at all Mom. Don't worry about it."

Dad was equally concerned, "Hurry up Bob, I'm hungry."

"Hang on, it'll be right out of the oven."

"The oven." Mary said in surprise. "What on earth can you cook in the oven, in twenty five minutes? Especially when it take ten minutes just to heat it up."

Mike started to look disappointed. "I sure hope that it isn't pork."

Bob merely shook his head and went back into the kitchen, grabbed the pizza and pulled it out of the box. It was sitting on a round cardboard insert, which, he thought would make a dandy serving dish. Into the room of fine dining Bob went, carrying his chef's surprise. Placing it in the centre of the table, they all admired the feast and the setting - how elegant.

Mary looked at Bob, straight-faced. "That's dinner?"

Mike simply smiled, from ear to ear and said with true

style and grace, "Pizza, yum, let's eat."

Bob thought he heard his father's stomach say, "Thank you." Bob too was starving and couldn't wait to dig right in.

"Oh, these aren't hot peppers, are they Bob?" Mary said with disappointment.

"Don't worry Mom, just pick'em off."

Mike jumped in, "Give them to me, Honey. I'll eat them."

She looked at him and said, "Oh, you'll eat anything, Mike."

After dinner, Bob helped Mary with the dishes - three plates and three forks. As it turned out, she rather enjoyed the change, and Mike was more than helpful with her hot peppers. Bob had decided to slip out to Del's and have a beer before going to see Lynn.

When Bob was finished in the kitchen, he quickly brushed his teeth and headed out. It was six-thirty by the time he got to Del's. There wasn't any room at the bar, so Bob sat at a table. Del must have read his mind, for it wasn't long before he walked over and put a Budweiser in front of Bob.

"Thanks Del."

"No problem Bob. I'll run you a tab."

He sat there simply watching everybody having a good time. It was quiet time for himself and he was enjoying it. After a half hour of sitting alone, in walked company.

It was Russel and he was by himself. He walked in and looked around, then he noticed Bob. He walked over shaking his head and smiling.

"What? Do you live here or something, Hills?"

"How's it going?"

"Not too bad. You here alone?"

"Yeah. Pull up a chair."

"Thanks. I will."

"What brings you here, Russel?"

"My wife kicked me out of the house for the evening.

She's having a Tupperware Party."

"I bet you didn't argue with her there?"

"You're right."

"Russel. What's your first name, anyways?"

"Russ."

"You're kidding?" It was difficult, but Bob managed not to smile.

"No, I'm not."

"So Russ, I understand you had a little excitement at the college this afternoon."

"Yeah. Some damn dick-headed asshole tried to burn down the R.O.T.C. facility in broad daylight with a molotov cocktail ... and missed."

Del dropped by with a beer. "Here you go Russ."

"Thanks Del."

"You're welcome." He smiled and went back to the bar.

Bob was still chuckling over what he had said. He couldn't believe anyone was that stupid.

"I bet that with your experience in Vietnam, you could do a pretty good job of it yourself."

Bob smiled. "I think so. Put it this way, they wouldn't see me coming and I sure as hell wouldn't miss."

"Yeah, I bet."

Bob smiled again, "And it'd be a good bet."

"Well Rob."

"It's Bob."

"Sorry. Bob, I saw your buddy today."

"Oh yeah. What did he have to say?"

"Not too much. We talked about his love life a little."

Bob gave him a puzzled look and asked, "What?"

"As it turned out, it wasn't very exciting. But I think I convinced him to keep his distance from you."

"Thanks Russ."

"Don't thank me, I love playing social worker."

Somehow Bob knew there was a lot of hidden sarcasm in all that he said. It must be hard to be a cop and take verbal abuse as they do every day. Having a sense of humour would help. It must be his way of dealing with the frustration. He certainly had a comical way of putting things.

"So how did my buddy look?"

"Oh, just fuck'n lovely. I think he would look better though, if he replaced the bandages with an athletic support."

Bob couldn't help himself and he broke out into laughter. "Yes, wouldn't he look cute?"

"Tell me. How bad was Nam, really?" Bob could see the curiosity in his eyes.

Suddenly Bob wasn't laughing any more, "Everyone seems to be interested in getting all the gory details."

"Hey Bob, I'm sorry ......"

"Na, that's okay. Actually it was pretty bad. It's particularly rough when you first get over there and you don't know anything. You're just one more N.F.G."

"An N.F.G.?"

"New Fucking Guy; a cherry. We lost two guys I stepped off the plane with in the first two weeks I was there. My best friend that I grew up with died in my arms. He was a month short of getting the fuck out of there."

"Hey, I didn't want to screw you up with a lot of bad memories. I wasn't thinking."

"Hey, no sweat. It's probably better to talk about it than keeping it all inside anyways. Get it off my chest and out of my mind, if that's possible. I'm just glad that I can confront the past and try to deal with it."

"Yeah, not everyone is able to do that. Do you think about it a lot?"

"Yeah. Especially at night when I sleep. We lost a lot of

good people over there. It's hard not to think about it. When you leave the Nam, you leave part of you behind."

Russ looked at him sympathetically. He obviously could sense that the emotional wounds of the war ran deep.

"Hey Bob, buy you a beer?"

"Sure, I've got time for one more."

"What's this? You got a hot date or something?" Russ was smiling now and motioned to Del, to bring over some beer.

"Sure. A good looking guy like myself. Why not?"

"Just don't marry them. It'll cost you a fortune in make-up and Tupperware."

They both laughed. Del brought over a couple of beers. "Hey you two, what's so funny?"

Russ was still smiling, "Women, Del, women."

Del simply smiled and shook his head. "Yeah, if they're not making you laugh, they're making you cry. Especially when the credit card bills come in. Enjoy your beers fellows." Then he turned and walked away with a grin on his face.

Russ said, "That Del, he's one of a kind."

"Yeah, he's a pretty good guy."

"I don't understand how his wife puts up with all the hours that he puts in here."

"Del's married?" Bob was surprised.

"He certainly is."

"Does he have any kids?"

"Hell no. I told you he spends all his time here."

They laughed, talked some more and sipped on their beers. Then after about forty-five minutes it was time for Bob to go and see Lynn. He was anxious to see her in her tights.

"Well, I've got to get going Russ. It was good running into you here. We'll have to do it again."

"It's been fun, Bob."

"Hope your wife didn't spend all your money. Hey Russ, just think you'll probably be drinking your next beer out of a Tupperware stein. Hell, you'll probably go home to a set of six of them."

"Wrong, it's a set of four and she bought them at the last Tuperware party she was at."

Bob laughed and shook his head. "See you later Russ."

"See you around." Russ watched as Bob Hills walked away. There was something about Bob that made Russ like him. Maybe it was his sense of humour, or maybe it was that he was one of the few people his age that still had respect for the police. But there was something else that really played on Russ. It was knowing that Bob Hills was an innocent victim of a radical student who might be capable of doing anything. One thing was for certain and that was that Russ had a bad feeling about Bob's future. It was a feeling he simply couldn't shake.

After paying his tab, Bob left Del's and headed towards the downtown YM-YWCA. He was almost there when he pulled up next to an old sixty-two, dark blue, Dodge with one red door. They were stopped at a traffic light. Bob looked over to the car and noticed the passenger was his old flame, Sue Lucas. He couldn't help but stare at her. Then she looked over and saw him. Her eyes widened as she looked at the car. Then, when she looked back at him, he gave her a big grin. The light changed and Bob laid a strip of rubber that just wouldn't quit. Bob said to himself, "See ya later, bitch."

Bob got to the Y at about ten-after-eight and received instructions of where the group was from the front desk. When he walked in, he found Lynn in the middle of practising a dance number with the rest of the group. She looked better in those tights than he had imagined. He could have watched her forever, with her dressed like that.

When the number was over, she walked up to him and said, "Bob, you made it."

"Lynn, that was very impressive."

With a big dazzling smile, she said, "Well, thank you. I'm glad you enjoyed it. Have you ever been to a ballet?"

"No. But I'm sure I will in the near future."

"I'm sure you will."

"I love that outfit, Lynn." Bob's eyes were almost bulging from his head.

"Thanks again. You're full of compliments tonight." She was flattered by his comment, and the expression on his face. Everyone wants to feel they look attractive and she certainly did. "You'll have to excuse me, for about fifteen more minutes. I've got another number to do. Have a seat on the bench over there and I'll be back."

It wasn't just the way that she looked that caught his eye that night. She had a real talent for dancing. You could see that she put her whole heart and soul into it. The type of talent she had was the type that you're born with; she was a natural. Bob couldn't keep his eyes off of her. He found her dancing almost sensual. She certainly was special and he didn't want to let her get away. Whatever had caused Sue to change, he hoped it wouldn't happen to Lynn.

She finished up for the night shortly before nine. Lynn was in a hurry to leave, but not until she introduced Bob, to some of the other dancers. Lynn suggested that they go for a drive, so he agreed. They drove around for what seemed like minutes, but was actually more than an hour. It was a nice night out and the music was good. For Bob, it was great just being near her.

Then he took her to a municipal water-front park. She remarked how peaceful it was there as he parked the car in the vacant lot, facing the water. The reflection of the stars and the moon illuminated the river. It's light allowed him to gaze at her beauty, as she looked onto the water. There was a cool breeze coming off the river, causing Lynn to snuggle to Bob for warmth. The console in the Camaro was a definite negative. She looked at him passionately and kissed him, ever so gently. He embraced her and returned her affection. They kissed and teased one another with their lustful advances for a while. Trying hard to regain control of the situation, she suggested it would be best if she went home, before they went too far. Bob wasn't sure why he didn't coax her to stay, instead he agreed. In that instance, it was probably best, as from that moment on, Lynn truly felt that she cared for and trusted Bob. From that moment, their relationship began to bond and grow.

When he dropped her off that night, he felt heavy-hearted. How he wanted to spend the night with her. The situation and his feelings were getting out of control. Bob's emotions were running wild on him and he questioned whether he was doing the smart thing. Should he get involved, or should he keep it simple. Bob walked back to the car after their goodnight's and drove off.

On the way home, Bob ran into another sorry sight. That was two in one night. It was more than anyone would care to bear. First it was Sue, now it was his pal Kevin, and he was coming out of a convenience store. The dumb shit never saw Bob. He just jumped in behind the wheel of his old tan Ford and drove away.

When Bob got home, he noticed some of the lights were still on. His parents were waiting up for him.

"Hi. How was your evening?" Bob said as he walked into the living room and saw them.

Mary looked up at him and said, "I got a phone call from Sue tonight."

Bob looked at her, shook his head and said, "What in the

world did she want?"

"She wanted me to tell you that you had better stop following her around."

Bob started to laugh, "She wishes. Forget that call. That's nothing to get too upset about."

She looked up at him with a strange look on her face, "That's not the one that upset me."

"What are you talking about, Mom?"

"Some guy called and said some terrible things about you and what you had done in Vietnam."

Bob didn't say a word. All he could do was stand there in silent rage. It was Kevin and he knew it. He was going to break more than just his nose. If Bob had known about the phone call when he had spotted him, Kevin would be in intensive care right now. That little bastard was going to pay for this.

Mike turned to her and said, "Mary, it's getting late, let's call it a night."

Bob slowly looked up at his parents. He could see the hurt in their eyes and he began feeling guilty for their dilemma. "Don't worry about it Mom, I'll take care of them."

"Don't do anything foolish, Bob. That's what they want you to do." she said.

"Don't worry I won't."

The two made their way upstairs to their room for the night. Bob sat in the living room in darkness, sipping on a beer, for close to an hour. He then called it a night.

Bob had problems falling asleep when he finally went to bed. Kevin and his past deeds occupied his mind. Thoughts of violent revenge ate at him like a cancer. It was only an hour after Bob finally fell asleep, when he was awakened by another nightmare about South East Asia. He felt the knot of fear that was so much a part of the Vietnam experience, form in his stomach. His trembling hands wiped the cold sweat from his face. Why was it he couldn't get it out of his head? Bob wished it would stop. It wasn't fair that not only him, but his family as well, had to suffer the war that nobody wanted. It's cruel after effects were unbearable. Mary had been a victim of not knowing what was happening to Bob when he was overseas and now she was a victim yet again. A victim of vicious and hateful people. Was there ever going to be an end to it all. Bob stared at the ceiling for what seemed like hours before falling asleep once again.

CHAPTER NINE

Bob awoke that morning still tired from the night before. The entire night, he had tossed and turned. Between his dreams and lying awake thinking about getting back at Kevin, it was a wonder he had slept at all. Kevin was looking for someone to blame the world's problems on, a scape goat; and Bob was it. Bob kept thinking of what the Army had taught him about hand to hand combat and how much he wanted to use it all against that son of a bitch, Kevin. That's when a part of Bob would take over and he would say to himself, "No... it's not right. The law will take care of him and anyone like him." Bob was sure that justice would prevail and Kevin would get his.

Mike had already left for work by the time Bob was showered and dressed. He stood in his room, looking at some of the memories of yesteryears. There was a picture, sitting on his dresser, of all the kids on the ball team he played for, when he was ten. Of course Jimmy was standing right next to him in the picture. He was all smiles, with his hand on Bob's shoulder. They had just won the league championship and Jim had gotten a trophy for the teams best player. Bob wasn't sure who was the most proud that day, Jimmy or his father. How Bob missed him; how he wished things were different.

Looking in the dresser mirror, Bob examined the circles that had begun to form around his eyes. There was also a pretty scruffy looking beard on his face. The way he felt that morning, he thought it best to have a coffee before attempting to shave. He went downstairs and grabbed a cup of coffee from the coffee percolator. Then, he went into the study to phone Russ. Not that Bob thought there was anything he could do; but he did want him to know that something did happen.

"Hello, Russel here."

"Russ, it's Bob Hills. I've got problems."

"Again? What happened now?"

"My parents received a phone call from someone last night. That person, decided to tell my mother what they felt my role was in Vietnam."

"Jesus Christ."

"My feelings exactly."

"Well Bob, we could tap your phone if you had a number of these calls. But it wouldn't be any more effective than you getting an unlisted phone number."

"That's what I thought you'd say."

"Sorry, Bob."

"That's Okay Russ. I thought I'd let you know so you could add it to your list of events."

"I'll make note of it."

"You know it was probably Kevin."

"No, I don't. But if I find out it was, I'll handle him my way. You leave this to me. That's what I get paid for."

"Anything you say, Russ. Just get this shit to stop."

"Hey Bob, I like you. And I hate to see you getting screwed around like this. But there isn't anything we can do right now. Understand that. Until we catch someone actually doing something, our hands are tied."

"Well, when he burns down the house I'll let you know. I better let you go Russ."

"Bob ..... give me a chance to catch him. And let me know if anything else happens."

"I will Russ, thanks." Bob hung up the phone.

After he finished his coffee, he got up and went into the kitchen to get another cup. It was going to take two coffees to get him to the point were he would trust himself shaving. Mary was sitting at the kitchen table, sipping on a coffee, when Bob walked in.

"Good morning."

"Good morning, Bob."

He could tell that she was still upset over the calls she got the night before. Kevin wasn't the only one Bob wanted to talk to. He was anxious to talk to that bitch, Sue, as well.

"Can I make you some breakfast, Bob?"

"No thanks. I think I'll have another coffee and drop over to see Dad."

Bob poured another coffee and headed to the washroom to shave. Breakfast would have been nice, but Mary didn't seem to be herself. So Bob thought he'd simply get a donut at the coffee shop on the way. Once he cleaned up, he began to walk out the door when Mary stopped him.

"Son, please take care of yourself and stay away from those people."

"What people?"

"You know. Susan and that fellow that you hit ... Kevin or whatever his name is."

"Okay, don't worry, I will." Bob kissed her on the cheek and walked out the door.

Bob drove to the coffee shop thinking he'd enjoy his modest breakfast in his favourite booth. The place was pretty quiet. Looking around, the only customers in the entire place were two women seated at the booth next to where he wanted to sit. Bob thought it might be rude if he sat there, when he had the whole coffee shop to choose from. But then he thought, it's not as if he's going to listen in on their conversation. He'll merely sit with his back to them, have his doughnut and look out the window. Besides that booth was very special to him. So Bob took his coffee and doughnut and sat down at the booth.

They were so involved in their conversation with one another, that Bob doubted if they even noticed him. He was seated with his back to them and not that he wanted to, but he couldn't help but hear everything that they said. Bob thought about moving, then decided not to draw any attention to them or himself. The minute Bob finished his doughnut he planned on leaving, so they could talk in private.

"Joan, did you find anything that really bothered you, being a nurse?"

"Gail, don't tell me that you're having second thoughts about being a nurse, already. You've only been into nursing for six months. Give it a chance. If you're still not happy with it in another six months, then consider quitting."

"I just find it so hard, emotionally, sometimes."

"Why's that?"

"It's working in geriatrics, I find it so depressing. Those old people, lying there, waiting to die."

"Gail, nursing is helping people who need help. The old need help every bit as much as the newborns in the nursery, or the kids in paediatrics."

"It's not what I want to do, Joan. What I really want is to become a surgical nurse, like you. There you're helping the surgeons repair a damaged body. Not giving out medication, or taking someone's body temperature. I'm fed up with old men trying to grab my ass."

"Being a surgical nurse isn't all what you might think it is, Gail. It can be tough. You see some pretty bad things in an operating room."

"I think I can handle it."

"I hope so."

"I've had my fill of terminally ill, old folks that are beyond medical help."

"And you don't think you'd see that in an operating room,

with car accidents and people trying to kill themselves or somebody else?"

"At least they're not all on their last leg. Joan ... I know I can handle it."

"Yes, well maybe so, but I had my stomach turn on a few occasions."

"I wouldn't think you had a weak stomach. What was it, a cancer patient? I know that some of them can get pretty bad."

"It isn't always just the surgery, it's the circumstances. For instance, a young, very pretty, college girl, came in for emergency surgery because she went to some butcher for an abortion. He really made a mess of her. They had to bring her in by ambulance, from her friends apartment. She could have died, poor kid. Now it doesn't look as though she'll ever be able to have children."

"You're kidding? When did this happen?"

"It was about ten months ago, I'll never forget that poor girl. It must have had a hell of a psychological effect on her. Such a young and pretty girl too. She somehow managed to pay for the hospital bills on her own, probably to hide it from her parents. I wonder if she had. That poor kid, Susan Lucas."

Bob's heart jumped up to his throat, along with his doughnut. He wanted to turn around and say something, but he couldn't, or at least he knew he shouldn't. It took everything in his power, not to turn around. Bob took a sip of his coffee and left his doughnut with only one bite out of it. He wasn't exactly hungry after hearing that. In a way, he felt sorry for her, having had gone through that. But in another way, he was furious, because of the way she attacked him for his part in Vietnam. Bob guessed that she felt that taking the life she took was not as bad as what he had done. Bob got up from the booth to leave. The nurses, still talking, didn't give a second thought to his presence. He made a pact with himself as he walked out the door, not to mention this to anyone except Sue; at least for the time being.

As Bob entered the hardware store, he noticed Mike talking to one of the cashiers. He walked over to him and put his hand on Mike's shoulder.

"Hi Dad."

"Bob. I'll be with you in a minute."

"No rush. I'll be in housewares."

"Sure. I'll see you there in a bit."

Bob walked over to houseware to see Lynn. She was busy stacking a shelf with sixty-minute timers. He carefully sneeked up behind her, with a smirk on his face.

"So this is where Betty Crocker shops when she's not making movies?" He laughed.

She turned around. "Come on ... Betty Crocker never played in a movie."

"Not even in Alice's Restaurant?"

"Not even in Alice's Restaurant. So don't tease me or I'll hit you with one of these cooking timers." She had a smile on her face and a twinkle in her eye.

"Now you're threatening me."

"And rightfully so. So how are you?"

"A lot better after seeing your violent side."

"Bob, I don't have a violent side."

"Are you sure?"

"Yes, I'm sure." She gave him a devilish smile. "So, what are you up to today?"

"Not too much. I thought I'd drop over to see my father and talk to him about my working here."

"You've got to be kidding? That'd be great. When would you be starting?"

"Perhaps Monday, if he wants me."

"That'll be great having you around, Bob."

"So what are you doing tonight, Lynn?"

"I'm supposed to go to my aunt's. But I could probably get out of it though. Why?"

"I thought maybe we could go out for dinner."

"Dinner, as in a restaurant, or as in burgers and a movie?" She was waiting for his response.

"A restaurant, of course."

"Sounds great. Where do you want to go?"

"How do you feel about Italian?"

"I love Italian."

"How about Mario's?" Mario's was one of the nicer restaurants in the area. The type of place that required a tie and a fair amount of money.

Her eyes lit up. "Mario's?"

"Sure. Why not?"

"Great!"

"I knew you'd approve. Let me call them first. We'll probably need reservations."

"You're really not kidding?"

"No I'm not. Then it's settled. Let's say I pick you up at six. If there's any problem with getting reservations, I'll find somewhere else as nice."

"Let's hope there's no trouble with getting into Mario's." She was all smiles.

Mike walked over. "There you are."

"Hi Dad. I was wondering if I could talk to you for a few moments."

"Yes, of course. Will you excuse us Lynn?"

"Certainly, Mr. Hills. I'll talk to you later, Bob."

"OK, Lynn."

The two went up to his office to have their talk. When Bob got there, he looked around in surprise. Mike's office, once again, resembled a functional office instead of a warehouse.

"Is this your office?"

"What are you talking about? Of course this is my office. Whose else would it be?"

"It's so neat and clean."

"Very funny."

Mike sat down behind his desk and Bob sat across from him.

"So what's up Bob?"

"I was thinking of working here, if you want me?"

"Sure. When did you want to start?"

"How about Monday?"

"I thought you were going to take some time off for a little relaxation?"

"I think I will have had enough time off by Monday. Besides, I'm starting to get bored and it'll keep me out of jail." There was a smile on Bob's face.

Mike laughed. "Yeah, you're probably right, it would keep you out of jail."

"I overheard you and Mom talking about maybe going on vacation. That's great, and with my working here, perhaps after a few years or so, you could retire. Wouldn't that be a vacation?"

"Even if I only worked a couple of days a week, Bob, that would be nice."

"I hoped you would like the idea."

"I do, I do. It sounds good to me. Monday sounds good too. I'll have you work with John Perry. He'll be able to teach you a lot. You better enjoy your time off now, because as of Monday, I'll be working your tail off." He had a smirk on his face.

"Just take it easy on me, at first."

"So, what are you up to today?"

"I'm going to work around the house. The lawn needs to

be cut, and the garage needs to be cleaned out. Basically just get caught up on small jobs around the house."

"You don't have to do that, Bob. Take it easy. You could use the rest, you said so yourself."

"No, that's OK. I don't mind, really." Bob stood up. "Well I've got to get going."

"I'll see you tonight at supper."

"Actually Dad, I have a dinner date."

"Oh brother. Do you ever take a break? This is the fourth night in a row."

"Come on Dad, lighten up."

"Right. Well, if you're ready to leave then I'll walk you to the door. There's a few things I wanted to show you."

Mike walked Bob to the front door of the store. As they walked, he pointed out some of the shelving changes he wanted to make. After a brief conversation at the front entrance, Bob left for home. Once there, he did all that he told Mike he was going to do. He even found time to straighten the basement out.

By the time Mike made it home from the store, it was five-fifteen. Bob had already showered and changed. He was wearing a sports jacket with his best shirt, tie and slacks. He didn't think his cheap after shave would cut it, so he used some of Mike's good stuff. Looking in the mirror, he said to himself, "I look good, I smell good; hell, tonight I should do good."

When Mike walked into the house, he commented on the work that Bob had done around the house that day. Bob told him that it was nothing and that he was happy to help out. The expression on Mike's face showed how much it was appreciated. Then he sniffed the air and asked, "What smells so good?" Bob said it was his wife's own corned beef and cabbage. He said, "No," that it was Bob and his cologne. Bob turned a pale shade of pink and was gearing up for the onslaught of kidding he was about to get, but the kidding never came. Mike only commented on his being dressed up and looking so nice. Bob reminded him that he was going out to dinner with Lynn, Mike had forgotten all about it. When Bob told him where they were going, Mike raised his eye brows and said something to the affect that he hoped that she was worth it. Bob assured him that she was. He simply smiled and shook his head. Bob was walking towards the door when he called out to the kitchen, "I'm leaving now. See you later." Mary stuck her head out the door and said, "Have fun." Mike slapped him on the back and told him to have a good time and enjoy his dinner.

Bob left and started to make his way to Lynn's. On the way there he spotted Kevin in his tan Ford. Suddenly all that happened to him and his family, at the hand of Kevin and his kind, flashed back to him as though it had just happened. Bob started to follow him. He turned down a side street and stopped at a mail box. Bob stopped about fifteen yards behind him. Kevin didn't notice him at all and got out of his car to mail some letters. Bob got out of his car and walked towards him. By the time Kevin mailed the letters and turned around, Bob had reached him.

"What do you want, warmonger?"

"Your ass!" Bob grabbed him and threw him on the hood of his car. "If you ever bother me or my family again, I'll make you wish you had been stillborn. You got that, asshole."

"Let go of me!"

Bob threw him on the ground. "You better take heed, shit head. I'm not fucking around with you any more. Now I mean it. Next time you decide to do something cute, you'll be shitting out your ears, cause I'm going to rip your head off and shove it up your ass. You got that."

Kevin, who was struggling and trying to get up, looked up at Bob with contempt and said, "What's wrong? Mommy didn't like hearing the truth."

Bob pulled back and punched him in the face. "There's some truth for you. That's just to let you know I'm not full of weak threats and a lot of bull shit. Now you sit there like a good little boy and shut the fuck up."

He now had a fat lip to match his bandaged nose, and it looked good on him. Bob motioned, as if he was going to kick him, but stopped short. "Leave my family alone. This is your last warning." Bob turned and walked back to his car, while checking his clothes for wrinkles. When Bob got into the car, he looked back at Kevin still sitting on the ground, glaring at him. Bob glared back then shook his head and drove off.

"I'll get you, you God damn warmonger! You bastard!" Kevin yelled.

Bob smiled when he noticed he was waving to him with a closed fist. "I never realized how sentimental you are Kevin." Bob thought to himself. "Good bye, little buddy." Hills said waving back, with only his middle finger extended. Bob hoped that Russ would never hear about his little talk with Kevin. Bob was sure that he wouldn't approve. The one thing that he was certain of was that if he didn't approach Kevin himself, he would think that he could get away with whatever he wanted. If he went unchecked, he simply wouldn't stop harassing him and his family. Bob wasn't about to let that happen.

Bob got to Lynn's place at about six. When he knocked at the front door, her mother answered. She smiled when she saw him standing there, all dressed up.

"Bob."

"Hi Mrs. Hathaway. Is Lynn ready?"

"Not quite. Come on in."

"Thank you." He walked into the house and into the living room. He didn't notice anyone else around.

"Have a seat Bob." She said making a gesture towards the sofa. "Can I get you something to drink?"

Bob sat down and said, "No thank you. I'm fine."

"Your father tells me you're coming to work at the store, on Monday."

"That's right."

"It'll be nice to have you around."

"Thank you. I certainly hope that everyone feels the same way when they find out. I wouldn't want to step on anyone's toes."

"Oh, don't be ridiculous Bob.........So, where are you going for dinner tonight?" As if she didn't already know.

"To Mario's. I made reservations this afternoon."

"That's quite a nice place. I'm sure that you'll enjoy it there."

Just then Lynn walked into the room, looking simply beautiful. She was wearing a tight navy blue skirt that showed off her great looking buns, and a very dressy, white blouse. Like a fool, Bob merely sat there and stared.

"Are you ready to go Bob?" She said with a smile.

It took him a moment to get an answer out. "Sure. Anytime you are."

"Great, let's go. See you later Mamma." She kissed her mother on the cheek.

Mrs. Hathaway smiled softly. "You two have a nice evening, and enjoy your dinner."

Bob smiled and said, "Thanks, I'm sure we will, and you have a nice evening too."

"Thank you Bob."

Bob started to walk out the door with Lynn following him, when he heard Mrs. Hathaway whisper to Lynn. "He's a nice boy. I like him better than the other one."

If she knew what Bob was thinking every time he looked at her daughter, she wouldn't be saying that.

They drove to Mario's, a large restaurant with a formal looking canopy that stretched from the building to the street. The parking lot at the side of the building was full closer to the main street, so they parked in a spot closer to the back alley. Once inside, they were greeted by a gentleman wearing formal attire. Bob and Lynn felt special, simply walking in the door. The gentleman smiled and greeted them with a soft and friendly "Hello", which made them feel at ease. It was as though they were regulars that very much belonged there.

They had a choice table located near the large fireplace. There was a candle on the table and the candle holder and cutlery looked to be real silver. The tablecloth was white, with a red overlay and the napkins were white linen. Their napkins were placed in the long stem wine glasses that were meticulously placed next to their pewter plates. The plates had the name, "Mario's" written in script and cast right into them.

Lynn sat there and looked at the table with widened eyes. The waiter also had formal attire on, as well as white gloves. When the waiter came to the table, he asked Bob if he would care to examine the wine list first or order a before dinner drink. Bob smiled and said he preferred to order the wine. He left it for him to look at, and walked away.

"I'm not old enough to drink Bob." Lynn whispered in a nervous tone of voice.

"Come on Lynn, one glass of wine won't hurt you. It's expected in a place like this."

"Under the circumstances, I would. But I don't want to get caught."

"It'll be alright, don't worry about it. I know what I'm

doing, simply follow my lead."

The waiter returned. "If you are ready, may I take your wine order Sir?"

Bob smiled and nodded. "Yes, could we have a bottle of your Chianti Bello please?"

The waiter paused for a moment, looked at Lynn with suspicion, then looked at Bob and Bob smiled. "Of course Sir, excellent choice." The waiter smiled and nodded back. "And would you like that now or with your dinner?"

"Oh, I think we would like to have it now, don't you think so Lynn?"

"Now will be fine." Lynn's expression was that of relief and she was smiling from ear to ear.

The waiter nodded and said, "I'll go to the cellar and get that for you, right away, sir."

The waiter left and Lynn was gazing into Bob's eyes. "It's beautiful here Bob."

"I'm glad that you like it. We'll have to make this our special occasion place."

She took his hand. "Yes, we will. Thank you for being so thoughtful, Bob."

"You're welcome, but the pleasure is all mine."

The waiter returned with the wine and asked if Bob would care to sample the wine. Lynn looked at Bob, not knowing if he knew what to do or say. He motioned to the waiter that he would sample the wine. After all, Bob was well versed in wine etiquette, having seen it done many times before on television. He showed Bob the bottle, it read Chianti Bello on the label. Bob smiled and nodded with approval. Lynn was impressed. The waiter then uncorked the bottle and gave Bob the cork. Picking the cork up, he sniffed it. Bob was a natural, and even began impressing himself. He then carefully plucked Bob's napkin from his glass and laid the napkin across Bob's lap. Then he poured a small amount of wine into his glass and Bob sucked it back, like it was a shot of Kentucky bourbon.

Bob smiled and said, "Ahhhh yes, great year. That will do nicely, thank you."

The waiter just looked at Bob with a strange, almost unbelieving expression on his face. He poured their wine and then, placing the bottle on the table, went to leave.

"Waiter," Bob said in a soft voice, trying to impress Lynn, "could we have our food menus now?"

"Sir?"

"The food menus?"

"I'm sorry Sir, I'm not your waiter. I'm the Wine Captain. I'll get your waiter for you immediately." Off he went, shaking his head. Bob had the feeling he wasn't overly impressed with Bob's wine etiquette.

"I knew he was the Wine Captain. I meant to ask him to send the waiter over."

Lynn tried to hold back her laughter, but wasn't doing a very good job of it.

The waiter was by to show them the menus. He was very helpful in explaining the different dishes and Bob thought it best not to try bull-shitting his way through that. He'd hate to order Lynn sugar glazed goats eyes by mistake. They made their selections and the waiter was off to the kitchen. Moments later a bus boy was by with glasses of water and a basket of bread.

Lynn smiled and raised her glass to toast their evening. "To a magical evening." she said with a sparkle in her eye. Then she sipped her wine, Bob thought her eyes were going to pop out of her head. She put her glass down and her lips were still puckered.

Bob looked at her with concern and said, "Lynn, is the wine too dry?"

"No Bob, it's fine."

Her thoughtfulness impressed him. He was sure she wasn't big on the wine, but she drank it just the same. He had certainly found a real prize in her.

After dinner they had an espresso coffee and talked for a while about the store.

Then Bob said, "So, what would you like to do now?"

"Well, we could go back to my house for a while. My parents are at my aunt's."

"Sure, sounds good to me."

Bob paid the cheque and they walked out towards the car. She clung to his arm whispering soft thank you's to him. When they finally reached the car, the two of them just stood there, staring. Bob was in total disbelief. Someone had smashed every window in the car. Even the head and tail lights were smashed. Bob was unable to speak. Lynn stood and watched him circle the car, looking the damage over. First Bob felt violated and hurt, then it turned into rage as he felt himself about to explode. Lynn walked over to him and held his arm, telling him not to worry.

"Come on Bob, let's go inside and call the police."

"My car, Lynn look what they did to my car."

"Come on Bob, let's go back in."

"Why? Why is this happening?"

"Come on, Bob."

"It's not fair."

"I know, Bob."

Bob looked down at all the glass scattered across the pavement and in his car.

"Come on Bob." Lynn managed to lead him away and back to the restaurant.

"Jesus...why? What did I ever do to them?

"We'll find out who did it, Bob."

By the time they got back inside, Bob had partially gotten

a hold of himself. One look at them and the host knew something wasn't right. He came over to them right away and asked, "Is there anything wrong, Sir?"

Bob looked up at him and said, "My car has been vandalized, the windows were all smashed.....headlights and tail lights too. Please, could you call the police for me."

The expression on the host's face turned to shock. "Right away; please, have a seat while I call." He motioned to a row of velvet covered chairs near the front entrance. Then a few moments later he returned and said, "They'll be here shortly. The owner, Mr. Terino, would like to offer his regrets. Can I get you anything, a drink perhaps, it's compliments of the house."

"No, thank you, not for me. Lynn, perhaps you would like something?"

"No thank you."

"Thank Mr. Terino anyways."

"Certainly Sir." He left them alone realizing they didn't need an audience, at that time.

A moment later, a distinguished looking man in a silk suit walked over to them and said, "I'm very sorry. My name is Aldo Terino, I'm the owner. This is very disturbing. Nothing like this has ever happened here before. Is there anything at all I can do for you? If you need transportation, anything at all please don't hesitate to ask."

The tone of his voice was very sincere and the expression on his face confirmed the honesty of his offer. Bob just shook his head and he left.

Five minutes later, a uniformed officer walked in and the host nodded in their direction. The officer said, "Was it your car that was damaged."

"Yes," Bob said, "we were in having dinner. When we went out, we found the car all smashed up."

The officer, in a low sympathetic voice said, "Perhaps we

should go out to the car."

They followed the officer who led them out to the parking lot. His partner was looking the car over and taking notes. The police cruiser was parked behind the Camaro, it's driver's door open. The sound of the police radio receiving different coded calls, filled the air.

"Do you have the vehicle registration, insurance and your driver's licence, Sir?" the officer asked.

Still in a daze, Bob said, "Yeah; sure." He reached into his jacket pocket and pulled out his wallet. Handing him the papers he had asked for, Bob said, "I can't believe it. I've only had the car a couple of days."

"Have a seat in the back of the cruiser, Mr. Hills, and I'll be right with you." The officer was soft spoken and sensitive to Bob's predicament.

Lynn and Bob sat themselves in the back of the police car and the policeman sat himself in the front. He opened a briefcase and pulling out a pad and pen, he began to take a statement. Lynn sat close to Bob and held his arm. It took about ten minutes in all, for the officer to take the statement. When he had finished, he asked Bob, "Do you have any idea who might have done this to your vehicle Mr. Hills?"

"Yes."

The officer looked up from his writing pad and said, "And who might that be, Sir?"

"His name is Kevin. Detective Russel knows all about him. Ask him."

"I know Russ. You say he knows this guy, Kevin?" the policeman asked.

"Yes, he does. This Kevin and I are having a bit of a problem. Russ was made aware of it, officially."

"Can you remember his last name at all?"

"I believe it's Patterson. You'd have to double check that

with Russ. He's driving an old tan Ford."

"I'll let Russ know what has happened. Meanwhile my partner and I will try to follow up on this, as best we can. It's been a busy night."

"What about my car?"

"You don't have any lights."

"But I can't leave it here."

"Look, you live about ten blocks from here, so I'll follow you home in the cruiser."

"How about Lynn here? She's got to get home."

The officer just shook his head and said, "I'm sorry Sir. I can follow you to your home, but it is getting dark and you have no headlights. You'll have to send her home in a cab. At least your vehicle will be on your property."

"Thank you. I do appreciate it, officer."

"You're welcome Mr. Hills."

Lynn and Bob got out of the police car and walked over to the Camaro. They opened the doors, brushed off the glass from the seats and got in. Bob was glad that the damage was limited to the glass on the car. At least he could drive it home. As they were pulling out, a bus boy was headed towards the parking lot with a broom, cardboard box and a dust pan. What should have been a wonderful evening out, turned into a nightmare.

The police followed them to Bob's house and he parked the car in the garage. Bob was surprised to see his father's car was not home. The police drove off and the two locked the car in the garage and walked into the house.

"Can I offer you something Lynn?"

"No thanks." She was quiet for a moment then decided to change the subject. "This is a nice house, Bob."

"Thanks."

"Where are your parents tonight?"

"I'm not sure. Actually I'm surprised myself to find them

not at home tonight."

"Well, let's go back to my place and we can talk, Bob. I'm certain it'll be a while before my parents are back. This way we can be alone."

"Sure, I'll call a cab."

Bob phoned for a taxi and a moments later, a cab was in the drive, beeping it's horn. Bob locked up and they headed over to Lynn's. When they got there, Lynn insisted on paying for the cab. It was a real shot to Bob's ego, but there was no arguing with her and she paid the fare.

Once inside she asked, "Would you like something to drink, maybe a beer?"

"Yes please. I need it." He sat down on the sofa.

She called from the kitchen, "Do you want a glass for your beer Bob?"

"No thanks."

She brought in a bottle of beer for Bob and a coke for herself. "Here you go Bob." She sat beside him, looking at him with caring eyes. She handed him the beer, then placed her hand gently on his knee.

"Thanks Lynn."

She shook her head and said. "I can't believe all this is happening to you."

"Neither can I." He said with a ripple in his voice.

"I really can't understand any of it, Bob. What brought all this on?"

"Nam."

"I don't buy that. It's got to be more than that." There was frustration in her voice.

"No. It's Nam. Someone's upset that Americans are over there and that there was a bunch of people killed." Bob had his elbow resting on the arm of the sofa and his head was resting on his hand. Bob was staring at the floor, not looking at anything in particular. "I think someone is holding me personally responsible for the war in South-East Asia."

"That's outrageous! It's not your fault! You didn't kill anyone over there. Did you?" She was looking at him, expecting him to say that he hadn't.

"Yes ... yes, I did."

She looked at him as though he had told her that he was a child molester. "You're kidding Bob?" She said in a low and nervous voice.

Bob began to get very defensive. The sensation of being dirty ran through his mind, but he had done nothing wrong. He felt rage and hurt at the same time. She obviously didn't understand. Bob tried to keep his cool but he wasn't doing a good job of it. "Lynn, when Nathanial Victor is coming at you with a Russian made A.K. 47 automatic rifle, you had better kill him before he gets a chance to kill you. And he certainly wouldn't have any qualms about doing it, either."

"Bob, who in the hell is this Nathanial Victor?" She seemed to be frightened and confused.

"The North Vietnamese." Now Bob was getting all the more frustrated and thought that for sure they were finished. In her eyes as well, he must have been a monster. Bob could feel tears forming in his eyes. "They're little, slant-eyed, yellow bastards, who get their kicks out of listening to you scream while you squirm in the mud, dying. The media is quick enough to say that we're killing innocent civilians, but they never tell you that those same civilians have been recruited by the damn V.C., complete with weapons and a cause." He started to shake as he wiped his face with his hands. "No one's overly concerned about what we were going through... not as much as they were about passing judgement on us."

Lynn's expression turned from horror to sympathy as she put her arms around him and much to his surprise said, "It's OK Bob........... It's alright."

"Sure it is, Lynn. But not for those poor bastards that I killed, right? But I'd still rather have them lying dead out there than me being stretched out, face down in that damn jungle. Somehow I just don't think I'd look so good, laying there."

"Bob, you did what you had to do, just to survive. I don't blame you at all. Not in the slightest." she took his hand. "You have to believe me, I really am sorry, Bob."

"For what?"

"For you having to go over there in the first place. For all that you went through when you were in Vietnam. I'm sorry too, for what your family has been through and they weren't even involved in the war. But mostly I'm sorry that I don't understand. For me to understand that, I would've had to gone there, myself. All I know is that this whole thing isn't fair, not at all. If the person who is doing all of this to you, knew the half of what you went through, there's no way they'd be doing this to you now."

Bob looked at her and thought how she was really, truly, trying to understand. And in her eyes Bob saw a warm, and caring human being, full of compassion. He leaned over and kissed her on her cheek and said, "Thank you for trying to understand."

"I care a lot about you Bob." Then she wrapped her arms around him and they kissed. Suddenly, Bob found myself escaping the problems he had a moment ago. She felt so warm, so good. Lynn was what he needed in his life, right at that time. As they stopped kissing and their eyes opened, he smiled.

"You're one heck of a woman, Lynn."

"You're something pretty special yourself."

He grinned and said, "Ah, I bet you say that to all the guys."

She shoved him aside and said with a smile, "I do not;

you little shit."

They talked for a while longer and then Bob decided that it was time to go. He walked over to the telephone and phoned for a cab, so that he could go home. They embraced and kissed some more until finally the taxi arrived. Before he left, she made him promise that he would see her the next day at work. Not that he'd tell her, but he fully intended to anyways.

On the way home in the taxi, all he could think about was Lynn. Tender visions of her, accompanied by a familiar love song, occupied his mind. It wasn't until the cab pulled into the drive, that Bob started to think about the Camaro again. Mike's car was in the driveway now. What would he say to them? How could he tell them what had happened? They'd be worried sick, if they knew. Most of the lights were out in the house, so he quietly went in, assuming that they were asleep.

As it turned out, they had gone to bed almost an hour earlier. So he sat in the kitchen and had a couple of beers, thinking about what had happened that night. Bob came to the decision, that he would let the insurance handle the car, and the police could handle Kevin. How he hated the Nam and how it affected his life, and the lives of those around him. He took his last swallow of beer and retired for the night.

There in the comfort and sanctuary of his own bed, he was transported through space and time . Back...... back to the hot, damp jungles of Southeast Asia. He was walking through the jungle with his rifle at the ready, just as he had so many times before when on patrol. The difference this time was that aside from Jim Wheeler and himself, no one else was on that patrol.

Jim was about twenty feet ahead of Bob, with his rifle at the ready, his head and eyes scanning the jungle as he moved.

"Jimmy." Bob whispered.

"What do you want?" He called back in a low voice.

"Where is everyone?"

"Who?" Jim replied with an annoyed look on his face.

"The rest of the squad."

"It's Just you and me on this one, Bob."

All of a sudden Bob heard a noise coming from a small clearing to his left. Bob called cover to Jim in a muffled voice, as he went to ground. He looked over to Jim, but he was nowhere to be seen.

"Jimmy, where are you?"

Suddenly there was another sound from the clearing. There seemed to be a fog rolling in from that direction and in behind the fog was a light. That's when he saw the two figures walking out from the jungle and into the clearing. Bob raised his rifle to fire, as he waited for them to get closer. The light cast a detailed silhouette of the two. Bob was surprised to see that one was a G.I. and the other was a girl with a cone shaped hat on. The silhouette of the G.I. called out, "Bob....... Don't shoot, Bob. It's me Wiener."

The voice was unmistakably Jim Wheelers. "Jim, what are you doing out there?"

"I've got someone here who wants to tell you something."

As they walked towards Bob, they left the fog behind them. The two stopped ten yards in front of him. It was Jim and the girl from the village. Both stood there in blood soaked clothes, with their wounds fully exposed. Bob began to experience the pain he felt that day when the girl died.

Jim, realizing Bobs pain, smiled sympathetically and said, "It's Okay Bob..... it's Okay."

With tears in his eyes, Bob said to her, "I'm sorry........... please forgive me?"

She smiled a gentle, peaceful smile and said, in American. "I forgive you, Bob Hills......... I do forgive you."

A great peace filled Bob as he looked on at the sincerity that was written in her face.

Then, all at once three more silhouettes emerged from the clearing, out of the fog. This time they were North Vietnamese soldiers. They screamed their battle cry as they ran towards them, firing their A.K.47's. Terror filled the faces of Jimmy and the girl. Bob looked on with horror and in anger as bullets riddled the two. Their bodies reacted to each round that pierced them. Their movements were as if time had caught them in slow motion.

Bob stood up and began to scream back, "NO!" as he returned fire.

Suddenly he found himself back in his room, half out of bed. He was soaked with sweat and his heart was pounding like a base drum. With wide open eyes' he looked around the room, his mind racing a thousand miles an hour. He consciously tried to correct his shallow and rapid breathing. It was like he was going out of his mind. Was it this room, or his dreams, that were reality. He got up and stood in the hall, listening to whether or not he had wakened his parents. When he was satisfied they were still asleep, he went down to the kitchen.

Bob opened the fridge and grabbed a beer. Turning the light in the stove's exhaust hood on, he sat at the kitchen table to drink his beer. As he sat there he thought of the young Vietnamese girl and what she had said in his dream. How he wished what she said was true and how he wished that she knew how sorry he really was. As he sipped on his beer he looked over to the clock. The time was four forty-three. He fought with the idea of going back to bed, but he knew he had to get some sleep. He finished his beer and returned to his room.

CHAPTER TEN

The next morning Bob could hear his parents talking to one another downstairs. The smell of coffee, bacon and eggs filled the air. He got up, showered and dressed. When Bob went downstairs, the two of them were smiling and talking about the wonderful time they had with the Wheelers the night before.

"The two of you seem to be in pretty good spirits. How was your evening?" Bob said, trying hard to smile.

Mike said, "Fine. The Wheelers had us over for a game of gin rummy. It was a lot of fun."

"That's good. Bill is really funny when he gets going. I trust the two of you won?"

Mary said with a grin, "We sure did. And how was your dinner at Mario's?"

"It was fine."

Mike looked at him suspiciously, "What's wrong, Bob?"

Bob hesitated for a moment. "While we were in the restaurant, someone trashed the Camaro. They smashed every window in it; along with the head and tail lights."

"What?" Mary said with anger in her voice.

Mike stood up from the table and said, "What are you talking about?"

"The car was vandalized while Lynn and I were inside having dinner. Someone must have followed us there."

Mike said, "How do you know someone followed you? It could have been some punks out doing dirt."

"My car was the only one touched. Who ever did it selected their target."

Mike was visibly upset and said, "How about witnesses? Did anyone see anything?"

"No one. No witnesses."

"Who would do that to you?" Mary said.

"The same person who phoned you about my morals in the war, not to mention the art work on the garage door."

Mike walked over to him and said, "So you know who did this to your car?"

"That's right. But, if there's no evidence, there's not a lot that I can do about it. Unless, of course, I went out and kicked the living crap out of him."

"BOB!" His mother wasn't impressed with his solution to the problem.

"I'm just kidding Mom." But really he wasn't. At this point, it was a definite consideration.

Ringgggggggg.

Bob started towards the phone, "I'll get it." Picking up the receiver he answered.

"Hello."

"Bob."

"Yes."

"It's Russ."

"Russ, I take it you heard?"

"Yeah, I did. Larry Turner left me a note on my desk this morning. He was the officer that responded to the call last night. Bob, you didn't do anything to provoke someone into doing this, did you?"

"Well actually, I ran into Kevin last night. He admitted to having called my mother the night before."

"And what in the hell did you do about it?"

"I gave him a fat lip."

"You what?"

"I gave him a fat lip. Now he looks like Mick Jagger with a broken nose."

"This isn't funny, hot shot. I never heard what you said. Bob, this conversation never took place. By all rights I should be down to your house arresting you."

"Sure, Russ, I understand. Meanwhile he's free to do whatever he want's to."

"Understand this, Bob. You are pissing me off. I thought I told you to stay away from him?"

"I know, it was stupid of me. Russ, this guy worries me. There's no reasoning with him. He's vindictive."

"That's why I want you to stay away from him. He's not wrapped too tight. I'm telling you right now, if you don't back off this guy, the seriousness of this situation will only escalate and you'll wind up getting the worst of it."

"Yeah, I know."

"You know all right. For the last time, stay away from him. If I get a chance I'll talk to him about it. But you realize of course, I'm not the one actually doing the investigation at this point."

"Thanks Russ."

"Don't thank me, I haven't done anything yet."

"I do appreciate anything that you can do."

"Call your insurance company and let them take care of the damages. Everything done to you so far, can be fixed. Let's not let this get into some sort of, out and out, blood feud between the two of you. These things can easily get out of hand.... and this guy's probably capable of anything."

"Alright."

"I've got to go. I'll call you if I find anything out. Meanwhile, if something happens let me know right away. Talk to you later."

"Thanks again. Talk to you later." Bob hung up the phone and turned around. His parents were staring at him, waiting to hear what was up.

"Was that the police?" Mike asked.

"Yes it was."

"So what did they say?" Mary inquired impatiently.

"Not too much. Simply that they were looking into it and when they find something out, they'll get back to me."

Mike said with disappointment, "That's it?"

"That's it."

Mike walked over to Bob and said, "Who did you hit?"

Bob looked at him defensively. "The creep that grabbed me during that damn demonstration. The same guy that's behind most of what has happened to us."

Mike was calm but firm. "I want you to stay away from him, Bob."

"I will Dad."

"So what now?" Mary asked.

"Yeah, what about your car?"

"I call the insurance company and they get the car fixed. The police will take care of the rest."

"If you need my car, just let me or your mother know. We don't use it too much during the day."

"Thanks, Dad. I'll drop by to see you a little later. First I have to call the insurance people."

"Why don't I wait for you to phone. This way I can follow you to where ever you're taking it to get fixed." Mike said.

"Yeah that might be alright. I don't need my head lights and if you're following me, I really don't have to worry about the tail lights either. This will work out pretty good. I'll give a call right now."

"Wait a minute Bob. Let me phone John Perry first. He's got a set of keys to get into the store and I want him there a little early to let the staff in." He phoned John and made his arrangements.

Bob went into the den and phoned the insurance company. They asked about the police report and some of the details. Then Bob was told to take the Camaro into Gravenhurst Auto Glass, where they have all their glass repairs done. They asked about any other damages that may have occurred when the windows were smashed. Bob told them the only damage was to the windows, head and tail lights. Then they told Bob that he'd have to take his car into the Chevy dealer to get the lights fixed, but that wouldn't be until the windows were all replaced. Bob agreed and hung up.

"Well Bob," Mike said, "what did they have to say?"

"I've got to drop the car off at Gravenhurst Auto Glass. I should have asked them where it's at."

"No problem, I know where they are." Mike said.

"Great. Do I have time for a quick coffee Dad?"

"Sure. I'll join you."

"Can I make you breakfast Bob?" Mary asked.

"No thanks."

"Are you sure? It'll only take me a minute."

"With all that's happened, I'm really not very hungry. Thanks anyways."

Mike and Bob had their coffees, then headed over to the repair shop with the car. Mike followed Bob in his car while Bob drove the Camaro. Tiny squares of glass covered the floor and back seat of the car. When they dropped the car off, Bob asked the manager when he could expect the work to be done. He was told that, he might have it completed by tomorrow, Monday at the latest. They left and went over to the hardware store.

When they got there, they went straight up to the office. Mike said he had something he wanted to show Bob, if he didn't mind hanging around for a little bit. Bob said that he didn't mind. Mrs. Hathaway was talking to John when they walked in.

"Oh Mr. Hills, you're in." Mrs. Hathaway said.

"I sure am, Dorothy, good morning. Good morning John."

"Good morning Mike, Bob." John replied.

Bob made an attempt to smile at John and Dorothy, as he walked by them.

Mrs. Hathaway looked up from behind her half glasses and said to Bob, "I'm really very sorry to hear about your car, Bob. It's a terrible shame."

"Thank you Mrs. Hathaway."

"Bob," Mike said, "if you're sure you have an hour or so to kill, I'd kinda like to show you our new inventory control system. It really can wait until Monday, if you're busy. It's really very easy to learn and makes our job so much easier."

"Sure, I don't mind."

Just then a heavy-set man, with a beard and glasses walked in, carrying a very large briefcase.

"Mr. Reinharte, Gold Line Electrical Products. I almost forgot about you." Mike said to him. "John, could you take Bob into the staff room and run over the inventory control system with him, please?"

"Sure thing Mike, no problem." John replied. "Come on, Bob, this won't take long."

John walked over to a filing cabinet and opened the top drawer and pulled out a bunch of papers. He made a gesture to the papers in his hand, "It looks worse than what it is." Then the two men walked out of the office and over to a room down a hall marked, "Staff Room".

The room was about fifteen feet square, with a large table in the centre. A number of wooden chairs surrounded the table, which must have been eight feet long. There was a kitchen counter with a sink and upper cupboards against one wall. A refrigerator was located on another wall near the counter and next to it was a stove with a hood fan. A few pictures dotted the walls and a sign hung over the sink. It read, "PLEASE CLEAN UP WHEN YOU ARE THROUGH". A coffee percolator with fresh coffee in it, sat on the counter-top, along with a sugar dispenser and a jar of coffee whitener with a spoon it. Disposable coffee cups were neatly stacked next to the coffee maker.

"Would you like a coffee, Bob?"

"Sure, I wouldn't mind one at all."

"All we have is this powdered whitener though. Sorry."

"Oh, that's Okay John."

John placed the papers on the table, arranging them into several, specific stacks. Then they walked over to the counter where the coffee was.

John said, "Nice of someone to have made a fresh pot." He poured them each a cup. "I was sorry to hear about your car being vandalized, Bob."

"Yeah well, these things happen."

"Damn kids. They don't have anything better to do?"

The anger began to build in Bob, as he hesitated before commenting on John's remark. "Not quite, but I do have a good idea who is responsible and so does the police."

"You're kidding?"

"Proving it might be another story."

"Why? Why would someone destroy another persons property like that?"

"Because he's a sick-o John. He's got it in for me because I was in Nam, if you can believe that."

"I find that pretty hard to swallow."

"There's a lot of nuts out there. Believe me, it can happen a lot easier than you think."

"Well, Bob, I don't believe in wars, but I certainly wouldn't blame the poor bastard who had to fight the damn thing for causing it. That's if that's the way this guy thinks."

"To tell you the truth, I'm not quite sure how he thinks. He's definitely twisted though."

"He should have a lot more consideration for what you've been through."

"I wish everyone thought that way."

"I think most people do. It's a loud minority that you're seeing and hearing about. And that minority, too, is a pretty darn small one."

"Yeah, I guess you're probably right. Were you ever in the service, John?"

"Oh, yes. That was something I could have lived without. Too young for World War II, and too old for Vietnam. But I did find myself in the Army in fifty-one, just in time for Korea. That was no treat, I can tell you. I remember a winter, it got so damn cold and the ground was so hard, that we couldn't bury our dead. We had to tie them to the sides of our vehicles, including our tanks. The poor bastards. It got pretty tough, up at the front. Did you ever fight at the front, Bob?"

Bob looked at him with a puzzled look on his face, then looked away and thought for a minute. "I was in Quang Tri Province near the D.M.Z., but we never considered it to be the front, as such. Certainly not as you might think."

They took their coffees, after adding the sugar and whitener, over to the table, and sat down.

"You must have had a front somewhere, Bob. There has to be a strategy or battle plan of some sort that the enemy would follow. A direction of advance."

"We didn't have a front and that's what people back home failed to realize. It wasn't like fighting any other war we've ever fought before. The front as you called it, was in front of you, a half mile to your right, a mile behind you and five hundred yards to your left. And, just as nuts as that sounds, there were times when that was exactly the way it was. The front was the seventeenth parallel, Cambodia, Laos, and in the streets of Saigon. The main enemy supply route runs right through Laos and Cambodia, ... it's called the Ho Chi Minh Trail. You never knew who the Viet Cong were. They could be a bunch of farmers, or an old lady, or even a ten year old boy. You simply never knew and one was just as deadly as the other. There were no safe places to be over there. The only way to understand what it was like John, was to have been there yourself."

He nodded and said, "It would be rather hard to fight an enemy like that. And you're right Bob, you would have to have experienced it, to fully understand what it was like. But your firepower was definitely superior."

"Sure, when you had them all bunched together. There you're looking at a mass assault by N.V.A. regulars. That wasn't an everyday occurrence. How about all the hit-and-run attacks, or V.C. snipers, and let's not forget they loved to use underground tunnels too. You have to remember, when you're trying to kill an enemy, seeing where they are, helps."

"But Bob even the rifles and machine guns you had were a hell of a lot better than what these peasants had to fight with. You should have had no trouble with them."

Bob was frustrated by his ignorance of the situation over there. "First of all John, these so called peasants were extremely motivated. Don't forget, it was us in their front yard setting up shop. And when they came at you with whatever they happened to have to fight with, they meant business. It was that determination that made Charlie so dangerous. He doesn't give a shit if he lives or dies. And as far as weapons go, we resorted to some really unusual ones ourselves. We had canisters filled with nails that would fit into pods that were installed on some of our choppers. They would fire these nails at the enemy. A couple of canisters would cover an area about the size of a football field. They're a French-made weapon called Flechettes."

"You saw these being used?"

"Hell no. You wouldn't want to be anywhere around,

where they're being used. I heard all about them though. We used shotguns in the field as well. They were pretty effective."

He looked surprised. "Shotguns? I can't imagine a shotgun being as effective as an M-16."

"Well they were. They were usually used by the man on point, in a patrol. If he sees something move, he lay down a screen of fire as he dives for cover. This screening fire also gave everyone behind him a chance to go to ground and find cover. Charlie was a little reluctant to stick his head up when there was a few shot gun bursts coming his way."

"Jesus Christ Almighty. You must be some glad you're out of there."

Bob's mind began to take him back again. "Yeah, but I do miss some of the guys. You tend to get rather close to people that you went to hell and back with. I met some awfully fine people over there. You learn a lot about a person when you're under fire or you're cooped up in a foxhole with them for hours on end."

"Well, Bob, your war may have been different in a lot of ways, but one thing that remains the same, and that is good people get killed for what quite often amounts to nothing. That much hasn't changed since man first started waging war against his neighbours in the beginning of time."

"The big difference though John, is the welcome we got when we came home."

He looked down at his coffee and said, "Yeah, you're right." Then he looked back up to him. "And it's not fair, that all of you weren't given more recognition by the public for what you've done. After all, it was the publics' own elected officials that sent you there."

"Yeah, well, I guess the way the American public is

viewing this is that we're not exactly coming home the victors."

"Perhaps you're right. Do you think we'll ever win the war over there, Bob?"

Looking into space, Bob shook his head and said, "I don't think so. We weren't doing all that great when I was there and I can't see where things are going to get any better."

"Maybe we should pull out?"

"Maybe we should, John."

The conversation then turned to the inventory-control system, and John began explaining how it worked. Mike was certainly right, it was fairly simple and it wasn't taking John long to show Bob, all about it. It was already planned that Bob would act as John's assistant and John was comfortable with that decision.

Russ Russel pulled up in front of the College Administration Building. As he got out of his unmarked police car and started walking towards the building entrance, he spotted Gregg Kiser just walking out.

"Captain Kiser, I was just on my way to see you."

"Russ, what can I do for you?"

"I've got a copy of the report on that ridiculous fire bombing. I'd appreciate it if you kept my witness's name under wraps." Russ handed Greg the report."

"Oh sure. I really appreciate this Russ."

"Good, you owe me a beer."

"Anytime. Well, everything here seems to be quiet now. It was probably a single individual, trying to make a statement. He probably didn't even want to do any damage. What do you think of that theory Russ?"

"I'll stick with my original one. An idiot with a lousy pitching arm. Gregg ... have you ever had any trouble with a student by the name of Kevin Patterson?"

"Off hand, the name doesn't ring a bell, but I could

always check my files. Why?"

"He got into some trouble the other day. It was during the demonstration."

"Right, I heard something about that. That was the fight on the street, right?"

"That's right."

"But I thought it was just a minor incident?"

"It was, on the surface. Kevin grabbed a Vietnam veteran, by the name of Bob Hills and ever since then, Hills and his family have been harassed. Some of it has been quite serious. I'd sure like to nail whoever is doing it."

"And you think it's this Kevin?"

"Yeah."

"I'll keep my ears and eyes open for you."

"Thanks."

That's OK. If it's one of the students doing it, I want him out of here. We don't need an individual like that around. Besides I owe you."

"I was glad to help you with that, Gregg."

"Thanks again Russ."

The two shook hands and Russ left, while Gregg returned to his office with the report.

John had finished showing him the inventory system and Bob had gone back to the office to see Mike. When he got there, Mike was busy talking to yet another salesman. Bob decided to go and have a short visit with Lynn until Mike was finished meeting with his suppliers.

Bob couldn't get that damned Kevin out of his mind. As sure as Bob was living and breathing, Kevin was responsible for everything that was happening to him. As Bob looked for Lynn, he passed by the guns in the sporting goods department.

He stopped, turned and began to stare at the rifles and shotguns displayed on the wall. He kept thinking of Kevin and how he wanted to frag that miserable bastard's ass. His mind started to drift into another world, one of violence. Bob just kept thinking about getting his revenge. As he stared at the weapons, his mind drifting, he could hear the choppers in his head. They were distant at first, but kept getting louder and louder. Then they appeared in his mind, looking like dragonflies silhouetted against the sky. Bob could hear the troops yelling commands to one another and the radio messages being transmitted. Someone was franticly calling in a fire mission. Then the artillery started. Soon the rifles and machine guns opened up. The cracking of gun fire seemed so real. It was wrong; so very wrong. Bob saw Jimmy lying in the foxhole, begging for help and asking for God's forgiveness. He could hear him call, as though it was that horrible day, all over again. Then Bob felt a hand touch him on the shoulder. It startled him and he spun around.

"Are you OK Bob?" It was Lynn. She was looking at Bob with a concerned look on her face.

"Yeah ... I'm fine."

"Are you sure? You're kinda pale."

"Really I'm fine. Just a little tired is all."

"How did you make out with the car?"

"Not too bad. It should have all the glass in by tomorrow, Monday at the latest. Then I'll be bringing it over to the dealer for the lights."

"That's good. So what are you doing tonight?"

"I'm not really sure just yet. Why, did you have something in mind?"

"Not really. I've got company coming over. My parents are having my Uncle George and Aunt Ruth over tonight. Uncle George is my Godfather and he's in poor health, so I think I'll stay home and have a visit with them. It's a case of doing what you should do and not what you want to do."

"Yeah well, I think I'll just go to bed early tonight. I probably could use it."

"That's right. You've been through a lot and you could probably use the rest."

"Well Lynn, I've got to get up to the office."

"Bob, there's a movie on T.V. tomorrow night. If I make the pop corn, will you bring the Pepsi?" She had a cute, irresistible smile on her face.

"Sure."

"Oh and Bob, my parents are going away for the weekend, they're leaving tomorrow morning. And I'll be able to use my mother's car. That sort of worked out well."

"Great. I feel guilty using my Dad's."

"It'll be a lot of fun. I'll pick you up tomorrow night around six and we can order a pizza for supper. I owe you a dinner anyway. We can even light some candles while we dine."

"How romantic."

"The dinner last night was romantic." She was looking at him now with such tenderness.

"I've got to go. I'll talk to you later." Bob kissed her on the cheek and walked away.

Bob was so embarrassed, to think of how she found him, standing there staring into space with his mind a thousand miles away. Bob was still fighting a war he thought he had left behind in Southeast Asia. As much as he felt that the war had left it's scars on him, he knew there were one hell of a lot of other vets out there a lot worse off than him. At least he still had all his limbs and was able to function as a person.

When he got to Mike's office, he was alone. The salesmen had left their samples and catalogues. Mike was busy looking them all over. The door to the office was open so Bob knocked and walked right in.

"Bob."

"Are you free now?"

"Yes, finally. It was one salesman right after another, this morning."

"Great. Maybe we can get some lunch now."

"Sure sounds good to me Bob."

"Where do you want to go?"

"I don't know. How about a deli sandwich?"

"That sounds good. Where would we go for that?"

"There's a new place called O'Neal's. You'll love it Bob. They're just around the corner. Once in a while I'll meet your mother there for lunch."

"That's fine with me. Let's go."

The two left the store and headed over to O'Neals. They were able to walk it in just a few minutes. The bright coloured awning on the outside was a real eye catcher.

"It would be pretty hard to miss this place, wouldn't it." Bob said looking the place over.

"Yeah, it would be. Come on Bob, I haven't too much time to spare today."

The deli, from the inside, looked more like a donut shop with a meat counter, than anything else. You could order your sandwich with whatever kind of meat or cheese you wanted. The only thing missing was the liquor licence. They got their sandwiches and sat at a table.

Bob took a bite of his sandwich and said after swallowing, "Good idea coming here. You get an "A" for this one."

"I thought you'd like it here."

"I'll have to bring Lynn here for lunch one day."

"Bob ... I've got to talk to you about all that's been happening to you."

"Don't worry about it. It'll work itself out."

"Bob," the concern was written all over his face, "this is getting serious. I don't think the police are doing enough about it."

"Their hands are tied Dad. They have to have evidence before they can make an arrest."

"Even if they can't arrest him, can't they protect you and your property from this guy?"

"They're not going to have me tailed so that nobody smashes my car or spray paints snappy slogans on the house. This shit-head hasn't tried to kick the crap out of me. It's not like he's threatened me with physical violence."

"I just don't like it."

"Quite honestly, neither do I."

"He's got to be real sick, Bob."

"Eat up Dad and don't worry about it. There's not a thing we can do about it right now, anyway."

"I just wish the police would nail this character. The sooner he's caught, the better."

"They'll catch him. That I've got a gut feeling about. And they'll catch him, red handed."

They finished their lunch and talked a little more. Then Bob walked him back to the store.

"Are you coming in?"

"No, I think I'll take advantage of what time I have left on my holidays. Monday will be here soon enough."

"I suppose. Enjoy your day off."

"I will."

"Oh, do you need the car?"

"No thanks. I'll see you later Dad."

"Okay, Bob."

Bob started to walk to Del's when he passed a drug store and he decided to go inside to get a magazine. Spending the afternoon in the quiet of Del's place, reading a magazine and sipping on a couple of beers, appealed to Bob. Besides he needed to get caught up on world affairs.

The magazine rack was near the front entrance. Standing there for a moment, Bob examined the latest issues of Time, Penthouse, Life, and Playboy. Bob grabbed one, not really concerned about which one it was. As long as there were articles of interest somewhere in it. He paid for it, then left for Del's.

Bob walked into Del's and found it to be as he expected, quiet. There were only two of the locals, sitting at the bar. Del looked over to him and smiled. Smiling back, Bob continued to walk to a table near the back in plain view of the bar.

"Could I have a Bud and a shot of Jack Daniels whenever you get a minute, Del?"

"Coming right up."

Bob sat down at the table and started to glance through the magazine. A moment later, Del walked over and dropped off the drinks.

"There you go Bob. Running a tab?"

"Yes please." He left and Bob knocked back the Jack Daniels; then a took a big slug of beer as a chaser. Now this was relaxing. He took another smaller sip of beer.

Bob started reading a story about Nixon. Somehow it didn't seem to be overly flattering. At that time, Nixon wasn't overly popular with most people. Bob finished off the beer and Del called over to him.

"Bob, you want another?"

"Sure."

"How about the Jack Daniels?"

"Sounds good."

He dropped by with the drinks. "So what are you reading about there Bob?"

"Nixon."

"No wonder you're drinking shots."

Bob laughed and said, "Thanks." as he was walking away.

The second shot went down a lot easier than the first and the beer was tasting pretty good too. Bob finished the article about Nixon, around the same time he finished his Bud. Then he ordered another round; this time with peppermint schnapps instead of Jack Daniels. Del brought them over. He was looking at him, a little strange.

"Here you go Bob. You must be on a real howl today. What's the occasion?"

"No occasion. I just feel I deserve to get out and tie a good one on."

"Well, enjoy it."

Bob started looking through the magazine and came across an article on Vietnam. There were pictures of Saigon ... Bien Hoa, and some of the troops in the field. They were Army, American Army, members of the Twenty-Fifth Infantry Division. Looking at them brought back memories that weren't really all that old. He downed the schnapps and took another look at the pictures. Bob could hear the choppers in his head. It was like a repeat of that morning's episode at the store. It seemed so real. There was the sound of gunfire in the distance and troops yelling out to one another. The memories of past patrols came back to him. The more he thought about it, the faster he drank. Bob could visualize the fire fights and enemy soldiers, arching their backs and yelling in pain; their lifeless bodies falling to the ground. The sounds of the chopper blades, slapping the air, got louder and louder. Bob was suddenly jolted back to reality, when Del yelled to him.

"Bob, you ready for another round?"

"Yeah, the exact same please."

"Coming right up." He brought the drinks over. "I sure hope your not driving."

"Nope, I'm walking."

"That's a smart move. I just hope you can still do that, when you're done."

Bob smiled. "Don't worry about me."

Del left and he downed the schnapps and took another slug of beer. He could feel the shots and beer really starting to take affect now. He meant to look for another article, but something drew him back to the same one. Looking at the magazine, he was back in the bug infested jungles of Vietnam. He was so involved in the article, that he never noticed the other two patrons leaving. Del brought him over another round. It was getting closer to four'o'clock now and Bob was getting visibly drunk. He kept looking at the pictures in the magazine and reliving Nam. He was on an ambush with Jimmy and the rest of the guys. It all seemed so very real to him. Bob was there, back in Southeast Asia. He could feel the adrenaline racing through his body.

Two well-dressed oriental gentlemen walked in and approached the bar. Bob hadn't noticed them at first, not until Del spoke up and asked them, "What can I get you?"

"A couple of scotch and sodas, if you don't mind. And maybe some pretzels."

Bob looked up and glared at them. They sat at the bar and Del put their drinks in front of them. The very sight of them made his blood boil.

Bob yelled to them, "What in the hell are you doing here?...... Answer me.... What do you want here, Charlie?"

Del and the two orientals turned around, looking to see who Bob was talking to. The look in Bob's eyes was so intense, that there was no mistake as to who he was addressing.

Del still puzzled said, "What are you talking about, Bob?"

"Them ... Nathanial Victor. They know who in the hell I'm talking about."

One of the oriental gentlemen started to chuckle and said, "Hey, he thinks we're Vietnamese."

"Damn straight, you fuck'n gook!"

"BOB! EITHER YOU SHUT YOUR MOUTH, OUR YOU'LL HAVE TO LEAVE." Del was furious.

Just then Russ walked in with Carter. They could feel the tension in the air. Russ took one look at Del and said, "What's going on?"

Del motioned to where Bob was sitting. "He's drunk and I want him out of here."

Then Bob said, "You want me out of here, how about the fuck'n slopes."

Russ walked over to Bob, shaking his head and said, "Come on, I'll take you home."

"How about those bastards over there. You're going to let them stay."

"What about them?" Russ now getting angry.

"They're V.C. I can smell it."

Russ now glaring, "You can't smell shit. Now come on Bob,... like..... right.... now."

Bob got up and followed Russ. As they walked past the two oriental men Bob eyed them, turning as he walked, making sure that his back was never turned towards them. They just grinned and shook their heads. Del frowned at Bob, with disapproval.

Russ said to his partner, "Have a beer on me. I'll be right back, OK?"

"How about chips partner?"

"Fine, have some fuck'n chips."

Carter was all smiles. Russ wasn't smiling at all. "Hey, thanks partner, you're a sport."

Once outside, they got into Russ's car. Russ pulled away from the curb and said, "Jesus Christ, Bob. What in heavens name was that all about?"

203

"What are you talking about?"

"That V.C. shit. Where in the fuck do you think you are anyway, fuck'n Saigon! You asshole, you're really pissing me off, Hills. BIG TIME!"

"Sorry pal."

"You get this straight, I'm not your pal. But I don't want to see you get in shit, either. Now I don't know what your problem is soldier boy, but you better either control it or get some help. And I mean it!"

"I'm OK Russ."

"Like hell you are. I saw you in there. You were in another fucking world, asshole! Psychologists have fancy names for this shit, and if I were you, I'd be seeing the V.A. about getting some kind of help."

"Yeah well, I'll think about it."

"You better do more than just think about it."

He got Bob home and asked, "Are you Okay?"

"Yeah, I'm fine ... thanks for your help, I do appreciate it."

"Just get some help, Bob."

He got out of the car and Russ pulled away. Bob walked into the house and called out, " I'm home."

Mary came out of the kitchen and said, "Dinner will be ready soon."

"I'm not hungry. I think I'll just go to my room and have a nap."

"Are you alright Bob?"

"I'm fine, just a little tired."

Bob went straight to bed and a moment later he was fast asleep. Again he dreamed about Nam. This time he and Jimmy were in a foxhole and Jimmy was telling him to keep an eye out for the enemy. He kept saying the enemy was close. Bob had his rifle at the ready and kept asking him where they were. But Jim just kept on saying they were close. Bob tossed and turned in his sleep, until he suddenly sat bolt upright in bed, wide awake. He was soaked from body sweat.

Bob showered, shaved and put on fresh clothes. He kept thinking about what he had done that afternoon and how he was so ashamed of himself. Bob had to go to Del's and apologize to the poor guy, for his inexcusable behaviour towards his customers. He must have thought that Bob was some sort of nut. He left there and didn't even pay for his drinks. Maybe Russ was right, maybe he did need help? Perhaps he should contact the V.A. about getting some counselling? He was now staring in his bedroom dresser mirror, and he didn't particularly like what he saw.

Bob went downstairs and found his parents sitting in the living room, watching T.V. "What's on the tube tonight?" Bob said as he walked into the room.

Mike turned and said, "Well, there you are. It's eight-thirty, we weren't sure if you were even planning on getting up tonight. Did you sleep well?"

"I sure did."

"Do you want some dinner?" Mary asked.

"No thanks. I'll just make myself a sandwich."

Mary said, "There's no bread."

"Well I'll just go out and grab a burger."

"When you're out, can you stop somewhere and pick up some bread, please?"

"Sure Mom ... no problem. Can I borrow the car, Dad?"

"Yes of course. The keys are sitting on the table, by the front door."

"Thanks Dad." He walked over to the table, grabbed the keys and left.

He drove over to the Burger Palace to get something to eat. While he sat at a booth eating, he thought of what was happening to him. It was then that he decided to give himself a few weeks to see if he was going to get over the nightmares. If he was still having problems, he was going to the V.A. for help. Bob also decided to quit drinking, at least for a while. He was sure that wasn't helping his situation at all.

Bob finished his dinner and headed over to Del's. When he got there, he found it difficult to go inside. The shame Bob felt was eating away at him, like a cancer gone rampant. How could he ever face Del? Bob embarrassed him as well as himself; in front of his customers. Finally he mustered up enough courage to go inside. Now was the time to account for his actions.

There wasn't more than a dozen people there that night and there were only two people at the far side of the bar. Del was serving them and hadn't noticed Bob walk in. Bob went to the end of the bar and waited for Del to see him.

Del, who was smiling at the time, turned and saw Bob, and his facial expression changed. He looked at Bob straight-faced and said, "What do you want, Bob?"

"I'm here to pay my tab and apologize to you. I'm very sorry for what happened this afternoon."

"You were drunk, Bob. Don't worry about it."

"I wish I could apologize to the two oriental gentlemen I hassled as well."

"Actually you did. You bought them their drinks. I put it on your tab. Hang on I'll get it for you." He went to the cash register and came back with a slip of paper. He handed it to him and said, "Can I get you anything?"

"No thanks, I think I've had enough to drink for a little while."

"You might have something there, pal. Just don't quit completely, I need the business."

Bob smiled and paid his bill. "Thanks, Del, and again I'm sorry. I'll see you later."

Giving Del a forced smile, Bob walked away leaving the bar, feeling as though a burden had been lifted from his shoulders. One thing for certain though ... he never wanted to go though that embarrassment ever again. He appreciated Del's understanding attitude, not to mention Russ's help as well. He felt indebted to them both.

On the way home he stopped off at a variety store for the loaf of bread, Mary had asked me to pick up earlier. As he was walking towards the entrance, he noticed a blonde woman walking out of the store. When she was out on to the side walk, she turned towards him. Bob saw that it was Sue Lucas. She was as surprised to see him, as he was to see her and their faces showed it.

"What are you doing; following me around?" She was abrupt in her tone of voice.

"Following you around? Why you conceited piece of shit. You only wish." He was angered, remembering the conversation she had with his mother on the phone. "Don't you ever ... I mean fucking ever... call my parents again."

"You can go to hell, you killer. To think I actually felt sorry for you. Ha. That was short lived." She looked at him with absolute disgust.

"You upset my mother needlessly, Sue."

"If I upset your mother, then I'm sorry. But that's life, isn't it."

"Listen, you have a lot of nerve, calling my mother and asking her if I was home. I saw you looking at Lynn that night at the box office. M*A*S*H, remember the show you didn't see? I thought you were going to rip Terry's arm off. You couldn't get away fast enough. Then you call her to tell her that I was following you around, because I happen to pull up next to you at a traffic light.I"

"Go to hell, Hills. You're an asshole and nothing but a common murderer. I don't give a shit about you or your damn family." She was visibly losing her temper and her ability to rebut.

"You're calling me a murderer! You've got your nerve, you piece of shit. At least anyone I killed had a weapon in their hands. That's more than what YOU can say. You're the damn fuck'n murderer. You murder an unarmed being, only a very small fraction your size and that's alright. Then you're right there, to condemn someone else."

"Just what are you talking about Hills? I don't know what you're talking about." She was beginning to break down.

"You know exactly what I'm talking about. It's morally wrong for me to kill communist soldiers, but you... you pathetic piece of trash... you on the other hand, can go out and have an abortion. In the eyes of some people, you've murdered an innocent, unborn child."

"Where did you hear that? Who told you, you son of a bitch? Who told you?" She was in tears now, and raising her hand to strike him on the face.

"Don't even think of it bitch. People like you make me sick. Sue, you're a hypocrite. If you felt that you needed an abortion, that's fine. That's your decision and you'll have to live with it. But don't you dare attack me and my morals. You gave up your right to question anyone's morals when you had that abortion."

She covered her face and began to cry. "You have no right, no right at all, you bastard."

"You ever call my parents again Sue, and I'll be making some calls of my own. I'm sure mummy and daddy would have kittens if they knew all about their little Suzy Q's morals. Don't you think so? Maybe now you'll think twice before shooting your big fat mouth off." Bob looked her up and down. "You know, I have absolutely no respect for you." He started to walk away and stopped to say, "Oh and don't think for one moment that I'm following you around.

There's just no way I could be attracted to someone like you. Inside, you're as ugly a person as I've ever met."

Bob left her standing there and walked into the store to get the loaf of bread. When he came out she had gone. He got into his father's car and drove home.

When he got into the house, Bob found Mary sitting in the living room.

"Hi."

"Hi, Bob."

"Where's Dad?"

"He's gone to bed for the night."

"Well, I guess he's up early tomorrow and could use the extra sleep."

"Oh, thanks for picking up the bread."

"No problem." Bob went into the kitchen to put the bread away and grab a can of Coke from the fridge. Sipping the Coke he walked into the living room and stood at the door entrance, leaning on the door casing.

"Is something bothering you Bob?"

"No."

"Something is bothering you. Now what is it?"

He paused a moment, then said, "I ran into Sue. I had a bit of a fight with her."

"What did she say?"

"I think I'd have to say that it was more of a case of what I had to say to her."

"And what was that?"

"I found something out about Sue, quite by accident; a regular skeleton in the closet. When I heard about it, I promised myself that I wouldn't mention it to anyone except Sue. Not until I had a chance to tell her that I knew."

"So it's a secret. Why did you even bother to bring it up then?" She was getting frustrated.

He smiled and said, "Well, I did tell her what I knew about her. I feel that if she had no qualms about telling you things about me, then I should have absolutely no qualms about telling you, or anyone else, things about her. Keeping in mind that not only was the things about me supposed to make me look bad, but it was also the distorted truth to the point of being a lie. This, at least, is the truth and I'm not running to her folks with it, yet. That of course, all depends on her."

Mary got up out her chair and said, "FOR PETE'S SAKES BOB, WILL YOU TELL ME WHAT IT IS!"

"Shhhhhh, you'll wake Dad," He slowly took another sip of his Coke. "About a year ago Sue had an abortion."

Mary couldn't speak. She just stood in the centre of the floor with her mouth wide open.

"I'd appreciate it if you would keep this to yourself. I have nothing against Sue's parents and this would kill them."

"Yes ... I guess it would, wouldn't it?" She shook her head. "I don't understand why she took such a strong stand against you."

"Neither do I Mom ... neither do I." Bob finished the Coke and said, "I think I'll call it a night."

"Good night."

"Good night, Mom." He kissed her on the cheek, then went to his room. He sat in the chair, in the corner of the room, much like Mary must have done on so many occasions, thinking of all that was happening. Much of it was unbelievable, even after having experienced it. Bob thought of what toll the war may have really had on him, and man, that was scary. There could be things wrong with him that he was not even aware of yet. That, he'd have to deal with, using counselling through the V.A., like Russ suggested. One thing that was for certain, things had to change and he had to change them. His life needed a big turn around.

Bob finally went to bed and a short time later fell into a deep sleep. It wasn't long and he was back in the Nam again. Jimmy and Bob were in a foxhole, just like in his earlier dream.

"What are we doing here Jimmy?"

"Trying to stay alive Bob."

"Is anyone coming?"

"The enemy."

"Come on Jimmy, I don't see anyone."

"They're there."

"How do you know?"

"I can see into the future, Bob."

"Yeah ... and I'm the Pope of Rome."

"Don't laugh at me, Bob. You'll be sorry."

"Come on, Wiener."

"Stop calling me Wiener; we're not kids any more, Bob."

"Lighten up, Jim."

Just then Jim yelled, "It's happening, it's happening." He raised his rifle and began firing.

As that happened Bob sat up in bed and woke up. He looked at his arms. They were out stretched as though he had a M-16 in his hands. His palms were sweating and he could feel his heart pounding. Bob laid down and tried to get himself together. There, awake, Bob laid for the better part of an hour before falling asleep again. He could only hope to forget Nam long enough to allow him to get some decent rest.

CHAPTER ELEVEN

All that was happening was weighing heavy on Bob's mind the next morning. What Bob had to do was take charge of his life with it's problems and get it all straightened out. The police would take care of the harassment and he planned to give up drinking, at least for the next little while. The booze wasn't going to help him deal with his problems: it would only add to them. The car was getting fixed so that was no real issue, and he was sure that time would take care of the nightmares. Bob still lacked something to make his life ... for the time being anyway, more complete. He only hoped that his folks would understand. What he needed was his independence; he needed his own place. It would give him the flexibility of having anyone he wanted over, for as long as he or she wanted to stay, and to do whatever they wanted to do. At this point, he was thinking about Lynn and where their relationship was headed. He was hoping it wouldn't remain platonic for much longer.

Bob got showered and dressed, then went downstairs. He knew Mike would already have left for the store. He always tried to get in early on Saturdays. This would give Bob a chance to talk to Mary alone, about him getting an apartment.

"Good morning." He poured himself a coffee.

"Well, good morning, sleepy head." She said with a smile.

"I must have been tired, I can't believe it's ten-fifteen already."

"You must have been and it's no wonder. Can I get you some breakfast?"

"No thanks."

"Bob, you haven't been eating properly lately. Besides, breakfast is probably the most important meal of the day. You should eat something."

"I'm simply not hungry Mom."

"What am I going to do with you?"

"Actually, now that you mention it, I think I can help you out there."

"What are you talking about?"

"I'm thinking about getting my own place."

"Why? Aren't you happy living here at home?"

"Yes, I am, but ... I just need my own space."

She appeared to be upset now. "Why? Do I bother you? Does your father bother you?"

"No, that's not it at all."

"We try not to pry into your life Bob. We do try very hard, to respect your privacy."

"I know you do."

"Then why?"

"Because I feel that I have to."

"But why?"

"This is something that I'm doing for myself. I owe this to myself. All this would be is establishing my independence. It's not an issue against the two of you, or the way I was treated. I could never say enough good about the fair and understanding way that Judy and I have been treated the entire time we lived here under this roof. But I feel that I have reached a time in my life, when I should be completely on my own. I'm not a child any more; I'm an adult. In the past you always managed to see my side of things, I'm asking you to please understand now."

She sat at the kitchen table in silence for a moment. There was nothing she could say or do. His mind was made up and she knew it. "I really don't understand, Bob, but I guess if you feel this strongly about it, then you had better do it."

"Thanks. I'll still come here for dinner once in a while. It's not like I'm leaving town."

"Great, you haven't even moved out and already you're planning on dropping in for freebies." You could tell she wasn't thrilled at all, but she put on a smile anyway.

"Ha, Ha."

"So when did you think you'd want to do this?"

"Soon. I was going to pick up a paper and start looking around this morning."

"My, you are in a hurry."

"I simply feel that now I've made the decision, I should just do it."

"You're probably right, Bob."

Bob finished his coffee and went into the study to phone Gravenhurst Auto Glass. They were full of good news. They hadn't even begun to fix the car and now it wouldn't be ready until Tuesday. He wasn't overly pleased at that, but at least the car was being fixed by the insurance and other than the deductible, it wasn't coming out of his pocket. Bob tried very hard to maintain a positive outlook on everything. With all that was happening, it was difficult.

He then phoned the hardware store. Mrs. Hathaway answered in her usual cheerful manner.

"Hill's Hardware."

"Mrs. Hathaway?"

"Yes."

"It's Bob. Is my father available?"

"He sure is. I'll put you through."

"Mike Hills."

"Hi."

"Bob, what's up?"

"I was wondering, if you're not to busy at noon, could we get together for lunch?"

"Sure, but it won't be until twelve-thirty."

"No problem. I'll meet you at the deli at twelve-thirty and I'll buy this time."

"Free lunch? I'll be there."

"Oh yeah, there's one other thing. May I borrow the car this morning?"

"Sure, in fact John picked me up this morning. The car should be in the drive."

"Thanks. I'll see you later."

"Sure thing, I've got to go. Talk to you at lunch Bob." He hung up.

Bob walked into the kitchen and had another cup of coffee with his mother.

"Do you need the car today Mom?"

"No. If you need it, take it."

"Thanks."

"Do you have any idea where you want to move yet?"

"Probably somewhere around the store. That's if there's something available in the area. This way I could just walk into work."

"That's good. So, that would mean you would be within walking distance from here."

"Yep, you're right. That also means I won't have too far to go for a decent meal."

Mary shook her head. "You're awful. What are you going to do about furniture and dishes?"

"Now that's half the fun ... getting things you need as you go along and can afford them. This way anything you buy is special to you. You're buying it for yourself to use in your own place. I'm looking forward to it."

"Well, Mister Independence, I can still make your curtains and drapes for you."

"You sure can. I certainly wouldn't know how in the heck to do it." He kissed her on the cheek and said, "I've got to go, I'll see you later."

"Will you be back for lunch?"

"No. I'm meeting Dad for lunch. I want to talk to him about some things."

"Well the two of you enjoy your lunch. I've got to get some of my old sewing books out and find some ideas for curtains."

"Hey ... nothing frilly and I hate pink."

"Get out of here you brat."

Bob grabbed the keys off the key-caddy on the kitchen wall and left. The first stop he made was to a drug store to pick up the morning paper. He was lucky, they only had one left. As he turned towards the cash register, he noticed the magazine rack. It reminded him of what an ass he had made of himself at Del's, the night before. After paying for the paper, he headed for the coffee shop to look over the ads in the paper.

Sitting down to a coffee, doughnut and the paper, he began scanning the ad section under apartments for rent. He wanted one that was unfurnished so that he could start to accumulate furniture. He already had bedroom furniture. All he really needed right away would be a kitchen table, television and a stereo. Maybe he'd get a stereo with an eight track player so he could use the car's tapes in the apartment as well. Bob thought, "Let's face it, the tapes wouldn't go to waste and eight track is here to stay."

Several of the ads caught his eye. One in particular seemed just perfect. It was an older building with an apartment above a music store. A block and a half from the hardware store on the same side of the street. It couldn't have been more convenient. The price was right and it even had a working fireplace. What more could a suave bachelor want? Bob went to a pay phone in the coffee shop and called the number in the ad.

A woman answered the phone. "Hello, Masters Music Centre. May I help you?"

"Yes, I'm calling about the apartment you have advertised in the paper for rent. Could you tell me whether or not it's still available?"

"One moment please and I'll check."

A well-spoken man came on the phone. "Hello. How may I help you?"

"Yes. I'm calling about the apartment."

"Yes of course. Would you care to see it?"

"I certainly would, Sir."

"When would be a good time for you to drop by."

"Well I'm only about three minutes away. How about now, if that's convenient?"

"That would be fine. If you'd like to drop by the music store and ask for me. I'm Mr Masters."

"Very good Mr. Masters, I'll see you shortly."

He hung up and so did Bob. He picked up his paper and drove right over to the Music store. It was a pleasant looking store dealing mainly in pianos. A young, neatly-dressed and attractive woman approached him.

She smiled and said, "May I help you?"

"Yes please, I'm looking for Mr. Masters."

"And what is it concerning?"

"The apartment he has for rent."

"One moment, please." She walked away and entered a room in the back.

An older gentleman came out of the room with the young woman. He was short with white-hair and wore a beard. He looked to be in his sixties. His suit was conservative, and tastefully coordinated with his shirt, tie, and a handkerchief tucked so neatly into his jacket pocket. He looked very distinguished walking towards Bob with his walking stick in hand.

He put out his hand to shake Bob's. "Good day. I am Victor Masters."

Bob shook his hand, "I'm Bob Hills. I telephoned you about the apartment."

"Certainly. Would you care to examine it?"

"Yes, please."

He reached into his pocket and pulled out a key, then started walking to the front of the store; Bob followed. They went outside to a door entrance next to that of the music store's. The outside door was naturally finished oak, with very ornate brass fixtures. Once inside, they found themselves at the foot of a tall, oak staircase that lead to a single door at the top. They climbed the stairs and unlocked the door at the top, then went inside. There was a hall that ran from the back of the apartment on the left, to a pair of leaded-glass french doors near the front. They walked to the back where they came across a narrow sitting room with windows that went right across the back wall, giving the room a solarium affect. The next room was the single bedroom. It was large with a walk in closet. Walking out of the bedroom, Bob found the next room in line to be the kitchen. It was a bit small, but adequate. It led into the dining room.

"Go ahead," Mr. Masters said, "look at the kitchen. The appliances are included."

"Thank you." Bob had forgotten about appliances. It was a good thing that they were included; he'd hate to live on takeout food until he could afford to buy a fridge and stove.

They walked through the kitchen and into the dining room. A small bathroom was on the left and the living room was on the right. Bob went into the living room and found the huge flagstone fire place that occupied almost the entire wall on Bob's left. A row of large windows looked over the front of the building and the street below. The apartment was beautiful, no question about it. Bob was sure he would be happy there.

Mr. Masters broke the silence and said, "If you walk this way through the french doors, it will take you back to the apartment entrance. There is a door buzzer that is hooked up to the lower door as well."

"I'll take it Mr. Masters."

"I'm sure you will, but not until I find out a little more about you. After all, Mr. Hills, I'm not about to let just anyone live up here."

"I understand."

"Where do you work?"

"Well, I was just recently discharged from the Army. I was in Vietnam."

He looked at Bob as if he had just wasted his time. "So you do not have a job presently."

"Yes, I do. My father has a business in town and starting Monday I'm going to be working with him."

"And what business is this?"

"Hill's Hardware."

"You're Mike's son?"

"Yes I am."

"All I need is first and last months rent and the place is yours."

Bob shook his hand and said, "Thank you Mr. Masters."

"Thank you. I am certain that you will take good care of the place and that you will find it very comfortable."

"I'm sure I will."

"And if you have any problems, I am always downstairs during business hours."

"Oh yes. In the paper it said that the fire place was in working order."

"Yes, it is. But please give me until the middle of next week before you use it. I'd like to get the chimney sweep in to clean it first."

Bob looked at his watch, it was almost twelve and he knew he had to get going. They talked for a short while and then they left to take care of the rest of their business in the store. As Bob walked out with Mr. Masters, he thought of how happy he would be there. The apartment was warm and homelike. It was perfect. They went into the store and Bob gave him a check for the first and last months rent, and he gave Bob the keys. Bob couldn't wait to tell Mike about the place. Finally he was getting his life in order... Lynn, the apartment, the job, and his car. Things were going to be great.

Mike had just ordered his sandwich when Bob arrived at O'Neals. Bob got his sandwich and when he went to pay for it, the girl at the cash said, "The gentleman over there in the corner said that you were buying."

He turned around and saw Mike sitting at a table in the corner. He had just taken a bite of his sandwich and was waving with a smile on his face.

"That's right." Bob paid for their sandwiches and went to join him at the table.

"Your mother called me."

"Yeah? Well I didn't think that she could keep it in. She was pretty disappointed when I told her that I was moving out of the house."

"What?"

"What do you mean by, what?"

"She called because she wanted the car this afternoon; something about sewing books at Heather Flynn's. Are you moving out of the house?"

"Oh shit, she didn't tell you? ... Yes I am."

"Any reason why, in particular?"

"No, not really. It's nothing to do with you and Mom; I simply need to be out on my own. All that I want is to have a place to call my own."

"You know Bob, I'll only be able to pay you a hundred and twenty dollars a week to start and I don't know when I'll be in a position to give you any sort of a raise."

"Hey that's great. That's plenty, my rent is only two sixty-five. The only thing I have to pay on top of that is the phone. My car is paid for."

Mike merely shook his head and said, "I guess that I really don't blame you at all. Hey, does this mean you'll be having poker nights every so often?"

Bob laughed, "I guess."

"So when are you planning on doing this?"

"Sooner than you think."

"Does this mean you've already found a place?"

"Yes it does."

"So where is it?"

"The apartment above Masters Music Centre."

"Victor's place."

"Do you know him?"

"Only through the Chamber of Commerce. We've both been members for a good number of years. So tell me all about this place of yours, Bob."

"It's got a lot of character. All oak wood trim with a fireplace. French doors with leaded windows and a sun room in the back. It's really nice. No woman will be safe there." Bob had a big grin on his face.

Mike smiled and shook his head, "No woman will be safe there. Oh, brother! Well, that's nice Son, and it will probably do you a world of good. You seem to be excited enough about it, especially when you mentioned the woman part. I'm sure that you'll enjoy the freedom."

"Thanks. I will."

"Listen, Bob, I never want you to be afraid to talk to either me or your mother. You know whatever it is that you want to tell us, we'll always do our best to understand."

"I know you will."

"I love you Son."

"I love you, too."

They finished their sandwiches then Bob said, "Do you have time to run over to the apartment and take a look at it?"

"I'd love to, but I'm short on time right now. Tomorrow I'm free, though."

"Great. Tomorrow I'll take the two of you over to see it. You'll love the place."

"I'm sure we will."

They left the deli and Mike returned to work. Bob took the car home. When Bob got there, he found Mary waiting for him in the living room.

"You're back."

"Yeah. Here are the keys." He handed her the keys.

"So how did you make out."

"I found an apartment."

"Already?"

"I'm taking you and Dad over to see it tomorrow."

"When are you planning on moving in?"

"I guess I'll start moving things in tomorrow. I'd like to take my bedroom suite if you don't mind?"

"Sure. I can't believe how sudden this is all happening. You get up this morning and decide to get an apartment. Noon rolls around and you say you think you've found one. You better be sure about it, before you give them any sort of deposit."

"Too late."

"Where is this place?"

"Above Masters Music Centre."

"That's just down the street from the store."

"Yeah, it'll be handy for work."

"So what are the cooking facilities like?"

"Great. There's the deli O'Neal's, Sal's Subs, the Pizza Palace, Del's and Wong's Chicken Hut."

"Bob, get serious!"

"Sorry. Yes, there's a kitchen. It even has a Refrigerator and stove. All I need is some paper plates."

"Fine. That's all I wanted to know."

"Hey. I even have a fireplace."

"You're kidding? How nice."

"I think things are really coming together for me now. I'm really excited about this move."

"I'm happy for you Bob. Just remember, if it doesn't work out the way you've planned, you can always come home."

"I know. Thanks."

"Well I've got to get going. I told Heather I'd be there fifteen minutes ago. Have yourself a good afternoon and I'll see you later, Okay?" She grabbed her purse and she was out the door. He barely had time to say good-bye.

Bob went through most of his belongings that afternoon deciding what to move with him right away. He spent quite a bit of time thinking about the past and the positive move he was now making. He couldn't wait to tell Lynn all about it.

Looking through his things in his room brought back a lot of memories. With each and every article he picked up, he picked up a piece of his past. A football brought back thoughts of the old school days, while a model car reminded him of a time when he received it so many Christmases ago. Bob opened the drawer in one of his night tables and found an old photo album. The pictures were from a Brownie Camera that Mike had bought for him when Bob was ten. A lot of the pictures included Jimmy Wheeler. It made him think of how much Jim's parents would appreciate having at least some of them. Bob decided to call Bill and Alice and tell them that he had the pictures for them. Perhaps he could even spend a little time with them. Bob was certain Jim would want him to. How they must miss him. Looking at the pictures made him realize how much he had missed him, too.

Bob went downstairs to the kitchen to get a can of Coke, then to the study to call the Wheelers. Bob was surprised to find that Bill answered the phone. Bob would have thought he would be working at that time of the day.

"Hello."

"Mr. Wheeler, it's Bob Hills."

"Bob, it's nice to hear from you."

"Thanks. I'm surprised to find you're home from work at this time of the day."

"Actually it's a late lunch. I'm running behind on this job and I'll probably be working late. But that's the way it goes sometimes. So what can I do for you?"

"Well I was just cleaning up my room; sorting through some stuff, getting ready to move."

"Move?"

"Yeah, I found a nice apartment a block and a half from the store."

"You're not having any problems with Mike and Mary, are you Bob?"

"Oh, heck no. They're great. I just felt that I needed my own space. In fact, I think Dad's got some idea to turn it into a Friday night poker house."

"Knowing Mike, that wouldn't surprise me. He's forever talking me into a game with the guys and he always wins."

"Well, he does like the odd game of cards."

"What else is up Bob?"

"The reason I called is that while I was cleaning and sorting out my things, I ran across some pictures of Jim I thought you might like to have. He was between ten and fourteen in the majority of the pictures. The photography isn't the best, but there's no mistaking who it is."

There were several moments of silence, then he spoke, "Yes, we would Bob. That was very considerate of you to think of us. It would mean a lot to us. Thank you very much."

Bob could sense the emotion over the phone. "It's ... Okay. I thought I'd drop them off to you later tomorrow afternoon. I won't be able to stay long tomorrow, but I thought next Sunday maybe we could get together."

"Why don't you come for dinner next Sunday. And maybe we can go out for a drink or something, just the two of us. ..... I'd really like to talk to you."

"Yeah, sure." Bob knew the time would come when Bill would want to talk about Nam and Jimmy's last few months alive. That was going to be hard.

"Good I'll tell Alice that you'll be coming for dinner on that Sunday then."

"I'll be there."

"Oh, and Bob ... Fred will be coming in for a visit next month and I'm sure he would appreciate it if you'd drop by to see him. He took the news about Jimmy pretty hard."

"Sure, no problem."

"Thanks again."

"You're more than welcome."

"I'll talk to you later Bob."

"I'll see you tomorrow with the pictures." Bob hung up.

It was hard not to sense the feeling of sorrow and loss that Bill Wheeler felt, even just talking to him over the phone. It would be difficult to measure the degree of anguish a parent would feel at the loss of a child, unless of course you were in the same position. I guess there's more truth than not to the old saying, "A child can always bury a parent, but a parent can never bury a child." Bob hoped that Bill would someday be able to prove that to be false. Not that Bob wanted Bill to forget Jimmy, but to come to terms with his death and remember the happy times they had together, rather than feeling only grief.

The afternoon passed and Mary came back from Heather Flynn's with the sewing books.

"How was your afternoon, Bob?"

"Fine. How was yours?"

"Very pleasant. The two of us had some coffee and a visit. I really enjoyed it; it was fun. Oh, and I drove past your apartment. It seems very nice from the outside. I'm really anxious to see the inside."

"You will tomorrow."

"Did anyone call for me while I was out?"

"No, but I called Bill Wheeler though. He'd like to have me over for dinner next Sunday. I have some old photos of Jimmy I thought they'd like to have. I think Bill wants very much to talk to me about Jimmy."

She stood in the centre of the room in silence for a moment then said, "Do you really think that's a good idea?"

"If he asks me about something, I'm not going lie. Jim was his son and he has a right to know everything that I know."

"Still, Bob...."

"I know pretty much how I'm going to handle the situation. I knew it would eventually come to this. Please, just trust my judgement."

"I guess so."

"I'll keep in mind that he's gone through a lot."

"Please do."

"I will."

A short while later Mike came home from the store. He was carrying a nicely wrapped box under his arm.

"I'm home."

Bob looked at him and smiled, saying, "Hi Dad. How was your afternoon?"

"Good. Where's your mother?"

"In the kitchen getting dinner for the two of you."

"Aren't you going to be here?"

"No. I'm going to Lynn's place for dinner."

"Oh? She can cook?"

"As well as I can."

"You having pizza?"

Bob put his arm around his shoulder and said, "You know, you should have been a detective."

"No thanks. I'm not that big on doughnuts. You know, I thought Dorothy said they were going away for the weekend." He stared at the floor, puzzled and thinking about what he had just said. Then his eyes widened and he began to smirk. "Enjoy your dinner and don't molest my secretary's daughter."

"Thanks. I'll probably be late tonight."

"No doubt. We won't be waiting up."

"Who's birthday is it?" Bob asked, pointing to the wrapped package.

"Oh, yes. This is for you. For the new place." He handed Bob the box.

"What is it?"

"I can't tell you. It's a surprise." Mike had a big smile on his face.

"It looks to be about the size of a toaster, Dad."

Disappointment was written all over his face. "Well you might as well open it, now."

Bob ripped the paper from the sides of the box. "A Toastmaster toaster. Thanks."

"I thought you could use it for your frozen waffles and pop tarts."

"Ha, Ha; very funny. I do appreciate it though, Dad. Thanks again."

"You're welcome Son."

They went into the kitchen to see Mary and to show her his new frozen waffle heater. Mike had a beer while Bob had a can of Coke. Bob was glad that the two of them were so supportive of his moving out. This was the second time he had moved. The first time wasn't by his choice, but rather Uncle Sam's. His parents weren't too keen on the first parting of the ways, neither was he. This was on a much happier note.

That afternoon Sue went to the student newspaper office. Terry and Jim were there when she came in.

"I'm surprised to see the two of you in here on a Saturday. What gives?"

"I was just getting caught up on an assignment. It's due on Monday." Jim said.

Terry, who was looking out of the window, turned around and said with a smile, "Hi Sue."

Sue, on the other hand, looked as though her best friend died. In a soft, barely audible voice she said, "Hi."

Terry looked at her with a puzzled expression on his face and asked, "What's wrong Sue?"

"Nothing. I'm only a little tired, that's all." She sat at her desk.

Jim Mueller could sense that something was up, so he decided not to say anything. He just sat back and watched, trying hard to blend in with the surroundings.

Terry said, "You're not ill are you?"

"No. I had a bit of a headache last night though. It made it difficult to sleep."

"Do you think we'll still be able to go out tonight? You look pretty tired." Terry asked.

"Oh sure. We've been planning this night for almost a

month. Linda's my best friend, I wouldn't miss her birthday party for the world."

"Well, alright. Just try to have a nap sometime before we go out tonight."

"Alright, I will. Oh, and Terry, did you get a chance to check out that last story I wrote?"

"Yes, I did; it's fine."

Just then Kevin walked in and said, "What's this a convention? I expected to have the whole place to myself."

"Hi Kevin." Jim said.

"Hello Kevin." Sue said while she opened her desk drawer, looking for something.

"Kevin, I'm glad you're here. I've got a couple of jobs for you to do for Tuesday." Terry said while walking towards him. "The first one is a story on prejudice."

"Sure," Kevin said nodding, "but you mean racism?"

"Not exactly Kevin." Terry replied.

Kevin looked at Terry as though he was up to something. "What do you mean by prejudice, specifically?"

"I mean this business of the fire bombing of the R.O.T.C. facility, specifically." Terry looked him right in the eye. "It's things like that fire bombing that are not only acts of senseless prejudice, but they also do considerable damage to our own Anti-War cause."

Kevin looked at him with disgust, "You're nuts. I'm not writing a story about your poor, mistreated, Gestapo friends."

"Look Kevin, they're not my friends. What they are though, are students just like you and me. They don't deserve to be treated like that."

Kevin, now angered said, "Look pal, I don't buy your bleeding-heart speeches and I sure as hell have no damn use for the military. I don't like anyone who was in it, is in it, or ever will be in it. So you can stick your assignment in you ear."

Terry now raising his voice said, "Kevin, you had better learn to forget your brother's death and start functioning like a normal person again."

"You don't know what happened to my brother." He was yelling and started to get emotional all the more.

"Kevin," Terry said, "we all know that your brother died in Vietnam and that he thought there were some illegal kills by American troops. You've only told us a thousand times for Pete's sake."

"Yeah." Kevin now was almost in tears. "I bet I never told you that when he was killed, he was caught in the middle of what the military refer to as a fire fight. He was caught in the crossfire. I bet too, that I never told you that when they found him that they pulled, not one, but two slugs out of him. I bet that I also forgot to mention that the slugs were .223 cal. The same God Damn size rounds as the M-16! Damn it Terry..... he was killed by Americans! The U.S. Army killed my brother! The American Government and the American Army are responsible for his death." Kevin eyes were now full of tears, and the agony of his brother's death was written all over his face.

Terry now found it hard to speak, but finally did. "I didn't know Kevin. I had no idea."

Jim said nothing, but sat quietly at his desk and watched everyone. He did, however, feel bad about the circumstances of Kevin's brother's death. But he wasn't totally convinced that it was an American that pulled the trigger.

Kevin, fighting back the tears, now said, "They had no right to kill him."

Terry tried to comfort him by saying, "You're right Kevin. Your brother's death was all wrong. They had no right letting him go into an area where his life would be in danger. The Army was wrong."

Sue cut in, and in a sarcastic tone of voice said, "That damn Bob Hills said that your brother probably got killed because he was interviewing the wrong side. Can you imagine the gall of that son of a bitch?"

Kevin screamed, "NO! THAT BASTARD! I'LL KILL THAT GOD DAMNED BASTARD!"

"Jesus Christ, Sue!" Terry said, "Why did you come out with a statement like that?"

Sue looked at Terry with fire in her eyes, "Because he said it. That's why."

"THE BASTARD'S DEAD, TERRY!" Kevin was now red and pacing the floor. "HE'S NOT GOING TO GET AWAY WITH THAT REMARK! NOT THAT MURDERING BASTARD!"

Terry grabbed Kevin by his arms and said, "Listen Kevin, take it easy. Flying off the handle isn't going to help anything. Just settle down."

Kevin threw his arms into the air, breaking Terry's grip and said, "You go right to hell, Terry! You go right to hell!" Kevin was pointing his finger at Terry's face. Then he turned and stormed out of the office.

Terry yelled to him, "KEVIN, GET BACK IN HERE! KEVIN!" Terry turned abruptly and glared at Sue. "Where do you get off getting him all worked up like that?"

"I just told him what the asshole said." She was trying to justify her actions. "It's not like I made it up. Why don't you ask Hills why he said it in the first place?"

"Sue the guy was crying. He was emotional. You could have put him over the edge." Terry said.

"Don't get so dramatic." She was now trying to down play what she had done. "You can be such a pain sometimes. Maybe I should go by myself tonight."

Terry looked her up and down with glaring eyes. "There's no fucking maybe's about it, you shit-disturbing bitch. As of right fucking now, we're through!" He charged out of the room.

Sue slammed her desk drawer closed and said, "Damn it, damn it all." Then she leaned forward putting her face in her hands and began to weep.

Jim stood up and stared at Sue. She raised her head and looked at him.

"What do you want?" She said abruptly.

"Sure as hell, you want Kevin to do something. You want him to execute your petty revenge. Terry's right, you are a bitch. If Kevin does something to Bob or his family I'll be letting the police know all about your part in it."

"What are you talking about?"

"You. You're the one who planted the seed in his head about Bob. That makes you partly responsible, or maybe even wholly responsible. Kevin can always claim temporary insanity. What's your excuse?"

Jim gave her a dirty look and left the office, slamming the door on his way out. He couldn't get Kevin's reaction out of his mind. It was almost a certainty that Kevin would try something stupid. He decided to go to the administration building to see if anyone was around who could help. The doors were locked when he got there, but old Harvey the janitor was just inside the door washing the floor. Jim banged on the door to get his attention.

Harvey, a slow moving man in his sixties, looked up, "Sorry, the offices are closed for the weekend. Come back Monday."

"Please; I have to talk to you."

The janitor approached the locked door cautiously and said, "What do you want?"

"I need to talk to someone. Is Captain Kiser in?"

"Maybe. What do you want him for?"

"It's an emergency. Please!"

"I'll see. Wait right here."

The old janitor left and returned a moment later with the Captain. Jim could hear Gregg saying to Harvey, "I told you I wasn't to be disturbed. Hell, I should be home with my family. It's the weekend." They reached the door and the Captain looked Jim over.

"Aren't you Jim Mueller, from the College Paper?"

"That's right Sir."

"What can I do for you?"

"Captain, can I talk to you?"

"Can't it wait till Monday? I shouldn't even be here."

"It's very important and it really can't wait. Please!" Jim looked worried.

With some hesitation Gregg said, "OK, but you'll have to be quick about it. Let him in, Harvey...... Shit."

Harvey unlocked the door and they walked into his office. It wasn't a large office, but it was neat and tastefully decorated. He had a large collection of cloth badges from different police departments nicely displayed in a dark oak frame. A ten by twelve picture of his family was in plain view on his satin oak desk. The room had dark green wall to wall carpeting. The room was very impressive.

"Nice office."

"Thanks, but I hope we're not here to talk about the appearance of my office."

"Sorry. Are you familiar with a student by the name of Kevin Patterson?"

Gregg thought for a minute, "Kevin Patterson, Kevin Patterson, right." He went over to the filing cabinet and began leafing through files in one of the drawers. "Here it is. Kevin Patterson. He's a journalism major. In fact he works for your newspaper. We've had a few problems with him; but mostly just disturbances at rallies. And according to these dates, all within the last year or so. Has this got anything to do with the fire bombing at the R.O.T.C. building?"

"No, it doesn't. But I'll tell you one thing, he's had a problem with a guy by the name of Bob Hills and I think he's out to get him. And in a big way." The look on Jim's face indicated the seriousness of the matter.

Gregg Kiser sat at his desk for a moment, staring at his brass desk lamp, thinking. He had heard the name Bob Hills before, but couldn't pinpoint where. "Do you think that this Kevin is capable of causing bodily harm to anyone?"

"I don't know. Possibly."

Gregg kept thinking to himself, that the two names were becoming more and more familiar. He had heard the names mentioned together, within the last day or so. "Jim, how do you know there is a problem?"

"I was at the student newspaper office when he had a blow up. I mean he went crazy."

Gregg was taking notes now and said, "Jim where do you live and what's your phone number? I may have to get a hold of you, if something comes up."

"I live at 2363 Franklin Drive here in the city and my phone number is 534-7589. If you need me, I'll be home all night tonight."

"Okay Jim, what time was it that all this took place?"

"I'd say about a half hour ago"

Gregg looked at his watch and wrote down the time. "Was there any indication what he might do to Bob Hills? Anything he may have said."

"He said he was going to kill Hills."

Gregg looked up right into Jim's eyes and said. "He said that he was going to kill him?"

"That's right."

"A lot of people get upset and say they're going to do something, but they really don't mean it."

"I think he meant it. If not to kill him, definitely to do him some bodily harm."

"Why? What happened?"

"It's like this, Captain, Kevin was really upset and while he was upset, someone said that Bob Hills had made a comment about his brother."

"Fine Jim. What kind of comment?"

"Well, Kevin's brother was a journalist in Vietnam and was killed over there. Apparently Bob had told this Sue Lucas that the reason his brother was killed was because he was probably interviewing the wrong side. When Kevin heard this, he started yelling and screaming; who knows what he'll do."

"And that was it?"

"Yes."

Gregg put his pencil down and standing up said, "Well I'll take it from here Jim. I certainly appreciate you coming over and telling me about this."

"You'll let me know what happens, won't you Captain?"

"Oh, sure." Gregg started to walk Jim to the door. "And you let me know if anything else crops up."

"I certainly will. Thank you Captain." Jim walked out of the office.

Gregg yelled to the janitor down the hall, "Hey Harvey, let this gentleman out please." Then he closed his office door.

Gregg sat back down at his desk. He wasn't sure whether the matter was anything to worry about, but Bob Hills' name still stuck in his mind. Then it came to him. "Russ Russel. Where in the hell did I put my note book." He rummaged through his pockets, then his desk. There it was in the top desk drawer. "Kevin Patterson grabbed Bob Hills at rally. Hills and family harassed since. Serious. .... SHIT!!!!"

He picked up the phone and dialled the police station.

When the switchboard operator answered he asked for Russ's extension.

"Jackson here."

"Yes, could I speak to Russ Russel please?"

"Sorry, he's not in right now."

"When do expect him to be back?"

"Not until Monday. No hold it. I'm wrong. He and his partner are covering for another two guys tomorrow. The guy went on some golf trip or something down south. So he'll be in about seven-thirty. Can I take a message for him?"

"Actually, if you could give me his home number I could call him there."

"Well we don't normally give out phone numbers of employees. What is it concerning?"

"I've got some information he would be interested in knowing."

"Well, I'll tell you what. Give me the information and I'll call him for you."

"Fair enough."

Jackson grabbed a pencil and paper. "Okay shoot."

"Can you tell him that Captain Gregg Kiser called, and that I had someone in telling me that Kevin Patterson ...."

The officer cut Gregg short, "Whoa, whoa, whoa. You're going too fast. That's Kevin Patterson, Okay go ahead."

"....is threatening someone Russ knows. A Bob Hills."

"Did he threaten his life; or did he just want to kick the shit out of him, Captain?"

"It maybe his life."

"MAYBE or IS, Sir?"

"Maybe. But it's worth checking into."

"Is that it?"

"Yes it is. You will give that message to him tonight, won't you?"

"I sure will. I'll call him right now; plus there's this written note on his desk as a reminder."

"Thank you very much." Gregg hung up.

Jackson looked up Russ's number on a roster in the desk, then dialled his number. The phone rang and at the other end children were running around the living room. The television blaring. Russ was calling to his wife, "Shelly are you getting the phone?" She didn't hear him because of the noise and was busy trying to get the children under control. The phone continued to ring. "Shelly, honey are you getting the phone?" The phone rang again. "I'll get it." He called. Jackson waited patiently at the other end of the line.

Just then another officer hung up the phone he was on and yelled to him. "HEY JACKSON, LET"S ROLL. WE HAVE A 2-11 IN PROGRESS AT HAMERSTEIN'S JEWELERY STORE ON 2nd STREET. Jackson hung up and put the note on Russ's desk as he left.

Russ reached the phone and answered it. "Hello." He was a moment too late.

"Who is it, Russ?"

"I don't know. They hung up." Russ didn't give it a second thought for the rest of the night.

Back at his office, Gregg sat at his desk, looking over Kevin's file. He was beginning to realize more and more, the potential for this situation to get out of hand. He was glad that he had called the city police and he was sure that they would look into the matter. After all, if Kevin did threaten this Bob Hills fellow, he should be told to keep his distance. Death threats are against the law. Convinced that he had done all that he could, Gregg left his office to call it a day. And so he should have; it was supposed to be his day off. As late afternoon turned to early evening, all seemed to be quiet.

Lynn picked Bob up at six as she said she would. She had

on a pair of tight fitting jeans and a light coloured sweater. Dancing certainly agreed with her figure. She looked as she always did ... great. They picked up some soft drinks at a near by store and went straight to her place. When they got there, she sat Bob on the couch while she turned on the stereo. The station she picked played soft rock, which was fine with Bob. Then she sat down beside him and put her hand on his shoulder.

She smiled and said, "I'm really looking forward to seeing the movie this evening. It's a little scary, that's why I need you here."

"That's all?"

"Maybe not just that." She leaned over and they kissed.

"Okay. I'll stay."

"You better. Are you hungry Bob?"

"Maybe just a little bit." Bob prayed that his stomach wouldn't growl.

She reached for the phone on the end table. "What would you like on it?"

"What ever you like Lynn."

"Do you like hot peppers?"

A smile came across his face. "Do I like hot peppers? Does the Pope go to mass every Sunday? I love hot peppers."

"I guess that means we're ordering hot peppers." She shook her head and smiled.

Bob had hoped he wasn't making an idiot of himself. He did want to impress her. He shouldn't have gone on about the hot peppers the way he had.

"Is there anything else that you want to have on the pizza Bob? Mushrooms, pepperoni, italian sausage?"

"Anything is fine with me."

She phoned for the pizza, then asked, "Can I get you anything to drink Bob? We have beer."

"Pepsi would be fine, thanks."

She got up to get them, their drinks and returned with them. As she walked back in with them, she said, "So, what did you do for excitement today?"

"Oh, not too much. I went out and found a new apartment."

"You what?" She had a look of surprise and excitement on her face.

"I got an apartment just above Masters' Music Centre."

"That's near your father's hardware store."

"Yeah, it's perfect. I'll be able to walk to work. It's pretty nice too."

"That's what I want to do, too. Get my own place. So when can we see it?"

"I've got the keys; so I guess anytime."

"Good, let's go."

"Wait a minute. The pizza is probably already on it's way. Let's eat first."

"Oh yeah. I forgot about that."

Lynn was all smiles, telling him about how she wanted to decorate her own place. She was anxious to see the place and get some ideas for when she set up house. The pizza finally arrived and they began to eat their dinner. Bob was just starting his second piece, when she suggested they take the pizza to the apartment and finish it there. She obviously had her mind made up, so they packed up the pizza and Pepsi, then left.

Bob gave Lynn the keys when they got there, so she could open the doors for him. This way he could carry the Pepsi and pizza in. She hurried up the stairs.

"Bob. Are you Okay with all that stuff?"

"No problem." He walked up the stairs fumbling with the pizza box and several loose cans of Pepsi.

She walked into the apartment and said, "Oh, Bob, this

is very nice."

Trying to catch his breath and juggle the pizza box, Bob said, "Thanks, I'm glad you like it."

She walked through the place, while Bob made his way to the kitchen counter with their gourmet delights.

"This place is great, Bob."

"Have some pizza, Lynn."

"No thanks. You know, I thought I'd like to have a place in a new building. But now I'm not so sure."

Bob shook his head and grabbed another piece of pizza. "What do you think of the fireplace."

"Oh, it's gorgeous. The whole place is gorgeous. I love the wood work."

"Can you picture us sitting in front of that fireplace, sipping on a glass of white wine. A fire gently warming us, the lights turned down low."

"Oh yes, and don't forget the soft music."

"Johnny Mathis would do, don't you think Lynn?"

"Aren't you the romantic."

"If I were such a romantic, I would have thought ahead and had the wine and music here tonight. And we wouldn't be watching T.V.; that's for sure."

She walked over to him and kissed him on the lips. "You're right, we wouldn't. But you didn't so let's go watch some T.V., and have some popcorn."

"Great." Bob said with disappointment.

"Come on, it'll be fun." She grabbed him by the arm and started to drag him off.

Leaving the pizza on the counter and taking only the Pepsi they left. She was holding on to his arm as they walked down the stairs and out to the car.

They went back to her place and began making popcorn for the nine o'clock movie. She had asked Bob if he really minded watching the movie. Bob felt that, since she was looking so forward to it, it was fine with him.

Lynn started making cute little gestures and noises, to set the mood for the movie they were about to see. She would sneak up behind him and yell, "Booo!" Along with other ghostly sounds Bob hadn't heard since he was twelve. Bob really enjoyed seeing the little girl in her. It was genuine, it was her. You know you're comfortable with someone when you can act like a kid and not be embarrassed. Lynn was so full of energy, so alive. The little girl in her made him enjoy her company all the more.

As they made the popcorn, they talked about the apartment. Bob told her about the new frozen waffle heater and she laughed.

She looked at him straight faced. "You really think highly of your parents, don't you Bob?"

"Yes, I do. They've always treated me fairly and listened to anything I had to say."

"I've never talked to your mother very much, but I have lots of opportunity to talk to your father. He seems to be a really nice man."

"He is." Bob stared at the stove for a moment. "So, Lynn, you never did tell me about this spooky movie that we're watching tonight. What is it?"

"A real chiller with Betty Davis. Hush ... Hush ... Sweet Charlotte."

"Never heard of it."

"Oh Bob, It was only at the show five years ago."

"I wasn't a movie buff five years ago."

"I don't think you were ever a movie buff."

"Ha, Ha; pass the butter."

They finished making the popcorn, then retired to the living room for the movie extravaganza. At least that's the way Lynn felt about it. Bob couldn't get over the size of the bowl of popcorn they had. Bowls like this, he thought, only existed in army mess halls. She had turned on the television just in time for the movie. They sat on the couch with their feet on the coffee table. Snug beside each other, they were hidden from all the dangerous movie characters. Harm couldn't find them, not with that popcorn bowl on their laps. Hell, they were lucky to see the T.V.

"Good popcorn Bob."

"Sure is. Do you think we have enough?"

"Ha, Ha."

They cuddled through the entire movie. She cuddled because of the movie, he cuddled because of her. Thoughts of what the evening could lead to raced though Bob's mind. He could only hope she was thinking the same thing.

He watched her more than the movie. A frightening scene would send her body crashing against his, seeking refuge from the evil movie characters. Her eyes would be glued to the T.V. while his would be looking over her sweater and jeans. He could only imagine how perfect her body must be. She smelled and felt so good. Lynn turned suddenly and caught him staring at her face. She smiled and excused herself, to go powder her nose, as she put it. A commercial was on and he hadn't realized it. If she would have looked at him a moment sooner, she may have caught him looking a little lower than her face. When she returned; Bob decided it would be best to pay attention more to the movie. Who knows, she may want to talk about it and he should have some idea what they had watched.

The movie ended and Lynn turned the television off and the stereo on. The same radio station was playing as before, except the disc jockey was playing all soft rock. He referred to his program as, "Pillow Talk". He couldn't have chosen a better name for his show. They danced in the middle of the living room to Brook Benton's "Rainy Night in Georgia" and the Righteous Brothers', "Ebb Tide". Then Bob sat down while she turned some of the lights off. She sat back down, beside him and they began to kiss. It wasn't long before they found themselves more than simply kissing. Bob's hands found all the curves of her body. It was when one of his hands, made it's way under her bra that she began to move away. She sat back and tried to catch her breath, as well as her thoughts.

"Perhaps I should go now, Lynn?"

She looked up at him with caressing eyes and said, "No. ... Stay with me tonight. ... Please?"

Bob looked at her pleading eyes and said, "All right ... I'll stay." They fell back into each others arms once again. It felt so right, so loving, so natural.

Out on the streets, Kevin had been driving around in search of Bob Hills. He was now determined to get his revenge for what he had said about his dead brother. Kevin was wild with rage. Bob Hills had no right to say what he had about his brother and now was going to pay the consequences. It was as though he had gone completely over the edge and had lost touch with reality. He drove around for better than three hours, passing Bob's parents house several times and stopping to look. On his last pass by the house, he noticed it was dark inside and it was quite evident that no one was home. So Kevin decided to park a few doors away, on the opposite side of the street and watch the house. Bob had to come home sometime and he'd be waiting for him. He looked at his watch, it was ten thirty-two.

All was quiet until eleven forty-five when a car approached Kevin's on the street. He ducked below the dashboard and peered just over the top to see who it was. The car pulled into the Hills' driveway and Kevin could see the silhouettes of two people inside. He could make out the outlines of what seemed to be a male in the driver's seat and a female in the passenger's seat. There was a fierce glare in Kevin's eyes and they focused on the driver. Then the driver's door opened and the driver emerged, facing Patterson's car, as he did. The car's interior light, illuminated the driver's face long enough to give Kevin a good look at him. It was Bob's father. He settled back down in his car seat once again and waited for his adversary to come home.

CHAPTER TWELVE

Lynn and Bob were sound asleep in her bed, both deep in dreams. She laid there very still with visions of love and marriage, racing through her head, while Bob was rocking back and forth in a cold sweat, worrying about staying alive. Once again, he was back in the Nam.

Jimmy and Bob were in the same foxhole as they were in previous dreams. The two friends were looking out over a tree line. There was some distant gunfire with the sound of the odd grenade going off. All Bob's senses seemed to come alive as though he were actually there.

Looking straight ahead Bob said, "Where's Charlie, Jim? Do you see anything out there?"

"The enemy's coming."

Bob kept his eyes on the tree line. "I don't see a damn thing out there."

"He's out there, Bob."

"Where?"

"Out there."

"How do you know?"

"I've got special powers."

Still looking at the tree line, Bob said, "What are you talking about Wiener?"

"Believe me, Bob."

"Sure thing pal."

"The enemy is ... out there, Bob."

"But where Jim?"

"Out there."

"Wiener, I'm scared."

"You should be. He's after you."

"Is it Charlie?"

"NO!"

"Well then who?"

"Kevin........ and he's crazy Bob."

"How do you know all this?" Bob turned to him.

Jim turned to look back at Bob, with the front of his uniform covered in blood. The bullet holes were where Bob remembered them to be. "I just know Bob. You'll have to trust me on this one; and please be careful."

Bob's eyes widened as he stood face to face with his dead friend. His heart began to pound uncontrollably, when suddenly he was jolted back to reality.

Lynn was shaking him and saying, "Bob, wake up. Are you alright Bob?" Bob was sitting up in bed now. "Wake up."

"Oh my God." Bob wiped his face with his hands.

"Are you alright?"

"Yeah ..... yeah, I'm fine."

"You were moaning and calling Jimmy."

"I was dreaming."

"Dreaming? I'd call that a nightmare."

"It was in Vietnam."

"What about Vietnam? Do you remember the dream?"

"Yeah, but it didn't make any sense." Bob stared into space trying hard to make sense of his dream.

Lynn was now looking at him with concern. "Can I get you anything?"

"No, I'll just have a shower."

"It's only six. Didn't you want to sleep in?"

"No...... I'm all sweaty anyways."

"I'll make you some coffee and breakfast."

"Just coffee will be fine Lynn. That I could use."

Bob got out of bed and so did she.

"Thanks, Lynn."

She walked over to Bob and kissed him. "You're

welcome." Lynn stood there looking into his eyes and smiled with a comforting expression on her face.

Bob showered while Lynn made the coffee. Soon after, he was dressed and had joined her in the kitchen. She looked good even in her house coat.

"Coffee's ready, Bob. Would you like a cup?"

"Yes, please."

She poured the coffee and handed it to him at the table. "Here you go."

"What time is it, Lynn?"

She turned and looked at the clock on the stove. "It's still pretty early, only six forty-five."

"I've got to be going."

"Why so early, Bob?"

"I want to pack some of my things and start moving into the apartment today."

"It'll take me a half hour to get ready. Have another cup of coffee and I'll go with you."

"How about if I take a cab home and you meet me there when you're ready. We can have dinner there tonight, we'll order chinese food."

"Great. But I wish you'd wait for me to drive you."

"It'll work out better this way. By the time you get to my place, I'll have a lot of the packing done. The sooner I get home, the sooner I can get packing."

"Alright. Did you want that cab now?"

"Please."

She phoned for the cab. It was seven o'clock by the time it got there. Bob kissed her and told her that he'd see her later. She stood in the living room window watching as the cab drove away. Her smile, and touch was still with him, even as the taxi drove out of sight. Bob found himself falling in love more and more, with each and every moment he spent with her.

In another part of town, Russ was just walking into the police station. His partner was calling to him.

"Let's go Russel."

"Hang on. I've got to check my desk for messages."

"Well, make it snappy."

Russ grabbed his messages off his desk and shoved them in his sports jacket pocket. "Okay, let's go Carter, you God Damn pain in the ass."

They went out to their unmarked police car and drove off with Carter driving.

Russ shook his head and said, "Fine, we're in a hurry, right. Where to?"

"The Doughnut Palace on Second. I need a decent cup of coffee and a doughnut."

"You mean to say you rushed me out of there like that for The Doughnut Palace? You better be buying."

"Hey, I'll even buy you a jelly doughnut."

"I hate jelly doughnuts."

"So have a honey dip. Besides, what were you doing that was so important?"

"Checking my messages. That reminds me." He reached into his jacket pocket and pulled out a few slips of paper. "Oh that's great."

"What?"

Here's one that's two days old. It's from my wife. It's says that she's going to be late tonight, as in two nights ago. Son of a bitch."

"So don't worry about it."

"Oh yeah, brain storm. I gave her shit for coming home late on Friday night. We wound up having a big fight over it."

Carter started to laugh. "You're kidding?" He turned to look at Russel and saw that he wasn't laughing, at all. "Sorry."

"Me too, Carter." Russ took the message from his wife, rolled it into a ball and threw in on the car floor. "Shit! That pisses me right off."

"Just explain to her. In fact, I'll even drop by and tell her what happened."

"She'll believe you about as much as she'll believe me and that won't do me any good." He looked at the next message in his hand; his eyes straining as he read it. "CALLED: CAPTAIN GREGG KISER. SAID KEVIN PATTERSON IS THREATENING BOB HILLS. MAYBE HIS LIFE. LARRY JACKSON."

"What's wrong Russ? You look like you've seen a ghost."

Russ just stared straight ahead.

"Hey ... earth to Russ. Are you Okay?"

"I've got a bad feeling about something."

"What are you talking about?"

"Just forget the Coffee and your stomach and head for Hampton near Crosby."

"Look, Russ, we're headed in that general direction; but we better not get caught sightseeing. We're supposed to be at the College first thing this morning."

"Carter, we're not sightseeing. THIS IS OFFICIAL POLICE BUSINESS. NOW MOVE IT!"

"Okay, Okay. Who did what?"

"Nothing's been done yet."

"Are you crazy Russ?"

"STOP QUESTIONING ME AND STEP ON IT. FOR FUCK SAKES, CARTER, LET'S JUST GET OUR ASSES IN GEAR AND HAUL IT!"

"Alright, alright! I've never seen you like this. And you owe me a doughnut."

"Will you stop worrying about your God damned stomach and start worrying about the road. Remember, we're in a hurry." Russ put the red flasher on the dash.

The car was speeding on it's way. "Give me a break Russ. I'm less than two minutes away. There's no call in on this and we're acting like I'm taking you to the hospital to have a baby."

"Good Carter, Good. Just keep up the good work and hustle your ass."

Carter glanced over to Russ and knew whatever it was, it had to be serious, so he floored the gas pedal for all it was worth. Russ had only wished that he had received the message the night before, but there was nothing he could do about that now. In any case, he'd have the chance to warn Bob in a minute. Then he'd be charging Kevin as soon as he got his witnesses together.

The cab had pulled up to Bob's parents' house. Bob was so busy thinking about Lynn that he hadn't even noticed. The cabby asking for his fare was what brought Bob back to reality. Lynn occupied his every thought, even as he fumbled with his wallet. He paid the cab driver and started towards the house. The cab backed out of the driveway and started down the street just as Bob opened the door of the house.

Kevin, who was still in his car, was awakened by the cab pulling away. He sat up in the car seat and noticed Bob, just as he entered the house. The sight of him renewed his anger. The door of the house closed before Kevin had a chance to do or say anything. He frantically looked for something to throw through the Hills front window. He grabbed an adjustable wrench that was sitting on the floor of the car and a .22 calibre rifle that was lying on the back seat. Finally, he was going to get his revenge and was going to kill a warmonger. He got out of the car and threw the wrench; it went right through the front window.

Bob was in the kitchen when he heard a terrible crash coming from the front room.

Mike yelled from the upstairs bedroom, "WHAT WAS THAT?"

Bob ran to the front room and yelled back, "It's the front window. We've got trouble."

He could hear his father scurrying in the bedroom, as he headed for the door. Bob was enraged. This was going to stop once and for all. He stepped outside and there was Kevin. He had a rifle pointing right at him. Bob started to dive to the porch for cover, when the first round hit him. It threw Bob back as the shot rang out, breaking the early morning's quiet. Bob heard a siren start to blare, almost immediately after. Then he felt the second round hit him. Bob was spinning around when he saw his father. He was screaming, "NO! .... NO.....GOD, NO......PLEASE NO!"

He could see the unmarked police car, with it's flashing red light, out of the corner of his eye. Russel and Carter came to a screeching stop swinging Russ's side of the car towards Kevin. Russ jumped out of the car with his pistol drawn.

"DROP IT!" Russ yelled.

Kevin turned to him with the rifle in his hands and a smile on his face.

"I SAID DROP IT!" Russ cocked his weapon.

"I got him!" Kevin started to raise his rifle.

Russel fired a single shot that knocked Kevin and his rifle to the ground.

Mike was holding Bob in his arms and rocking him. Bob could hear him crying and saying, "No, please God no... Please don't... God no... I'll be good. I promise I'll be good." To Bob, it began to sound distant and drawn out, as though things were happening in slow motion. Bob felt himself getting cold; so very cold. The tears from his Dad's eyes felt so warm as they fell on his face.

Mike looked down at his son in his arms, who was

straining his eyes, trying to look back at him. There was a small stream of blood running from the corner of his mouth. He could feel Bob's body shaking, so Mike held him all the closer to keep him warm.

Things around Bob were getting very hazy; and he became so very frightened. He tried to say something, but couldn't. Finally everything went a dark grey, then finally black and Bob felt as though he had been packed in a tub ice. That was when all went quiet.

After what only seemed a brief moment; Bob felt warm again. And there was a comforting bright light. Then he saw a familiar face and an outstretched hand. The face broke into a tranquil smile and spoke to him, in a soft serene tone.

"Hey pal, it's me, Wiener. All's been forgiven, I've come to take you home."

THE END